THIEF'S
COVENANT

THIEF'S COVENANT

A Widdershins Adventure

ARI MARMELL

an imprint of **Prometheus Books**
Amherst, NY

Published 2012 by Pyr®, an imprint of Prometheus Books

Cover illustration © Jason Chan
Cover design by Nicole Sommer-Lecht

Inquiries should be addressed to
Pyr
59 John Glenn Drive
Amherst, New York 14228–2119
VOICE: 716–691–0133
FAX: 716–691–0137
WWW.PYRSF.COM

16 15 14 13 12   5 4 3 2 1

Library of Congress Cataloging-in-Publication Data

Marmell, Ari.
    Thief's covenant / by Ari Marmell.
        p. cm.
    ISBN 978–1–61614–547–7 (pbk.)
    ISBN 978–1–61614–548–4 (e-book)
    I. Title.

PS3613.A7666T48 2012
813'.6—dc23

2011041551

Printed in the United States of America

Widddershins *adv.*

1. In a direction contrary to the apparent course of the sun
2. Counterclockwise

PROLOGUE

TWO YEARS AGO:

The girl watched, helpless, as the world turned red beneath her.

She clung—first to the walls above, where few could even have *attempted* to climb, and then to the rafters—terrified to move, to breathe, to *think*, lest she accidentally attract a murderous eye. No matter how she tried, no matter how hard she bit her own hand in a desperate attempt at silence, she couldn't entirely suppress her sobs. Her body shook with them; her face glistened. But any sounds she made were lost in the carnage below; any tears that fell vanished in the sheen of blood that covered the floor.

Blood that, minutes before, had pumped from the hearts of men and women she knew. Men and women she loved.

Long after the slaughter had ended, long after silence had fallen, Adrienne Satti could only clutch the rafters with both arms and legs, her eyes squeezed tight, and pray.

✸

Thin strands of mold clung to broken mortar along a wall of bricks. The watery tendrils of twisting underground estuaries and man-made sewers flowed beyond those walls, sweeping away the city's filth, twisting and wearing away at the brickwork, keeping it consistently damp. As easily find a museum without dust, or a tax collector without scars, as a cellar beneath the city of Davillon without mold.

Yet it was neither mold nor condensation weighing down the

chamber's stagnant air, obscuring the abstract designs on the burnished flagstones. Rather, it was blood—almost inconceivable quantities of it, mixing with the mold into a foul sludge, seeping through cracks in the floor, seeking a return to the primal earth. Scattered across those ornate tiles lay an obscene carpet of limbs and other, less recognizable bits that had so recently stood upright, talked and laughed and borne names.

With a gut-churning squelch, a booted foot stepped into the chamber of horrors. And there it remained, in mid-stride, until its wearer cautiously examined the floor to ensure he was not about to set foot on a corpse, or part of one.

A second glance followed, to ensure that his gauntlet had not picked up any of the stray filth that caked the walls. Only then did Sergeant Cristophe Chapelle of the Davillon City Guard carefully smooth his salt-and-pepper mustache (poking, in the process, at the camphor extract that he and the others had applied to their nostrils). A brief prayer to Demas moving silently across his lips, he grimly shook his head.

"This is a mess," he muttered irritably. "We're going to have to count heads."

"Sir? Sir, I—that is, I think . . ." The voice petered out as the younger Guardsman gagged, forcing something back down where it belonged.

Chapelle turned toward the speaker, a young recruit named Julien Bouniard. Soft, unassuming features and slightly drooping eyelids belied both wit and reflexes at least as keen as the service rapier that hung loosely at his hip. Like the sergeant, he wore the black tabard of the Guard, emblazoned with the silver fleur-de-lis, and a medallion of Demas, patron deity of the Guard, around his neck—a medallion he rubbed gingerly between thumb and finger, seeking comfort and strength. Only his ribbons of rank differentiated his uniform from that of his sergeant.

Well, those and the abstract patterns of blood on his boots.

"What is it, Constable?" Chapelle demanded, his face a gruff mask behind which his own revulsion cowered.

"I've identified one of the dead, sir."

Not a good sign. "And who might that be?"

"Sir, I believe . . . I really think you'd better see this for yourself. If I'm wrong . . ."

"Understood, Constable. Show me."

Accompanied by a chorus of nauseating sounds, they crossed the chamber, stopping beside one particularly hideous corpse. The other Guardsmen, scattered throughout the room, paused in their own investigations to see what their sergeant was about.

Chapelle crouched perfunctorily beside the body Julien indicated—no. No, this wasn't even a proper body. It was a shell, a suit of meat. Everything that gave life, everything that was supposed to be found within, was scattered around instead, ripped out through a gaping chasm in the abdomen.

It was the work of no weapon with which the sergeant was familiar. A bear, maybe, or a panther, if such a beast had somehow developed a sadistic taste for suffering.

Unable to put it off any longer, Chapelle turned his attention to the victim's face, blinked back a surge of pity at the horrified expression forever etched into the man's features. Clearly, the fellow saw exactly what was coming, and couldn't do a damn thing about—

"Demas!" he cursed as recognition finally set in. "It's Robert Vereaux!"

He lacked the wherewithal, as he rose to his feet, to reprimand his men for the shocked murmurs that swirled about the chamber.

And then, because things clearly weren't bad enough, one of the other Guardsmen shot to his feet. "I've another one, sir!" the Guardsman stammered. "I think it's Marie Richelieu!"

Chapelle cursed vilely, something he *never* did in front of the men. The Lady Richelieu was the young matriarch of a household that was, if anything, wealthier even than House Vereaux. Unmindful now of what he stepped on, the sergeant darted over. Sure enough, he recognized the pert features and ravishing blonde curls of Marie Richelieu, though a sizable portion of her left cheek was absent.

The old Guardsman, growing visibly older by the instant, could only shake his head, mumbling prayers beneath his breath. The House Richelieu was quite accustomed to scandal and slander, but *this* was not the sort of public affair with which the House was equipped to deal.

And if there were two, how many more? Sergeant Chapelle set his men to examining every face, and with each positive identification, his world tilted farther off its axis. Pierre Montrand. Josephine Poumer. Darien Lemarche. Gaston Carnot, the Marquis de Brielles. No, they couldn't put a name to every face, nor even a face to every victim. But every last soul they could identify hailed from the ranks of Davillon's rich and powerful; each name they recorded was another House about to become the stuff of rumor, another god bereft of a most eminent follower.

Swallowing his distaste, Sergeant Chapelle ordered a more thorough search of the room. If there *were* clues to be found, they could well be hidden beneath a carpeting of blood, and they weren't about to leap out and reveal themselves.

The Guardsmen applied an extra dose of the disease-shielding camphor to their noses, swallowed their rising gorges, and began to sift.

✳

A pair of fearful eyes in an oceanic shade, hovering indecisively on the cusp between blue and green, blinked open to watch the Guardsmen anxiously from above. The rafters atop which the blood-smeared figure had scurried—which were utterly unnecessary in the arched stone chamber, possibly left over from the days of construction —were thin, dusty, precarious. Yet she crouched among them carelessly, a human spider clinging to her perch, breathing through her mouth in a futile attempt to avoid the grisly fetor.

Her whole body trembled as a thrill of panic danced spastically up her spine, sending a trickle of dust raining from the rafters. Her own fear momentarily overwhelmed by this external, alien emotion, she twisted her head to glance over her shoulder, though she knew no one was present.

Not physically, at least.

"Stop that!" she hissed in a raw whisper. "This is hard enough without you distracting me!"

Through the fear, she sensed a faint but unmistakable tingle of sheepishness.

"Right, then." She glanced downward once more, fingers grasping reflexively at the wooden beam.

"I'm going down there," she decided suddenly. She didn't much care for the Guard; hated them, actually. But after what she'd witnessed, she was willing to break down and cry on any shoulder, even if it sported the silver fleur-de-lis, or the stern visage that was both the face and the symbol of Demas.

A spike of terror, one that came from the *other* rather than from her own soul, rooted her in place. An involuntary cry escaped her lips.

✳

One of the Guardsmen craned his neck upward, seeking uselessly to penetrate the shadows that clung to the ceiling in the lantern-light. Pushing back the brim of his plumed hat, he shook his head irritably. These new oil lamps were better than torches, but you still couldn't bloody well see a damn thing when you needed to.

When the sound failed to repeat itself, he shrugged and, with a muttered, "Rats, I suppose," resumed his grisly work.

✸

"Now see what you almost did!" the girl hissed at her unseen companion, slowly edging her way across the beam. "When we get out of this, we're going to have a serious talk as to who's in charge here. I—"

"Sergeant!" The voice reverberated from below. The rafter-borne figure tilted her head, gazing down at the young constable who'd identified the body of Robert Vereaux.

You think this is horrible now, she thought at them bitterly, blinking back tears. *Where were you while I watched it happen?!*

A swell of sympathy and understanding washed over her from the unseen presence.

"Oh, shut up," she snapped quietly.

"What is it, Constable?" This, weary-voiced, came from the older Guardsman.

"Sir," the young man replied, "I've found a loose stone in the wall here. There's a lever of some sort hidden behind it."

"Oh, figs," the young woman breathed.

✸

With an old, practiced eye, Chapelle studied the large brick that lifted easily, despite its apparent mass, from its housing; the lever, perhaps a foot long, concealed behind it; and finally, took a single all-encompassing glance around the room entire, as though trying to discern what the mechanism might do.

"Well," he said eventually, his tone even, "adventure fiction aside, nobody actually builds traps this obvious, just in the hopes that someone may be curious." *Nobody sane, anyway.* "All the same, I want everybody to leave the chamber and step back into the hallway. Just in case. Bouniard!"

The young constable snapped to attention. "Sir?"

"I want you waiting in the doorway. If something untoward *does* happen, I expect some modicum of effort to get me out of it." The sergeant smiled tightly. "I'm not expecting miracles, of course, since someone gets a promotion if I die in here. But at least make it look good."

Julien Bouniard smiled faintly. "I'll certainly appear to do my damnedest, sir."

"That's the spirit! All right, move!"

In moments, the room was emptied of all living inhabitants save the sergeant himself, and the unseen watcher above. A quick glance at young Bouniard—gravely returned with a nod—and Chapelle yanked on the lever.

A low grinding sounded from beneath the bloody tiles; deep, ponderous, as though they were witnessing the gestation and birth of the thunder itself. The room shuddered, sending faint showers of dust spilling from the rafters (and eliciting a second involuntary yelp that, thankfully, went unheard amidst the rumbling). Agitated from beneath, a few dead limbs flailed about in a profane dance.

The center of the floor opened up, revealing a hollow almost ten feet on a side. Several corpses dropped into the gap, landing with a symphony of wet thumps on whatever lay below. Chapelle, his face gone pale, realized that they had just lost the bodies of five or six of the city's elite.

But the procedure, whatever it was, was not complete. Something emerged, in rapid fits and starts, from the newborn pit.

The statue rose to its full height of eighteen feet, its horns almost brushing the rafters. It was carved in a crouch, as though it might leap to attack at any moment, bringing to bear the wicked axe slung over its left shoulder. Bedecked in furs that were carved with exquisite detail, sporting a beard so finely sculpted that it seemed possible to go and pluck a hair, it stared down at Chapelle with narrowed stone eyes. It looked for all the world to be a warrior of the ancient northlands, save for the horns that jutted from its otherwise bald scalp.

There was nothing inherently religious about the sculpture, but Chapelle knew an idol when he saw one; *every* citizen of Galice knew an idol when they saw one.

"Sir?"

"I'm fine, Constable. Bring the men back in here." Trusting that his orders would be obeyed, he continued his examination of the towering form.

It clearly wasn't one of the 147 gods of the Pact—or at least, not in any iconography recognized by the High Church. Sure, worship of an unrecognized god wasn't *technically* illegal, but every city, every government organization, every guild, and every noble house of any repute claimed as their patrons a member of the Hallowed Pact. For *all* of these victims—each one claiming a different house and thus, most probably, a different patron—to have participated in rites devoted to an unrecognized deity was another blemish to fuel an already scandalous situation.

Yet again, Chapelle heaved a sigh from the very depths of his soul. "Search the statue," he ordered, indicating a trio of guards, including Constable Bouniard. "The rest of you . . . keep counting bodies."

✴

In the rafters above, some eight feet from the leftmost horn, the filthy young woman again glanced over her shoulder. Pushing her matted and reeking hair from her face, she asked quietly, "This doesn't actually change *your* situation, does it? Them seeing your idol, I mean?"

A resounding sense of denial ran through her body. She grimaced.

"All right," she said, shifting her attention back to the events below. "This is bad. Still, I think we can talk our way—"

"Sergeant! I've found something!"

"This keeps getting better," she mumbled.

✳

Chapelle appeared beside the young constable, who was pointing toward a carefully concealed catch at the rear of the idol. "You seem to have a knack for finding these things, Bouniard," he said gruffly. He looked over the constable's find: a simple switch, set flush with the stone, just beneath the lip of the platform. With a leather-gloved hand, the sergeant flipped the switch.

A drawer, so expertly crafted as to have been all but invisible, slid from the stone. Within lay several small candles, a long quill, a jar of ink, and a wood-bound and velvet-wrapped ledger. Without so much as a pause for breath, Chapelle snapped up the book and flipped it open, eagerly scanning the pages for answers.

Even the most casual examination suggested the book could be nothing less than a roster of membership for this strange little cult, each page devoted to one individual. There were no names—gods forbid they make this easy!—but it did include dates, titles of rank or seniority that were pretty much meaningless to the old Guardsman, and a monetary value listed in gold marks, perhaps indicating donations.

Chapelle was quite sure that he'd just found the motive for the horrific crimes: The sheer quantity of gold in the sect's coffers must be staggering. Why, the first eight or nine entries alone totaled up to more than *ten thousand* marks!

More importantly, though, his men had managed a tentative count of the dead while he'd searched the statue and perused the ledger. And if that count was correct, the room contained twenty-six corpses—to the ledger's twenty-*eight* entries. At least two members were unaccounted for.

"Inside job," he said to Bouniard. "I suppose it would almost have had to be. I . . . ."

"Sir," Julien pressed as Chapelle's brow furrowed in thought. "What is it?"

"Didn't I hear Darien Lemarche listed amongst the dead?"

"Uh, yes, I believe so."

"How many of you," the sergeant asked, surveying the room as a whole, "are up on the latest gossip?"

Several Guardsmen exchanged glances and guiltily raised their hands.

"Was Lemarche still involved with Adrienne Satti?"

"Last I heard, yes, sir," one of them replied.

"Find her. Now."

They failed; no matter how they tried, they found no trace of the woman among the dead. Chapelle nodded with each report, his expression growing ever more certain.

Damned aristocrats! He could have told them it would end badly, with her. *Although*, he admitted to himself, *I didn't expect it would go this badly.*

"We'll have these bodies picked up, gathered, and . . . reassembled as best as possible," Chapelle told his men. "I'm fairly certain I know what's happened, but we have to identify them, all of them, to be sure."

"I also need a volunteer," the sergeant barked as his men fell eagerly in line to depart. "Someone to stay behind and ensure the room's not disturbed until the clean-up workers arrive."

Julien Bouniard moved forward, arm half-raised, only to fall back—eyes and mouth agape, obviously shocked to the core—as a blond-haired figure appeared before him.

"I'll stay, sir," volunteered Henri Roubet, a constable some few years older than Julien himself.

Chapelle quirked an eyebrow. "Resting Roubet," the others in the unit called him. "When Roubet volunteers" was, so far as they were concerned, roughly analogous to "When pigs fly," or "When hell freezes over."

Well, perhaps the surrounding scene of depravity had kindled some residual spark of responsibility in the man. Be a shame to squelch it before it could spread.

"Very well, Roubet. You're on watch. I don't imagine you'll be waiting too terribly long; shouldn't be more than half an hour. Report to the main office when you've been relieved."

"Yes, sir. Thank you, sir."

Chapelle pivoted on his heel and marched from the room, grateful to be away. Julien Bouniard fell in line with his compatriots, but his expression remained thoughtful, his thoughts clearly on the man who stayed behind.

✸

"Well, that's just dandy!" the young woman spat under her breath as the guards sorted through the ledger below. "What kind of secret cult keeps written records, can you tell me that?"

Judging by the sudden sense of disapproval—the emotional equivalent of a saddened headshake—she was fairly certain he couldn't.

"Don't you have any say over the doings of your own worshippers? Because I've got to tell you, the way they were running this thing . . ."

Her throat closed and her eyes widened, first in surprise at hearing the name "Adrienne Satti" spoken by the gravel-voiced sergeant, and then in mounting horror as the implications sank home. A hole opened in the pit of her stomach, just wide and deep enough for her soul to drop slowly and painfully through it. She watched, barely comprehending, as the bulk of the Guardsmen departed, leaving a trail of bloody bootprints in the corridor beyond the chamber door.

"Oh, gods . . ." Not even a whisper, now, but the faintest susurrus of exhaled breath. "Oh, gods, they think *I* did this!" For the second time in an hour, she had to blink hard to keep the tears from falling. "How could they possibly think . . ." Adrienne felt, once again, a touch of sympathy in the back of her mind.

"This is your fault!" she exploded at him, her fear turned suddenly to anger. "If you hadn't stopped me from going down to them, I could have explained it! I could have told them what really happened! Now it's too late! I—"

"Had better come down from there right now, Mademoiselle Satti, before I am forced to shoot you down."

Adrienne froze, cursing her own stupidity. She peered downward, past the dusty beams on which she lay, past the horned form of the god. The remaining Guardsman looked up at her, an odd expression plastered across his scruffy face. His rapier hung sheathed at his left hip, but in his right fist he clenched a gleaming flintlock pistol—a Guard-issued special with a frame molded of brass rather than wood, reinforced to function as a brutally efficient headbreaker. In her youth, before the aristocracy, Adrienne had more than once been on the butt-end of those so-called bash-bangs.

But rarely had she stared so squarely down the barrel of one.

"I'm not going to ask a second time," the Guardsman warned.

Adrienne slid off the beam. Limber as a double-jointed cat, she swung from the nearest horn and clambered down the statue without pausing for breath (or to acknowledge her incorporeal partner's sudden squawk of indignation at having his likeness used as a stepladder). In seconds, Adrienne stood upon the blood-slick floor.

Frowning thoughtfully, the Guardsman took a moment to examine his catch, difficult as she was to see beneath the filth and caked blood. She looked to be maybe fifteen, give or take a year or two; still somewhere in that nether realm between childhood and womanhood. Her hair, to judge by the few unsoiled strands he could see, was an earthy brown, and her eyes shone with a blue-green hue so liquid that he almost expected to see waves. A small, ever-so-slightly upturned nose sat in the center of a slender face. Impossible to tell precisely what her outfit had looked like; what remained of it gave the rather hideous impression that she'd fashioned her wardrobe from the scraps left over on a slaughterhouse floor.

"Do you normally find blood so fascinating?" Adrienne finally barked irritably. "Or am I special?"

"Rather clever of you to hide out here until we'd departed," Constable Roubet told her casually, flintlock aimed unerringly at her bloody cleavage. "A pity you didn't notice me, or it might've worked."

"I was distracted," she muttered, shooting an aggravated glower toward the statue. "But look at me, Constable. You can't honestly believe me capable of this, can you?" She pressed her right hand to her heart—more than a bit melodramatically—and blinked at him. "I only survived by hiding in the rafters. I can only thank the gods that the killers weren't as observant as you were, or else—"

"Shut up before I shoot you."

Adrienne's jaws snapped shut with an audible click.

"Even if I believed a word of it," the Guardsman told her, shaking his head, "it makes no difference. I'm not the man making the decisions here."

The young woman nodded slowly. "I think I'd like to speak to an advocate just as soon as possible."

Roubet smiled grimly. "I'm sure you would. If you hadn't tried to kill me during your escape, you might have lived long enough to do just that."

"What are you talking . . . ?" And then she understood, and her knees threatened to give way. "You're not a Guardsman," she whispered hoarsely.

"I am, actually. But I'm also a great deal more."

Frantically, she judged the distance between them. Twelve feet, give or take. She could cover that swiftly enough, but not so fast that he couldn't pull the trigger. And even if she reached him, she wasn't armed.

"So what is it, then?" she asked, stalling desperately for time. "Dead women tell no tales? You blame all this on me and the real killers go free?"

"Something like that."

Roubet's arm straightened, the bash-bang shifting until it came directly in line with her heart. The barrel gaped open before her, an endless tunnel to hell.

"I'm sorry, Olgun," she whispered, unable to look away from the pistol. "I tried."

She felt a brief surge of emotion from the near-dead god, followed by the faintest tingling in the air. She had just enough time to wonder if she'd imagined it before the flintlock's hammer crashed down with a deadly clank—

And detonated with a sharp crack and an ear-rending screech of metal. Shrapnel ripped through the soft flesh of Roubet's hand and arm, scored the stone floor in a staccato patter that punctuated the Guardsman's cry of pain. With a resounding thud, the remainder of the now useless weapon dropped to the floor, sending cracks shooting through a small blot of dried blood.

Roubet himself followed an instant later, clutching the bleeding wreckage of his hand to his chest and sobbing inconsolably.

"Well," Adrienne said finally. "*That* was convenient."

She felt a brief swell of satisfaction from her divine partner—but it was no match for her own sense of satisfaction as she darted forward and kicked the whimpering man in the head until he was well and truly unconscious.

"We've got to get out of here," she told the god seriously, limping on a vaguely sore foot as she moved toward the long passage and the stairs beyond. "They think I did this, and I sort of doubt that Lefty here is going to tell them otherwise. We've got to hide until I can figure out what to do, or how to get back to Alexandre."

Another questioning probe.

"I don't know," she admitted. "It doesn't matter, really. I grew up out there, remember? The Guardsman hasn't been born that can find Adrienne Satti when she doesn't want to be found!"

Olgun's doubt, when it came to her, was almost tangible. She concentrated on it, so she wouldn't have to confront her own.

CHAPTER ONE

Brick walls and wooden fences were the borders of her world, roads of dirt or broken cobblestone its fields, rickety staircases its trees. The city wasn't just "a big place" at her age, her size—it was all there was, all there ever could be.

She'd spent much of that day exploring the nearest reaches of that world, along with a number of friends who, like her, were ducking out on the various chores with which they were tasked. Rag-clad and dirt-faced, they moved in a feral pack, yipping and screeching and giggling. Their chins dripped with the juices of fruits they hadn't paid for; their wrists and arms and shoulders ached with the iron grasp of merchants who snagged them before they could run. But there were always more vendors, and those swift or fortunate enough to catch them were far less numerous than the shopkeepers who never knew they'd been robbed. The children pushed, slipped, shoved, and squeezed through barricades of flesh and cloth, making their way through the bustling markets and crowded streets. The heat of bodies pressed together in the throng was enough to make them sweat, despite winter's chill in the air and a light dusting of snow on the rooftops. They shouldn't really have been here unsupervised, so far from home, but their parents had long since given up forbidding them to go.

Futility was a common enough guest in the poorer quarters of Davillon. No sense in inviting him for an extra stay, no sense at all.

Young as she was, however, the girl had some vague sense of responsibility. While everyone knew that adults thrived on giving children meaningless busywork, there were *some* chores that needed doing. And of course, she wouldn't want her parents to worry. (The fact that it was growing late, and that her stomach—unsatisfied by purloined produce—was rumbling for dinner had, of course, nothing at all to do with her abrupt decision to head for home.)

A few shouted farewells, a few insults and protruding tongues, and she left her friends behind. She didn't quite skip along her way, for even if she'd been a happy enough child, the traffic on the roadways wouldn't allow for it. But she was, at least, as carefree as her lot in life would allow. Today, given her own limited frame of reference, had been a good day. She watched, with a delight that she hadn't yet outgrown, as clouds of dirt puffed up around her worn and ragged shoes.

The forest of legs thinned notably as she moved farther from the market, and she began to shiver as the season coughed and wheezed across her skin. She kept her head low, wrapped her arms about her chest in a quest for the warmth her tunic failed to offer, and mumbled aspersions upon her friends. It must, after all, have been *their* fault she'd stayed out so late.

It wasn't the change in the constant roar of the city's voice; people were always shouting about something or other. It wasn't the faint stinging in her eyes, or the almost dainty cough that kept traveling up and down her throat like a yo-yo. No, it was instead the sudden gust of warmth, a comforting yet confounding relief from winter's winds, that finally drew her attention from her feet.

She saw, at first, nothing but the various muted colors and shoddy fabrics that covered the legs and backs of the people before her in the road—more of them, in fact, than was entirely normal. Higher her gaze drifted, higher still, to the flickering glow and the plumes of smoke twisting their way skyward.

Even at her age, she knew full well the dangers of fire, especially in a neighborhood as poor as this. Should she run the other way? Find a place to hide? Offer, however small and feeble she might be, to help?

Mother and Father would know. Again winding between, around, and under a thicket of limbs, the hitch in her breath now as much fear as it was smoke, she wormed her way through the ever-growing crowd.

And then she was near enough to see precisely *which* building was on fire.

The frantic adults simply stepped over her as she fell to her knees in the middle of the road, and her scream was just another voice, lost amidst the many voices of the city.

✸

". . . and as ever and always, to your endless grace, Vercoule. To you, our most humble thanks for the prosperity you have brought us, the safety you have brought us. For Davillon, which is both your gift to us, and our greatest testament to you. In your name, above all, we pray. Amen."

Sister Cateline smiled shallowly at the dull, mumbled chorus of *amen*, already drowned out by the scraping of cheap wooden spoons on cheap wooden bowls, scooping up mouthfuls of cheap porridge (*probably* not wooden, but who could really say for certain?). Stretched out before her were a quartet of long tables, crammed to bursting with unwashed children clad in undyed frocks. There had been a time, oh so long ago, where Cateline felt horrible that the convent couldn't provide a more comfortable life for these unfortunate waifs; when she would've felt guilty that the blue and silver of her own habit was so much better kept than the clothes they offered these lost souls.

Once, but not now. Still she did all she could, but no longer lamented her inability to do more. She'd seen too many of them in her years, and she simply couldn't afford to care any more than she had to.

She strode forward, wending her way between the tables, and stopped just as swiftly, pinned in place by two tiny, red-rimmed eyes. The new girl—what *was* her name . . . ?

"You're not hungry, child?" Duty, more than genuine concern, but at least she'd bothered to ask.

"Who's Varcool?"

Cateline felt her jaw drop.

"You don't know Vercoule, child?" she asked, gently correcting the girl's pronunciation. Many of the nearby children had stopped to listen, some scoffing at the new kid's ignorance, others—just perhaps—hoping for answers to questions they'd never had the courage to ask.

When the girl shook her head, Cateline continued. "Why, he's our patron god! Vercoule, above all others, watches over Davillon."

"What others?"

"The gods of the Hallowed Pact, of course."

"What's the hollow pact?"

Good gods, was nobody *teaching these children anything? Little heathens, running the streets of Davillon.* The nun really wanted nothing more than to get the children finished up and put to bed, but even her cynicism recognized a spiritual obligation when it appeared before her.

"It refers to all the gods of the High Church, child. Uncounted gods ruled before our forefathers carved Galice from the lands of the barbarian tribes. The one hundred forty-seven greatest of them joined together over civilization, promising to watch over humanity."

"And Varcoo—Vercoo—"

"Vercoule."

"Vercoule's the biggest?"

Cateline smiled. "I certainly think so." Then, somewhat more seriously, "Here, in Davillon, he's the greatest. In other cities, he probably stands as the patron of only a single guild, or a bloodline— just as, for instance . . ." She cast about for a moment. "As Banin is the patron of two or three of Davillon's noble houses, but elsewhere, he might be the patron of a great guild, or even an entire city."

The girl nodded slowly as though she understood, though Sister

Cateline doubted that was the case. The nun had just begun to turn away, when—

"Can I ask one more question?"

Cateline repressed a sigh. "One more. Then you need to eat your supper."

"If Davillon has so many gods, how come not one of them got off his butt and *saved my mommy and daddy*?!"

Sister Cateline actually fell back a step, hand raised to her lips. A whisper of astonishment swept through the other children, but here and there, the nun was certain she heard a mutter of angry agreement from among the worst of the hard-luck cases.

Well, it was positively past time to nip *this* in the bud!

"Young lady, that is *not* an appropriate way to speak of the gods!"

"When they explain themselves to me, I'll apologize."

The nun had the girl by the wrist and was dragging her out the door before the second round of shocked gasps—and supportive murmurs—had finished making the rounds of the hall. "We're going to have to teach you some manners and respect, child!"

"Stop calling me *child*!" the girl spat, not even bothering to try to pull away as she was hauled off to gods-knew-where. "My name is Adrienne."

✵

Adrienne did *not*, as it happened, learn either manners or respect from Sister Cateline, or any of the other nuns either. Despite the chains, the locks, the heavy doors, and the fact that she frankly had nowhere better to go, she was gone from the convent after only a few days—before the welts of her lashing had even fully faded.

Sister Cateline wasn't truly sorry to see her go. That one, she was certain, would have been nothing but trouble.

CHAPTER TWO

NOW:

It was, all of it, enormous. The Doumerge property was enormous, the manor at its center was enormous, and the ballroom deep within that house was—no surprise, by now—enormous.

And the chaos within, slipping further out of control by the minute, was rapidly becoming enormous as well.

A cluster of musicians sat upon a raised platform off in one corner, isolated from everyone they were hired to entertain. Furiously they played, lobbing their music into the crowd like arrows, reproducing some of the most popular tunes currently making the rounds of courts and noble soirees throughout Galice. Their outfits—the musicians, that is, not the pieces of music, though those too were arguably gussied up and overdressed—were lavish fabrics in a hypnotic mishmash of garish colors. Tunics and vests hung haphazardly; wigs sat askance atop sweaty heads; abused fingers ached in protest. For five hours they'd played, with never more than a few minutes between songs, and the torment didn't promise an end anytime soon.

For all that their music accomplished, they might well not have bothered. The ballroom, packed so full that dancing required advanced planning and possibly tactical diagrams, hovered at a volume just shy of tectonic movement. Every voice was a bellow, each and every speaker struggling to be heard over every other. The music, to them, was nothing more than extraneous noise, an obstacle to be shouted over.

The table was long, and laden with a quantity of food not merely sufficient to choke a large elephant, but also to bury its remains. Every variety of animal, it seemed, could be found at some spot along that buffet, smothered in sauce or breading or dressing or gods alone knew what. Beef, venison, fowl of every possible variety, at least a dozen types of fish, eggs of both fish and fowl, escargot, every vegetable known to man—it was all here, and no matter how much the guests ate, a criminal amount of food would go to waste. The smell alone was heavy enough to satiate a smaller appetite without a single bite.

The house had been well prepared, in expectation of the night's revelry. Paintings and tapestries hung high on the walls, well beyond reach of drunken fingers or spilled foods. Most were pastoral or mythic scenes, but several depicted the golden pyramid of Geurron, patron deity of the d'Orreille line, and a scant few boasted the sun-and-crown of Vercoule, Davillon's High Patron.

Fires blazed happily in numerous hearths, determined to enjoy the soiree. Various herbs and scents were sprinkled upon the logs, filling the room with a bizarre combination of odors that spun around the guests before rising to cluster at the ceiling's arches and buttresses. The carpets, lush and thick, had been brushed in expectation of the guests' arrival. Servants, immaculately groomed, stood at attention or bustled about the rooms, preparing this, refilling that, and basically playing the part of so many trained hounds, always running and fetching.

And in the center of the maelstrom, buffeted on all sides by the constant eddies and swirls of humanity, stood an unlikely pair. Despite the press of partygoers and the constant blank smiles, polite waves, and spouted small talk, they exuded an aura of calm, a globe of peace that extended a scant few feet from them.

"I must say, my dear baron," the woman was commenting haughtily, "you've really outdone yourself. I can't recall when I've last attended festivities so elegant." Her expression managed to add *Other than those I've planned myself*, without the slightest aid from her tongue.

The gentleman bowed in gratitude, his face partially hidden

behind a loosely clutched kerchief held dangling from long, spidery fingers. "The duchess," he said, his voice thin and watery, "is too kind."

"She is, isn't she?" the woman replied.

Beatrice Luchene, the Duchess Davillon, Voice of Vercoule, landholder and ruler over all territories claimed by the duchy, province, and city of Davillon, was just shy of six feet, and broad of shoulders, hips, and features. Her hair, black-going-gray, was piled high above her head in a mountain of curls that failed utterly to soften a face grown taut with age. She wore rich purples and reds and blues, as well as a golden sun-and-crown brooch, and her face was powdered to within a shade of newly fallen snow.

Her host, by contrast, was a short, bony, shadow of a weasel of a man. Charles Doumerge, the Baron d'Orreille, looked perennially ill. His skin was near gray even without the benefits of powder, and his limp, straw-colored hair was thinning faster than a slug in a salt-shaker. Not even his finest outfit, of blues and browns, made him look any less the walking corpse.

Doumerge leaned in, his rodent's nose cutting through the intervening air like a prow. The duchess managed (barely) to refrain from pulling away.

"I'm grateful," Doumerge told her, his voice as low as the surrounding cacophony would allow, "that I've guests here with the appropriate—shall we say, refinement?—to appreciate my efforts." He furtively glanced around, as though ensuring he wouldn't be overheard, then, simpering, continued, "The truth is, I don't believe that everyone here is quite suited to this sort of thing. If I may be brutally honest with you, Your Grace, I'd not have chosen to invite, say"—he cast about quickly for a safe target—"the Marquis De Brielles. The fellow simply doesn't have what it takes to survive in our particular arena, you see? But, well, poor Francis has had such a difficult time of it of late, it would have been boorish not to offer him the opportunity to escape his problems. Still, I doubt that he's properly able to—"

"Francis Carnot," the duchess said stiffly, "has done quite well,

considering the title of marquis was expected to fall to his late
brother. I consider the gentleman a friend, and I look forward to the
day when he has managed to get his House back on its feet." She
peered down on her unpleasant little host, her expression lofty.

Floundering wildly for a distraction, the baron's gaze fell upon
another guest nearby, a pretty young woman currently standing
alone amidst the swirl of people, staring vacuously off into space.

"Umm—ah, Your Grace?" he asked, even as he reached his
stick-thin arms and wormy finger to grasp at the young lady's elbow.
"Have you met Mademoiselle Valois? No? Well then, I present to
you Madeleine Valois. Mademoiselle Valois, this is Beatrice Luchene,
the Duchess Davillon."

The young lady blinked twice, her only sign of surprise, and
curtsied elegantly. "Your Grace," she said, her voice throaty yet
demure, "I'm honored."

With an artfully concealed flicker of amusement at Doumerge's
clumsy diversion, Luchene gave the newcomer a brief once-over.

She was young, this Madeleine Valois, scarcely more than a
child, with a slender face, sharp features, and aquatic eyes. Her head
was piled high with lavish blonde curls; clearly a wig, but since half
the women in attendance sported wigs, this hardly mattered. Her
gown was a heavy thing of forest green velvets. All told, little about
the woman separated her in any way, shape, or form from a dozen
other ladies of quality.

And yet . . .

"It seems to me," the duchess said, having acknowledged the
young woman's genuflection with a shallow nod, "that I have seen
you somewhere before, my dear."

"Almost certainly, Your Grace," Madeleine told her, face mod-
estly downcast. "I've been privileged to attend several balls and din-
ners before tonight. But this is the first time," she added breathlessly, with a beaming smile toward their mousy host, "that anyone
has done me the honor of formally acquainting us."

"Ah." The duchess's mind was clearly already moving on to other pursuits. "Well, it's certainly been a pleasure to meet you, dear. Do enjoy the rest of the party, yes? Good Baron," she continued, abruptly swiveling toward the pale-faced lord of the manor, "I believe that you and I were in the midst of a discussion?"

✸

As the royals launched back into their debate regarding the values of particular guests, the young lady drifted, unnoticed, into the throng. "Well, *that* was interesting," murmured the woman who currently called herself Madeleine Valois. "I thought we'd been found out."

Heartfelt agreement, tinged with a patina of relief, flowed from her unseen companion, followed by a sense of inquiry.

"No, I'm not worried about the baron. That clown wouldn't comprehend a real threat if someone hid a manticore in his chamber pot. I was afraid the duchess might have recognized me, though. Thankfully, I'm not important enough for close examination."

Another surge of emotion, almost but not quite nostalgia.

Madeleine—who had once been Adrienne—nodded. "And it was a long time ago, yes. But enough worrying." Sliding through the forest of humanity, she continued to survey the house, absorbing every detail. "All right, he's not allowed any of his guests upstairs, so I'll wager that's where he keeps most of his valuables." Irritably, she shook her head, careful not to dislodge her wig and reveal the thick brown hair beneath. "I wish I had the opportunity to examine the layout up there," she complained. "It would make this all so much easier. Ah, well. We're only human, yes?"

Somehow, without the use of a single coherent word, Olgun growled something impolite.

Madeleine flickered a mischievous smile. Right. As if she would wake up one morning and just forget that she had a god riding around in her head.

Gradually, she allowed the flow of the party to edge her ever nearer the door. It was time for Madeleine Valois to make her farewells, preparing the way for a different and uninvited guest.

✳

Several pairs of eyes watched as Madeleine Valois made her graceful exit from the Baron d'Orreille's soiree. Most were potential admirers, sorry to see so lovely a creature depart from their midst.

One was not.

All the houses of Davillon boasted their own guards. Even if most never saw the slightest action, it was simply Not Done to go without. Some were veritable armies unto themselves, while others consisted of anyone who could stand up straight and look competent while making parade-ground turns in formalwear or old-fashioned armor.

Doumerge's guards were largely of the latter category, which meant that the baron's hiring requirements were rather more lax than those of the City Guard. And that meant that, though his ruined hand had cost him his commission in said Guard, Henri Roubet had never lacked for a position.

This wasn't the first party at which the crippled solider had spotted the Lady Valois, though she had never spotted him in turn; it was part of his job, after all, to remain inconspicuous and out of the guests' way. But tonight was the first time he'd gotten a good enough look at her to be certain that she was who he thought she was.

Madeline Valois was, indeed, Adrienne Satti. It was a bit of news for which his employer—his *real* employer, not the weaselly fool of a baron—would pay well.

✳

To those who dwelt outside the law, within the slums and poor districts, and among the population of the so-called Finders' Guild, she
was neither Madeleine nor Adrienne. She was Widdershins, a simple
street-thief like a thousand others. Tonight, Madeleine had done her
part admirably; now it was Widdershins's turn to take over.

Two blocks south of Doumerge Estates, sandwiched between a
large bakery and a winery, lay a narrow alleyway that was nigh invisible in the late hours. Filled with refuse from both establishments,
emptied once a week by underpaid city workers, it was ignored by
those few who noticed it at all.

At the moment, however, it boasted an abnormally large human
population: that is, one. Madeleine edged her way down the alley,
away from the boulevard. Knees bent, back pressed tightly against the
winery, feet pushing against the opposite bricks, she passed above the
reeking filth. Her gown lay in her lap, clasped tightly in her left arm;
she wore, now, a bodysuit of supple black fabrics and leathers that had
lain hidden beneath the forest-green velvet. At the end of the alleyway,
she reached out, straining to grasp the pack she'd stashed earlier that
evening. Though her entire weight shifted and she feared she'd dis-
lodged herself from her precarious perch, her fingers brushed against
the satchel. She quickly grabbed it and yanked it up.

Still without setting foot on the cobblestones, her nose wrinkled
against the stench of refuse, she stuffed the gown roughly into the
bag and removed a second, smaller bundle. This prize, carefully
unwrapped, revealed deerskin gauntlets, hood, thin shoes of black
leather, and a belt whose pouches and pockets contained, among
other things, a candle stub, a one-handed tinderbox, a tiny hammer
and chisel, and the finest set of skeleton keys and wire picks available in any market, black or otherwise. Finally, her tool of last resort:
a rapier, blade blackened with carbon and ink, the basket-hilt
removed so that the weapon could hang flat against her back.

The dark-colored sack in which her tools had been wrapped, she folded tightly and jammed through her belt. The larger pack—stuffed with the gown, jewelry, and everything else that identified Madeleine Valois—would remain ensconced at the end of the alley.

A few quick breaths to steady herself, and she reached over her head to grab the overhang. She tightened her fists and pulled her legs away from the far wall, lifting them smoothly up, her weight supported only by her hold on the roof. Her stomach muscles, though toned through years of practice, still screamed in agony as first her feet, then her knees, cleared the roof over her head and curled over. A final heave, arms straining, and she lay on her stomach at the edge of the winery's roof.

For a few minutes—more than a few, if truth be known—she simply lay, gasping as she regained her composure. She quirked her lips in annoyance at the question she felt from her divine passenger.

"Maybe, but this way was quicker," she whispered.

Olgun's response was amused, and more than a little teasing.

"No, I did *not* do that just to prove I could!" she snapped at him.

Some emotions were more easily translated into words than others. The one he projected now was definitely the equivalent of, "Yeah, right."

Grumbling, Widdershins rose to her feet—ignoring the twinges in her abdomen—and moved across the rooftops. A step to this roof, a leap to that, a quick scamper up a nearby wall. . . . Perhaps a quarter of an hour later, she settled on a building across a wide lane from the gates of the Doumerge Estates.

The boulevard was the border between two worlds. Behind, the square, squat buildings of the district's shops. They, like most of the city's newer construction, were of cheap stone or haphazardly painted wood, all business. Before her, a row of manors. Sloped roofs, ornate cornices and buttresses, fluted gutters and snarling gargoyles, all in marble or whitewashed stone, all old enough to have acquired an arrogance utterly independent of those who dwelt within. The straight lines and angles of poverty facing off against the graceful arches of wealth.

Widdershins had dwelt in both, and wasn't certain she was entirely comfortable in either. Crouching atop the flat roof, melding into the shadows, she settled in for what would surely be a long and boring wait.

✳

Long and *boring*, as it turned out, were ridiculously optimistic. *Endless* and *mind-numbing* would have proved more accurate. The hours lazily meandered by, and the impulsive thief found herself near to bursting with the strain of waiting. Finally, as the moon rowed her way across the sea of night, the manor finally began to excrete its guests in sporadic fits and spurts. The stars wheeled their courses across the nighttime firmament; bats and nightbirds flapped past overhead; cats fought in nearby alleys, hissing and spitting all the while; and time plodded toward morning.

Not long before dawn, when she felt she could take it no longer, the lanterns in the upper-story windows flickered and died, suggesting that Baron Weasel-face had finally retired to his burrow for badly needed (and blatantly ineffectual) beauty sleep. The downstairs lights continued to burn, no doubt for servants who, having stood and watched as rich people grew fat on fancy foods, were now compelled to clean up after the satin-wrapped and brocaded swine.

"Hsst!" she hissed, her throat vaguely hoarse from the yelling that had passed for conversation during the baron's party. "Olgun! Wake up!"

Her mind was filled with a sense of self-righteous—and vaguely drowsy—protest.

"Sure you weren't," she needled at him. "You were just practicing snoring, so you'd be sure to get it right later on, yes?"

Olgun's response very strongly resembled an indignant snort.

"Whatever. It's time."

She cocked her head in response to an unvoiced question.

"Of course I'd rather wait a bit longer," she lied, actually fidgeting foot to foot. "But the night's not just old, it's getting arthritic. We *have* to go now."

The faint scrabbling of loose shale shifting as she set foot on the roadway was the only sound of her swift and graceful descent. Had anyone been watching the wide boulevard in the faint light of the street lamps, he'd have seen nothing more than a quick wink of blackness, a wisp of shadow, no more alarming than a running tomcat and dismissed just as readily.

The polished stone wall surrounding the Doumerge property was near ten feet tall, and impressively smooth. No cracks or seams provided even the most infinitesimal handhold. A rope and grapple might have provided a solution, but Widdershins, who preferred to work light, carried no such thing.

She never needed one.

"Olgun?" she prodded, breaking into a dash as she neared the barrier. "Would you be so kind . . . ?"

As she drew within a few feet of the wall, her boot came down on something that simply wasn't there, an invisible step or perhaps the interlaced fingers of unseen hands. With Olgun's boost, she cleared the wall entirely, tucking in tight to avoid the short but wicked spikes that topped it.

The shock upon landing was considerable, though she tumbled into a forward roll to absorb as much momentum as she could. Half kneeling in the baron's dew-coated grass, she gingerly tested both ankles, both knees; as often as she'd done this, she was convinced each time that she'd injured something. Only when each and every joint proved fully mobile and free of pain did she rise and take in her surroundings.

Large, flowering bushes of diverse hue decorated the property at random intervals that someone had probably thought were tasteful.

A few trees grasped gently at the stars above, while sculptures and fountains of stone dotted the estate. Even in the dark, Widdershins could see two satyrs, a naked nymph, and a urinating cherub. The entire place emitted a sickly sweet scent, as though the combination of so many flowering plants and blossoms brought out the worst in each. No wonder Doumerge always appeared faintly ill.

It all just oozed excess. Widdershins felt her mouth curl in a faint sneer at what Baron Doumerge was—what she herself had almost become, a lifetime ago.

"Olgun?" she asked, her tone again little more than a breath. "Dogs?"

A pause, an answer.

"Ah. And do you think you should maybe do something about that?"

Self-satisfied gloating.

"You already did." It wasn't a question.

Another affirmative.

Widdershins sighed. "I hope you didn't hurt them."

Olgun sent a flash of horror running through her, so strong that she felt herself shudder.

"All right, I'm sorry!" she hissed. "I know you like dogs. I know you wouldn't hurt them! I wasn't thinking!"

The god sniffed haughtily.

"Look, I said I was sorry! Let's move on already, yes? We're running out of night."

At an easy jog, flitting from shadow to shadow, Widdershins crossed the property. She passed, on the way, a large brown hunting hound wearing a spiked collar. The dog sniffed once in her direction, wrinkled its nose with a slight yelp, and ignored her.

One of these days, she thought to herself, *I'm going to ask Olgun exactly what it is that he does to them—or what it is he makes me smell like to them!*

And with no more difficulty than that, she was at the wall of the manor. Dropping to her belly, Widdershins wormed her way below the first-floor windows. It'd be embarrassing to come this far just to be discovered by some lovelorn servant staring out at the stars. Only when she'd reached a stretch of wall unbroken by glass did she return to her feet.

Each mortared spot between the bricks was a rung, the entire wall a ladder placed solely for her own convenience. In less time than it takes to tell, she was ten feet above the ground, sidling sideways toward the nearest darkened window.

She took a moment to curse the craftsmen's guilds for making glass so much cheaper in recent years—this would have been much simpler in the days of open panes or oilcloth-covered windows—before her questing fingers produced a thin length of wire from her pouch. She inserted it between the window and the pane with one hand, clinging to her perilous perch with the other. Within seconds, she felt resistance, heard the faint clack as the strip fetched up against the window latch. It required a few tries, but finally the tiny metal hook lifted from its eyelet and fell away with a tiny ping.

In a span of seconds, the wire was back in her pouch and Widdershins was inside the darkened room.

That was the good news. The bad was that she'd just come to the end of any real knowledge she possessed about the manor's layout, as she'd never found the opportunity to examine the second floor.

"Keep your eyes and ears—or whatever—open," she told Olgun in her inaudible whisper.

After listening for a full minute, ensuring that her own heartbeat was the only sound in the room, she took the tinderbox from her pouch, along with a candle stub, and struck sparks until the wick caught. Keeping her back to the window, she quickly examined the small chamber.

Between the comfortably padded chair, the heavy mahogany writing desk liberally dusted with sundry scraps of parchment, and the overburdened bookcase that skulked dejectedly against the far wall, she knew this must be Doumerge's study. Moved by a sudden sense of idle curiosity that could just as easily have come from her or her empathic ally, the thief-turned-aristocrat-turned-thief leafed hurriedly through the nearest stack of writings. It contained little of any real interest: various calculations on the worth of this product or that market; some letters of identification, presumably for servants running errands in the baron's name; and a few attempts at romantic epic poetry so teeth-gratingly, mind-numbingly, soul-shrivelingly awful that it might have doubled as a form of interrogation. With a quiet "Bleah!" of disgust, Widdershins dropped the parchment back into place and moved to the door, as though afraid that the verses might leap off the page and pursue her screaming down the hall.

Her hand was on the latch when Olgun yelped a warning. Unable to repress a startled gasp, Widdershins fell back, instinct alone keeping her soundless as a snowfall as she snuffed the light of her candle and vanished, an insubstantial phantom, into the darkened study.

Muffled footsteps trod slowly down the hallway, pausing once for a brief instant by the study. Widdershins modulated her breathing, as motionless as the statues in the garden, until the footfalls resumed and slowly faded away.

"Thanks," she whispered to her unseen guardian. "Though you didn't have to yell."

Olgun's reply was more than a little perturbed.

"Yes, I *should* have been paying more attention!" she admitted, her voice rising slightly. "I made a mistake. It happens. I've already thanked you! What more do you—what? I did *so* mean it! All right, fine! See if I thank *you* again anytime soon!" Widdershins pressed her ear to the door, making absolutely certain this time. "Condescending creep," she muttered as her gloved hands once more worked the catch. "Thinks he's so much better, just because he happens to be a god. . . ."

Still murmuring—though low enough that none but Olgun

could hear—she drifted out into the hall. She was prepared, if necessary, to search room by room until she found what she needed, but here, at least, her task proved easy. No need to hunt down Baron Doumerge's bedchamber; the prodigious snoring was more than sufficient evidence.

At least, Widdershins assumed it was snoring. Judging by the sheer volume and variety of tones, the noise could just as easily have been a cold-stricken lumberjack chopping down a copse of trees with a wild boar.

"All right," she breathed, "here's where it gets tricky." Ready to dive in any convenient direction should she be interrupted, she crept toward the bedchamber.

The door opened inward, unfortunately, meaning that she couldn't grease the hinges. The baron *probably* ordered his servants to keep them oiled—little disturbs the idle rich so much as petty annoyances—but Widdershins hated trusting to luck. Then again, what was luck, really, but divine intervention?

"Olgun? Could you take care of any creaks or squeaky hinges?"

Petulance was his only reply; well, that and the emotional equivalent of a wet raspberry.

"Olgun," she coaxed in a breathy undertone, "you're not still mad at me, are you? It was such a *little* argument. . . ."

With an obvious roll of nonexistent eyes, the god twiddled his equally nonexistent fingers at the door. Widdershins felt the tingle of Olgun's power in the air around her.

"Thank you, sweetie," she teased. "I'll rub your tummy later, all right?"

Grumble.

Widdershins lightly pressed the catch and opened the door just enough to squeeze through the gap. The sound of the baron's somnolent rumblings intensified, and the young woman experienced the sudden sensation that she was stepping into the gullet of some fantastic beast that would gobble her down as an appetizer.

As the sensation faded and the chamber steadfastly insisted on remaining a chamber, she shut the door and consciously commanded each and every muscle in her body to relax as she waited for her vision to adjust to the near darkness. Thankfully, the window faced west (can't have the baron awakened by something as inconsiderate as the dawn, can we?), from which direction there currently shone a sliver of the vanishing moon.

The room was gaudy, the living space of a man who'd never outgrown the childhood conceit that *more* is always and automatically *better*. Paintings, bejeweled weapons, and even a few small tapestries jammed the walls, resembling nothing so much as a bargain bin at a market stall. A tacky chandelier in the shape of Geurron's golden pyramid hung above the bed. The dresser sitting beneath a large silver mirror was covered in knickknacks, doodads, and diverse baubles, from gilded brushes to jewel-inlaid boxes to haphazardly scattered jewelry.

Widdershins ignored it all. Anything stolen from Doumerge Estates would be too easily traced—anything except hard currency. A man as paranoid as the Baron d'Orreille would certainly keep a strongbox of coin close at hand for emergencies. It was this, and no other, that she sought in the man's bedroom, mere moments before the first stirrings of dawn. Sure and silent, she crept from corner to corner, eyes and hands roving, examining. The baron continued to snore, obliviously if not peacefully, as his room was methodically ransacked.

Drowned out by the sound of the baron's nocturnal symphony, all but smothered by the thick quilts and comforters of the bed, the room's *other* occupant almost completely escaped even Widdershins's methodical examination. Only as the thief reached the far corner of the bed did she spot the young woman—a high-class courtesan, to judge by the clothes carefully laid out on the floor and the smeared makeup that still smudged her face—slumbering beside the noble rodent. Widdershins went statue-still, but the woman remained asleep, if not deeply so. Her eyelids twitched as dreams pressed against them from within, and every few breaths a tiny portion of her voice would escape with a slight moan.

Widdershins, whose desperation had more than once driven her to within a finger's breadth of the profession herself, during her hungriest years, had to force down a sympathetic sigh.

At least she's got access to a high class of clientele. Somehow, though, that wasn't much of a consolation. Chewing the inside of her cheek, Widdershins resumed her hunt.

It was, perhaps unsurprisingly, under the bed that Widdershins finally found her prize: a heavy mahogany box, equipped with the finest steel lock that money could buy. She knew it was the finest, because it took her two full minutes to open it. Inside, hundreds of gold marks glittered, newly captured stars, wealth enough to live on for many months.

This was, by far, the most dangerous moment of her night: transferring the hoard, or as much as she could, into the heavy black sack.

Fortunately, unlike most people who worked alone, Widdershins never worked alone. Olgun would warn her if anyone approached, or if the baron began to awaken. Furthermore, her "plunder sack" was woven of a heavy cloth, intended to at least partly muffle the inevitable clank of coins. Nevertheless, handling the cache was a slow and arduous process, one that wreaked havoc on the nerves, and Widdershins was covered in a sheen of sweat by the time she was through. The sky had grown bright enough that she could see the stirrings of dawn even through the window's western exposure. It was time, and past time, to go.

She looked up, one last glance to make sure all was well—except that it wasn't. The Baron d'Orreille remained fast asleep, but his companion had sat halfway up in bed, clutching the sheets to her naked breast, staring in terror at what, to her eyes, must have been little more than an inky blot moving through the darkened room.

Widdershins was around the bed in a silent flash, one gloved hand covering the courtesan's mouth. The woman fell back with a terrifying squeak, but otherwise made no sound at all.

Still in absolute silence, Widdershins leaned in until her lips were practically on the woman's cheek. She felt the contours of a bony face—clearly, even with clients as wealthy as the baron, the job didn't pay all *that* well.

"I'm not going to hurt you," Widdershins breathed in a voice that even a whisper would have been hard-pressed to hear. "But I need you to keep quiet." She smiled, knowing that the other couldn't possibly see the expression, hoping maybe she'd *feel* it. "Fifty gold marks. All yours, for keeping your mouth shut." She couldn't just *give* her the coins—doubtless she'd be searched, thoroughly, when the theft was discovered. But . . . "The peeing cherub statue. Look in the water right under his—uh . . ." The thief was grateful that the darkness hid her sudden blush. "Well, you know."

The woman clearly had no good cause to believe what Widdershins said. But fifty marks was more than she'd make in *months*, and so far, the thief hadn't hurt her. Widdershins hoped that would be enough to convince her.

The courtesan nodded, her face barely moving beneath Widdershins's hand. Widdershins breathed a silent gasp of relief and vanished from the bedside.

Moving with far less speed and far more care—it is simply impossible, however eloquent one might be, to convince a sack of gold to be silent, and Olgun could only muffle the sounds so much—the black-clad intruder crept back up the hall, returning to the relative safety of the study. Widdershins glanced at the window, but found herself unwilling to leave just yet. Doumerge's tawdry display of excess had *really* rubbed her the wrong way, and she felt an overwhelming need to express her displeasure.

If she was also, perhaps, angry at the reminder of what her life *could* have become, well, neither she nor her divine companion chose to acknowledge the possibility.

With Olgun impatiently tapping a nonexistent foot, Widder-shins resumed her examination of the ledgers and parchments on the desk. No need for a candle now, for the sky was light enough that she could see clearly. She was pushing this too far, leaving it too close, but by the gods (well, by one god, anyway), she wouldn't leave until she was well and truly done. And despite his impatience, she knew Olgun would have it no other way.

Snatching up a nearby quill and dipping it deeply into the inkwell on the desk, Widdershins very carefully blotted out several dozen figures and totals throughout the ledger. It would take the greedy bastard days, if not weeks, to recalculate it all. Then, flipping several days ahead in the accounting ledger, she scrawled her mes-sage across the page in a neat but hasty hand:

Thanks for the gold, my lord. I'm sure I'll enjoy it more than you would. But look on the bright side. Now you won't be tempted to go out and spend it all, having fun, when you should be at home balancing your books.

Sincerely, someone a lot richer than they used to be.

A smirk crawling its way across her face, Widdershins closed the ledger and arranged the scattered chaos atop the desk, nearly as she was able, as it had appeared when she found it. Let the baron dis-cover her little thank-you in his own good time.

"Now," she told Olgun, stepping to the window and glancing outward, "the only issue is getting away from here, yes?" She scowled at the rising sun. "I don't suppose you could whip up some clouds, or maybe even a nice morning mist, could you?" she inquired doubtfully. Olgun scoffed.

"All right. Can you at least take a little of the weight off me?" She glanced meaningfully down at the sack full of gold marks.

The bag grew slightly but noticeably lighter.

"That's just fine. It won't need to be long." She opened the pane, stretched down as far as she could, and allowed her bag to fall the remaining few feet to the grass. She followed quickly after, scuttling down the side of the house. Glancing around warily to ensure that nobody was up early and working in the garden, she hefted the sack over her shoulder and then did the only thing she could.

It was one of the primary rules of thievery. When hiding, sneaking, and trickery are all out, the correct answer is "run like hell."

Whether some god other than Olgun watched over her that morning or whether she simply ran through a free-floating pocket of good luck, she made it across the Doumerge Estates without being spotted. (She even managed to make a quick detour and complete her promised delivery to the cherub fountain, despite Olgun's objections.) Then she was at the outer wall, leaped without slowing—again boosted by unseen hands—and vanished into the nearby alleys.

✳

Birds, squirrels, and other disgustingly pastoral creatures sang and chirped their greetings to the rising sun. The streets of Davillon's marketplace filled rapidly: merchants setting up shop, patrons looking for a good deal while the market remained uncrowded and the proprietors remained in a good mood. The trickles of humanity grew, first into streams, then veritable rivers. Flowing through the streets that were the veins and arteries of the town, these were the lifeblood of Davillon.

Above the growing throng at the market's edge, one woman rolled over in bed to face the window, blinking blearily against the sunlight. She'd taken to her bed only a few hours before, and had no intention of rising with the dawn. With a muffled curse, she slammed the shutters and drifted back to sleep, carried into dreams by the low tones of the bustling market.

She woke again around noon, gave some brief thought to staying in bed a while longer—she never opened the tavern more than four hours before sunset, anyway—but decided, reluctantly, that the place needed a good cleaning after last night. Grumbling under her breath, she rose to her feet, shivering as her flimsy shift failed utterly to keep the chill autumn air at bay.

Some hours later, washed, dressed, and breakfasted, she emerged into the sweeping tides of market-goers and allowed them to carry her a few doors down the street to her destination.

To the casual observer, Genevieve Marguilles was stunning. Luxuriant blonde tresses, the sort that most noblewomen tried (in vain) to achieve with expensive wigs, cascaded down her shoulders. Her eyes were a gleaming brown, golden in the right light; her features soft; her figure the envy of women ten years her junior. She wore today a long, burgundy skirt beneath a smoke-gray tunic and a snug bodice that emphasized attributes that, on her, didn't really require additional emphasis.

Yes, Genevieve was beautiful. And had that been the end of it, she'd already be twelve or fourteen years married to some aristocratic fop chosen for his political connections by her father.

But that *wasn't* the end of it. Her gait was uneven, leaning heavily leftward as she walked. From birth, her left leg had twisted slightly inward, bending awkwardly at the knee, and though the details of her deformity were hidden by the long, flowing skirts she favored, she could not hide its effect on her stride. It was something to which she'd long since grown accustomed, but for Gurrerre Marguilles, patriarch of the House Marguilles—and, not incidentally, her father—it was the touch of death for any political marriage. To offer an "imperfect" child to the scion of a noble house would have been an insult.

Sensing that she wasn't wanted (not that the proud Gurrerre had tried to hide the fact), Genevieve spent her childhood and teenage years associating with a "lower" class of people. She made many friends among the commoners of Davillon, and while it took some time to grow accustomed to a life where not everything was provided at whim, she ultimately persevered. She'd struck out on her own, taking with her enough of her family's funds to open her tavern. Her father didn't approve of his daughter working among the lower classes, and certainly wasn't happy with her chosen vocation, but neither could it be said that the old man was sorry to see her depart. He made the occasional attempt, for form's sake, to coax her back into the fold, and otherwise they happily left one another alone.

Today, Genevieve found herself in a jovial mood, no doubt due to the extra sleep in which she'd indulged. Waving cheerily at several market regulars, she climbed the five shallow steps to the door of the Flippant Witch. It was a squat building, fairly plain, nothing more than a large common room, a small storeroom, three tiny private parlors, and a kitchen. It boasted no decoration, save for a tiny blue stone with a white cross: the symbol of Banin, the Marguilles' household deity and one of the few portions of her old life Genevieve hadn't abandoned. But despite its modesty, it was a popular spot for those who couldn't afford the "prestigious" drinking establishments. Her prices were reasonable, the food and drink tasty, the staff friendly.

To Genevieve, it was more than her tavern. More so than the house in which she'd grown up, more so than the small cluster of rooms in which she slept, the Flippant Witch was home.

Which was why, when she stepped into the darkened taproom and spotted a trio of men sitting around the nearest table, her initial reaction was one of anger, rather than fear.

"Who the hell are you?" she demanded angrily, one hand darting to the steel stiletto tucked in her bodice. "How did you get in here?"

All three stood, largely concealed by the ambient shadow, and the biggest stepped toward her. Despite herself, Genevieve retreated until her back struck the wall. She thought briefly of making a run for freedom, but she knew the intruder could easily catch her before she managed to open the door.

"What—what do you want?" she asked, voice shaking. "I don't have much money here. We—we haven't opened for business. If—"

"Shut up." His voice was as deep and unfriendly as she'd expected. "We don't want your money. And," he added as Genevieve gasped and went deathly pale, "we don't particularly want to hurt you." He stepped nearer still, pressing the frightened proprietor tightly against the wall. She was near enough, now, to strike with her small weapon, but she knew better than to try. "All we want," he continued, "is for you to help us out with something. After that, we'll leave you alone."

"What do you want?" she asked again, staring up at this mountain in man's clothing.

"Just to find someone we hear is a frequent visitor to your lovely tavern. And it *is* a lovely tavern, by the way. Do you know a young woman who goes by the name Widdershins?"

✸

Hours later, the sun setting at her back, Widdershins wandered the crowded boulevard, whistling a jaunty tune. She wore a tunic of verdant green and earth-brown breeches topped by a green-trimmed black vest, a combination that made her look vaguely like an ambulatory shrubbery. Her chestnut hair hung in a loose tail, her rapier swung freely at her side (the intricate silver basket now reattached), and her coin purse overflowed with the smallest portion of the baron's liberated gold. All in all, the last couple of days had been magnificent, and she was determined to share her good cheer.

And, Olgun aside, the thief possessed only one close friend in Davillon with whom she might share it.

Widdershins had gone directly home after her escape from the Doumerge Estates, detouring just long enough to retrieve her pack from the filthy alley. The following day—or what remained of it after a well-earned slumber—she'd spent in circumspect travel to several bolt-holes scattered throughout the city, secreting a portion of her gains in each.

Now she fully intended to enjoy a moderate allotment of her newfound wealth. And so, ignoring the aggravated glares of passers-by who would now have the melody she was whistling stuck in their heads, she sauntered across the market, up the shallow stairs, and through the front door of the Flippant Witch.

A cheerful fire crackled in the imposing stone hearth. Lanterns hung at irregular intervals, lighting a common room that was crammed near capacity with thirsty market-goers and city-dwellers. The noise level was not much below that of the baron's party two nights past, but it was friendlier, somehow less abrasive.

Several regulars called or waved gaily as she entered, and she happily waved back, teeth bared in a wide grin—a grin that grew even wider as Robin sidled up to her with a shy smile of her own. The slender serving girl—a few years younger than Widdershins herself, with short-cropped black hair and drab wardrobe—was often mistaken for a boy at first glance. It was an effect she cultivated deliberately, due to some truly unpleasant experiences about which she rarely spoke.

The Flippant Witch, Widdershins noted, attracted more than its share of hard-luck cases.

"The usual, Shins?" Robin asked softly.

"Not tonight, kiddo," Widdershins laughed, ruffling Robin's hair. "Scyllian red, oldest you've got. I want to celebrate."

"Obviously," the girl gasped, shaking her head. "Shins, I can't serve anything that expensive without Genevieve's permission, you know that."

"Fine with me. Where is she, anyway? I wanted to talk to her tonight. I—"

They were interrupted by a raucous call from a nearby table whose inhabitants rather loudly demanded to know where their ales were.

"Gotta go," Robin apologized, sounding not at all contrite. "Genevieve's working the bar tonight. I'm sure she'd love to talk to you." With another smile, the girl slipped through the crowded tables, assuring the impatient patrons that she'd be right with them, and could they just give her one more moment. . . .

Still smiling, Widdershins amiably shoved through the intervening space, working her way toward the heavy oaken bar. Other than the fact that it was missing the compulsory large mirror—that would've been far too expensive, especially given the all-too-real danger of it being shattered by flying tableware during some of the Witch's wilder nights—it perfectly fit the popular image of the "typical tavern." On the left rose several hefty kegs of ale and beer; on the right, rack upon rack of bottled spirits. Between them stood the door to the storeroom. The kitchen was located away from the bar itself, along the left wall. The succulent aroma of roasting venison wafted forth, a benediction from various culinary gods.

And standing in the midst of it all, her face a mask of worry, stood Genevieve Marguilles, owner, proprietor, and one of Widdershins's very few friends.

"Genevieve!" the thief called happily, bellying up to the bar. "I've got to tell you about the other night! You won't believe . . ."

Her voice petered out, the last trickle of a drought-dried stream, and the grin fell from her lips at the look on her friend's face.

"Genevieve? What's wrong?"

Even as the golden-haired innkeep drew breath to speak, a hulking form rose from the nearest table, an impending avalanche looming ever nearer. Clutching tightly at her rapier, Widdershins turned about, and the last of her good cheer drained away.

In a voice that perfectly matched a body far taller and far broader of shoulder than any human should be, the colossus spoke. "Hello, dear Widdershins. If you think you can spare us a span from your hectic schedule, the Finders' Guild would really like a word with you."

CHAPTER THREE

SIX YEARS AGO:

In the hustle and bustle of the bazaar, nobody would even have noticed the girl as she passed between the rough-brick walls of the various shops, or the flimsy wooden panels of the far more temporary and far more numerous vendors. She looked like any other market-goer, if perhaps younger than most. Her hair was tied back out of her face, without any regard for the fashion of the day. Her tunic and gown, although faded by age and use from their former canary yellow and light lavender, were clean and well cared for. A heavy satchel hung at her side, and she all but skipped through the throng—just another low-class shopper, or perhaps the servant of a House fallen on hard times.

In point of fact, Adrienne Satti was neither. She had no regular home, be it house or House. Her face was clean because she'd scrubbed it so in a public fountain the night before, and her garments were clean because they'd been someone *else's* garments until that morning when they "walked" off a clothesline.

Adrienne moved through the market, and slowly her satchel started to accumulate various goods, a smattering of pastries, and the occasional coin purse lifted from an oblivious passerby.

All of which made it a decent day, but not a *good* one. She eyed the shops as she passed them by, hoping to see a till, or perhaps a heavier purse, left unattended at just the right moment.

For long hours, until her feet ached and her face gleamed with sweat even in the day's modest warmth, she prowled the shops, watching for an opportunity that never arose. A great many members and servants of the aristocracy were out today—Adrienne recognized more than a few House crests—but there never seemed to be enough separation between their eyes and their purses to be worth the risk.

And then, just as she thought about calling it a day and trying to find a halfway clean flop with the money she had, she saw them entering a leatherworker's shop. The elder fellow boasted a dignified, regal demeanor, exuding that pride which came only with fantastic wealth. Other than a thin tract of gray that ran across the back of his head, he was bald as a snake's belly. His features were sharp, hawkish, especially the beak he called a nose. His tunic was wine purple and ruffled, his half cape of midnight blue, his trousers a rich red. It looked as though a bruise had thrown up on him, but then *most* of the aristocracy, in Adrienne's experience, dressed as though they'd been painted in watercolors by a blind artist.

His servant was rather less remarkable: hair, tunic, hose, boots, belt, cloak all dull, muted browns and grays. He wore a goatee and a thin mustache, and his hair dangled in a single tail. At his left hung a suede pouch, most probably his employer's funds for the day's purchases; at his right, an old-fashioned cut-and-thrust sword, broader than a modern rapier. Over his left shoulder, he carried a gape-mouthed blunderbuss—not the most accurate of weapons, but brutal enough to shred any man unlucky enough to be on the business end when it discharged.

But what attracted Adrienne's attention was not the aristocrat's fruit-hued outfit, nor even the weighty purse toted by his well-armed porter. No, it was the noble's own weapon: a magnificent rapier, swinging from his left hip. The basket was convoluted, ornate, yet excellent protection against an enemy's thrust. The young pickpocket had seen fancy weapons, and more than her share of functional ones, but rarely had she seen the two combined with such a perfect elegance. Even allowing for the meager percentages offered by the average street-level fence, that rapier could fetch enough coin to keep Adrienne in comfort for months!

Leaning against a cart across the street (and ignoring the irritated glower of the vendor), Adrienne removed a shoe and rubbed at her sore feet, surreptitiously watching the shop. Within, the peacock and his servant engaged in an animated discussion with the proprietor, who lifted a long strip of leather from the rack behind him, holding it up for inspection. The elder aristocrat nodded once and removed his own belt, laying it carefully upon a small wooden bench beside him.

Adrienne froze, slack-jawed. Why didn't the man just *hand* the rapier to the nearest thief?!

Not that she was about to complain; gift horses, mouths, and all that. With nervous alacrity, Adrienne darted inside, keeping to the racks of uncut hides, invisible among the shadows and folds of leather. She could hear the conversation now: talk of the pedigree of the animal from which the leather was cut, negotiations over price. The thief crept nearer still, scarcely daring to breathe. She saw, glinting dully on the ring finger of the aristocrat's right hand, a signet of some sort. Diminutive as it was, the carving was of such exquisite quality that she could clearly identify the crest it bore: the head of a lion wearing a domino mask, the sort held on a small baton and so frequently exhibited at the aristocracy's masquerade balls.

And then her hand brushed against the smooth-worn surface of the man's discarded belt. Her fingers closed tightly, the edge of the leather biting slightly into her skin. Carefully, she drew it back, silently, silently . . .

Loud as a church bell at vespers, the basket of the rapier rang against the edge of the bench.

All conversation ceased, and three pairs of startled eyes swiveled toward Adrienne. With a muttered curse, she was out the door, thin legs pumping, the belt—along with the traitorous rapier—dangling from her right fist, streaming behind her like a pennant as she tore through the market.

A roar of outrage shook the air behind her, pursuing her across

the square on demonic wings; she heard it clearly, even above the
rumble of the crowd. Glancing over her shoulder, she saw the
nobleman's servant burst from the shop, his employer and the proprietor following behind. In a smooth, practiced motion, the man
slung the blunderbuss off his shoulder, bringing it up, muzzle
gaping wide, a ravenous beast.

And the rapier, perhaps determined that it not be sullied by a
petty street-thief, twisted as it swung, jutting suddenly between her
ankles.

With a terrible clamor, Adrienne fell, crying out as though she'd
already been shot. A small fruit vendor's cart loomed before her as
she tumbled, all but begging her to hit it. She obliged, plowing into
it headfirst, knocking it clear over and landing in a fruit-covered
heap amidst the splintered wreckage. Hands and knees stung where
rough cobblestones and splintered wood had peeled away layers of
skin, and a shallow gash across her forehead had already bled enough
to gum her left eye shut.

It was, by and large, neither the most graceful nor the most suc-
cessful escape she'd ever attempted.

Painfully, feeling that her entire body had become a single enormous bruise, Adrienne began to climb unsteadily to her feet, only to
freeze once more, half-crouched, at the sight confronting her.

Everyone between her and the leather-goods shop had cleared to
one side or the other, opening a corridor for her pursuers. The servant stood in the center of the street, blunderbuss aimed in stone-
steady hands. Adrienne found herself unable to swallow, to blink,
even to breathe as she saw the tiny fuse shrinking down to nothing.
It sparked, sparked once more, then vanished as it burned down to
the weapon's reservoir. Even from this distance, Adrienne heard the
muffled *whumph* of the black powder igniting.

"Claude, stop!" A fraction of a second before the weapon discharged, the old aristocrat appeared beside his servant and slapped
the barrel upward.

A crack of thunder reverberated across the massive courtyard, eliciting shrieks from the watching throng. The ugly lead pellets passed several feet above their intended target and slammed with a loud crunch into the nearest wall, where they sent a puff of powder and several slivers of stone raining into the street.

Adrienne stared, shocked to the depths of her soul, at the nobleman she had just robbed—the nobleman who had just saved her life from his own man. For a brief instant, their gazes met, hers frightened, bewildered, unaccountably grateful; his own unreadable.

And then she was gone into the nearest alley, aches and pains forgotten, leaving the chaos and confusion far behind.

CHAPTER FOUR

NOW:

It was not a pleasant place, this chamber. The walls, all *five* of them, were a dull ebon stone, set with equally dark mortar. The floor and ceiling, both black marble, were smooth and unbroken. The room possessed only a single door, and that substantial portal—constructed of a heavy, darkened wood—led to a small antechamber. An ingenious system of gears and pulleys prevented the outer door of that tiny vestibule from opening unless the inner door was firmly shut, and vice versa. Thus protected, and completely windowless, the shadowy inner chamber had never been exposed to the searing touch of day.

Really, *really* black, basically.

Standing within this room, lit only by a pair of torches that hung opposite the door, a visitor could truly believe he stood on the brink of eternity, staring into the primordial darkness that skulked beyond the borders of creation.

Between those flickering brands lurked the room's only other feature. Embossed into the otherwise blank wall were the head and torso of what, in the impotent lighting, might be mistaken for a man. The shoulders and arms were human in every particular, if perhaps too heavily muscled. The head was the proper shape, topped by an unruly mop of hair that billowed behind, carved into the wall with exquisite detail.

All of which was designed eventually to direct the viewer's attention to the figure's face.

The entity's features were hideous, terrifying as the fading mem-

ories of a recent nightmare, and equally as bewildering. Oh, this was
not the mask of some horrific monster; no fangs, no fur, no scales.
No, the face was human, beautiful even. It was also utterly devoid of
mortal emotion. Surely this was the bust of some madman, a being
incapable of experiencing, or even understanding, the urges, desires,
hates, and fears that should have been his birthright. It was the face
of pure need, pure hunger, an evil that sprung not from some cause,
nor any great malevolence, but pure predatory instinct. Beast it was,
wolf or serpent or lion, scarcely concealed behind a mask of man.

Before the great idol waited two figures. The first was Roubet,
his eyes wide with a pungent blend of fear and greed. They darted
between the graven image and the other man, a man clad in robes of
midnight blue that almost, but not quite, blended with the surrounding darkness. This was a man who had paid Roubet well, since
before he was forced from the Guard; a man he would address by no
name or title other than "Apostle."

Henri Roubet refused to admit, even to himself, that he knew
the Apostle's other name, for fear of how that knowledge would be
rewarded.

"You're certain they're coming?" the Apostle asked, glancing
irritably at the fane's outer door.

The soldier and spy neither sighed aloud nor rolled his eyes,
though he was tempted to do both at this third or fourth repetition
of the question. "I'm certain, Holiness. They'll be here. I imagine
they just need—"

A dull gong reverberated through the black walls, and the room
began to rumble with the sound of grinding gears.

"—a bit more time," Roubet concluded as the inner door slid
aside.

There were six of them, of varying heights, varying demeanors.
This one wore heavy leathers, stained dark and well creased; that one
dressed in the bright and jarring plumage of the Davillon aristocracy, down to the razor-sharp rapier at his side; and a third was

garbed entirely in black, nigh invisible against the ebon backdrop of the chamber.

They did, however, share a profession in common. And they were all quite good at it.

"Has Roubet explained why you're here?" the Apostle demanded without preamble.

"I'm willing to take a stab at it," the leather-clad man replied. His voice was deep, gravelly, thanks to the jagged scar that ran across his neck. "I'm guessing you want someone killed."

"If I want comedy," their host rejoined, "I'll hire a jester. Of *course* I want somebody killed, you blithering imbecile!"

The leather-clad killer shrugged. "Ask a stupid question—"

The nobleman—or the assassin garbed as one—stepped forward, cutting off his companion. "It's been some time since you've asked us to meet with you personally. And while your errant Guardsman was somewhat terse, I could hear the excitement in his voice. I can only assume you've located Adrienne Satti."

"Very good, Jean Luc. I'm glad to see there's at least *one* brain amongst you." To the group at large, he continued, "Indeed, I have found our wayward cultist—something, I must remind you, none of you has managed in *two years*." He met their eyes, reminding them one by one of his displeasure; and one by one, these hardened assassins turned away. "And indeed, I'll be calling on your talents to assist me with her final disposition. But for now, all I want you to do is locate her alias—Roubet will fill you in—so that you can find her when necessary. She is *not* your current target. I have an entirely other commission in mind for you."

A smattering of confused murmurs arose from the group. The chamber's bizarre acoustics bounced them back as a veritable hissing chorus.

"I'm sure, by now," the Apostle continued, rather than awaiting the obvious question, "that each of you has heard of the dignitary soon to grace our fair city with his presence?"

The room echoed again, not with puzzled whispers but a series of stunned gasps.

"I see that you have." The Apostle smiled, a gleam of white amidst the unrelenting black. "Let me tell you what I require. . . ."

✸

The door slammed behind her with an awful ring of finality, the snapping trapdoor of a gallows. The private rooms of the Flippant Witch were plain, simple: six chairs and a single table in each, and nothing more. Nonchalant, or at least trying hard to appear that way, Widdershins confronted the trio who'd shepherded her in here. A jaunty smile fixed on her face as though glued to her jaw, she hopped up to sit on the table, her legs crossed demurely and dangling over the edge.

"Brock," she greeted the hulking boulder of a man.

"I'm so pleased you remember me, Widdershins," he rumbled, a cruel little grin playing at the corners of his mouth.

"What? No, actually, I didn't. I just have a habit of cursing in High Chicken when I'm startled. Brock! *Brock*-brock-brock-brock-brock-brock! Bu-*caw*!" She blinked coyly. "See? Like that."

The grin slid from Brock's face, leaving a faint trail, and his teeth ground against one another. "Oh, you're *funny*," he growled.

"I am? Really? I'm so glad you told me. Based on your expressions, I'd never have guessed that—that—"

Her voice broke into a nervous gulp as the glowering twist to Brock's visage shifted even farther down the spectrum from "unamused" toward "homicidal." Widdershins decided that, just maybe, Brock-baiting was not the healthiest pastime to engage in.

With his short-cropped dark hair and rock-solid jawline, Brock might even have been deemed handsome, if someone of a far gentler persuasion had resided behind his face. Though a member in good standing of the Davillon Finders' Guild, Brock wasn't actually a thief. He was, rather, one of the guild's "negotiators"—or, in more mundane terms, a leg-breaker. He was no less a blunt object than the weapon he favored.

He stepped nearer the table, his tread shaking the floorboards into spitting tiny puffs of dust. Widdershins's eyes, of their own accord, flickered to the enormous hammer at his side.

In her agitation, and in spite of her determination not to taunt the man any further, she blurted, "Gee, Brock, I didn't know you were a blacksmith. What—what were you planning to forge with that?" She chuckled nervously, and wished now she hadn't sat atop the table. Her position offered little room to retreat. "You know, when they talk about members of the Finders' Guild 'forging' things, that's not really what they mean. See, most people in our line of work prefer pen and ink. It's really a lot more—"

"Shut. The hell. Up."

She did just that, leaning back ever farther as Brock loomed nearer, until it seemed that she might wind up lying flat on her back in order to meet his gaze. He finally stopped, however, no more than a foot away.

"You annoy me," he told her succinctly. "That's never a wise idea."

"It's a habit," she retorted instinctively. "What do you want with me?"

"What do I usually want from people, Widdershins? What they owe the guild. And you, girl, are a little behind."

His fellow thugs smirked at the entendre.

Widdershins scowled despite herself. Lisette again—it had to be. Nobody else would be riding her yet about a job she'd just completed *yesterday*.

He could, she supposed, have been speaking of other, older jobs, but she'd never held back on those. Well, not much; *everyone* held out a *little*. . . .

"I don't know what you're talking about!" she insisted, indignant. The others chuckled once more, having heard it a thousand times from a thousand mouths. Brock shook his head. "Of course you haven't," he said snidely. "This is all a big mistake."

"Well, yes, it is! And besides," she added quickly as his hand settled on the heavy mallet, "if you kill me, the guild never gets what I *supposedly* owe them! They'd be unhappy with you for that, yes?"

"I'm not supposed to kill you," Brock told her, his breath a caustic cloud mere inches from her face. "I'm not," he added, sounding vaguely put out by the whole thing, "even supposed to break any bones. I'm just supposed to make sure that you remember our conversation." He smiled an uneven, gap-toothed smile as his hammer slid loose with a slimy hiss. "I think you'll remember."

"Oh, absolutely," she told him, forcing a laugh through a dry mouth. "Never forget a word of it. You've set me straight, Brock. No sense in wasting any more time on me!"

"This will go easier," he told her, hefting the mallet, "if you don't fight."

"Probably," she agreed, slamming her shins with crushing force up between Brock's legs and into one of his few tender spots. "But 'easy' is *boring*." She smiled at the shocked expressions of the other enforcers, even as their boss slid to the floor with an agonized whimper. "Wouldn't you agree, boys?"

They needed only seconds to shake off their stupor, to advance on the tiny thief, snarls on their faces and blades in their fists. But in those precious moments of confusion, Widdershins rolled backward, rising to her feet in the center of the table, rapier in hand. The wood creaked beneath her weight, shifted precariously, but held. The blade carved tiny circles in the air as she waited, watching, as the thugs fanned out to flank the table.

Widdershins had time for precisely two thoughts. The first was a brief prayer of thanks for Genevieve's high ceilings; the second a tense whispered instruction to Olgun to "Watch my back!" And then there was no more time for thought at all.

The first enforcer, a scar-faced man with a scraggly blond beard and matching yellow teeth, lunged across the table's edge, attempting to cut Widdershins's ankles out from under her with a wickedly curved dagger. It was, at their respective heights and angles, an impossible parry. The sensible move would have been for Widdershins to step back out of reach.

Which, of course, would have put her squarely in line for a similar attack from the man's companion, a smaller, rat-faced fellow with pockmarked skin. And it would have worked, if Olgun hadn't been bellowing a warning in Widdershins's mind. She indeed stepped backward, but instantly kicked out behind her with her other leg. The thug's vision filled with a blur of soft black leather, and by the time he'd realized that what he saw was the business end of a boot, it had already spread his nose across his left cheek with an unfortunate snap.

The bearded man, having brilliantly reached the conclusion that things weren't going as planned, hurled himself up onto the table, rising in a knife-fighter's crouch. Widdershins, stooping slightly herself, circled warily. She stepped right and he moved to follow, neither looking away, neither daring to blink. Step, follow. Step, follow. Step . . . Widdershins could barely keep from grinning. Gods, but the man was a nitwit! Follow . . . The bruiser scowled, uncertain why this impudent bitch was smirking at him. Step, follow.

With a very brief cry and a dull thump, he stepped clean off the table to land, seat first, on the unforgiving floor.

Laughing openly now, Widdershins crossed the wood and delivered a sharp, swift kick to the man's temple. He collapsed next to his bloody-faced companion like a sack of very ugly grain.

"Well," Widdershins said snidely to the room at large, "I think you boys have accomplished your mission here. I guarantee you, this is an evening I'll remember for a very long *eeeep!*"

That bit of extemporaneous grammar was the result of Brock surging abruptly to his feet, red faced and roaring like a goosed tiger. His hammer slammed down, a thunderbolt hurled from the heavens, directed not at Widdershins but at the table. Wood splintered, the entire surface tilted sharply, and Widdershins, with a brief squeak, was on her back and sliding.

She found herself fetched up in a twisted heap at Brock's feet, rapier lying uselessly just beyond her grasp. A sick feeling roiling inside her gut, as though she'd swallowed a live and very frisky eel, Widdershins pushed the hair from her face, blinked the dust from her eyes, and peered up with a wan smile.

"Brock? You're a reasonable man, yes? I know that we can come to some sort of understanding if—Brock, your orders! You're not supposed to kill me, remember?"

Apparently, he did not remember. With an inarticulate bellow, he raised his hammer high, fully intending to pulp the young woman's skull between the weapon and the floor.

Widdershins kicked him in the groin again.

Brock couldn't have frozen any more utterly had he gazed lovingly into the face of a gorgon. For interminable seconds the tableau held: the massive enforcer standing above her, immobile as the earth itself; Widdershins, foot still buried someplace unpleasant, equally motionless. And then the air in Brock's lungs joyously escaped to freedom with a sudden *whoosh*. His pupils actually crossed, his grip went slack, and . . . well, Widdershins didn't see what else, since she had to scramble madly to remove her face from the path of the hammer that now tumbled from nerveless fingers. It hit hard, splintering the wood beside her ear and ripping several strands of hair from her head.

When Brock followed his weapon to the floor a moment later, she was forced to scuttle aside once more, this time to avoid being crushed by three-hundred-some-odd pounds of thug.

Battered and dust-caked, Widdershins bent to retrieve her rapier, clucking her tongue at the mess they'd made of Genevieve's furniture, and marched haughtily from the room. She felt a faint glimmer of satisfaction from Olgun.

"Oh, please. Like you helped." She frowned at his indignant protest. "Yes, you warned me of the guy behind me. Well, thank you *so* much. You couldn't maybe have actually *done* something about one of them? I almost got my head turned into so much carpeting."

Genevieve was on her in a flash, slowed only marginally by her bad leg. "Gods, Shins, are you all right?"

Widdershins probably would have replied, but her friend's violent embrace was only marginally looser than that of a hungry boa constrictor. Genevieve failed to notice the faint bulging around the thief's eyes.

"I'm so sorry!" the barkeep sobbed over and over. "Gods, I'm so sorry."

"Gen—" Widdershins finally managed to croak. "Air . . ."

"Oh!" Flushing an embarrassed crimson, Genevieve loosened her death grip and stepped back. Widdershins gasped in what might have been gratitude.

The other patrons of the Flippant Witch, she noticed, were staring at them with a fascinating mixture of expressions, and Widdershins decided that this probably wasn't a conversation to have in public, or even anywhere vaguely public-adjacent.

"Robin!" she shouted (after sucking in a few more deep breaths), summoning the small serving girl to her side.

"Is she all right?" Robin asked with a concerned glance at her employer.

Great, Widdershins grumbled silently. *I'm the one who almost got pulped into a pastry, and the brat wants to know if* Genevieve's *all right.* "She'll be fine, Robin. We just need to talk for a few minutes. Can you handle being in charge out here for a little while?"

"Oh, sure. I've run an entire shift before. But you tell me if you need anything." She looked up at Widdershins, expression iron-hard and insistent. The thief couldn't help but laugh.

"I'll do that," she chuckled, again tousling the girl's hair. Then, taking Genevieve by the shoulders, she led her disconsolate friend toward another of the private rooms, snagging a decanter of wine and a goblet from the bar as they passed.

"Did they hurt you?" Widdershins asked softly as they neared the door.

"What? Oh, no, not . . . not at all." Genevieve's eyes clouded again, and she sniffled loudly. "They just . . . they wanted to know when you'd be here next. I didn't want to tell them anything, Shins, I swear to Banin I didn't! But—"

"Hush, Gen. It's all right. I understand." She did, too. Brock was frightening enough to Widdershins, accustomed as she was to the sorts of people with whom she shared Davillon's shadows. For someone like Genevieve Marguilles, he'd be downright terrifying.

There was, however, one little detail she needed to know.

"Gen," she asked, voice calm, "you didn't tell them . . . that is, *about* me, did you?"

"Tell . . ." For an instant, her mouth quirked in puzzlement, and then her face fell. "No, of course not! Gods, I'd never—"

"I know," Widdershins assured her. "I just had to ask."

Genevieve, so far as Adrienne knew, was the only other human being alive who knew that Widdershins had once been Adrienne Satti. If she were ever identified and arrested, Widdershins knew she couldn't expect anything resembling a fair trial, or even a clean execution. When it came to vindictiveness, the aristocracy could have taught the Finders' Guild a thing or two.

But with that unpleasant possibility thankfully out of the way, there was nothing remaining but to comfort her traumatized friend as best she could.

When Widdershins released her hold on Genevieve's shoulders to shove open the narrow door, she discovered that their so-called private room was already occupied.

A short but impishly handsome fellow sat smugly in the farthest chair, his booted feet propped up on the edge of the table. The twinkle in his azure eyes vaguely belied the frown of concern that twisted his lips and jet-black mustache.

Genevieve, already as jittery as a wine-addled monkey, loosed a shrill cry. Widdershins merely put a comforting hand once more around her friend's shoulder and scowled at the intruder.

"What in the name of Khuriel's left shoe are you doing here, Renard?"

Renard Lambert rose to his full unimpressive five-foot-seven and bowed extravagantly. He wore today a long tunic of the finest fabrics, constructed in panels of white and sapphire blue, and trimmed in gold embroidery. His boots boasted bright buckles—and, Widdershins knew from experience, several hidden daggers—and he sported a deep purple half cape and a white flocked hat with an ostrich plume.

"Do the gods even *wear* shoes, dear Widdershins?" he asked her.

"If you don't tell me why you're here, and why you felt it necessary to frighten my friend half to death, you're going to be *eating* your *own* shoes. So spit it out!"

With a magnanimous gesture, the finery-bedecked man motioned for them to come in. *As though we needed his invitation.*

"It's all right, Gen," she said softly to her pallid friend, steering her gently through the doorway. "He's harmless." She cast a sideways glance at the smiling popinjay. "More or less.

"Renard," she continued, once she'd firmly shut the door behind them, "this is Genevieve Marguilles, the owner of this tavern and, therefore, your *host*. Genevieve, Renard Lambert, a friend—acquaintance—of mine, and an incorrigible thief. Keep an eye on your silverware, your coin purse, and possibly your hair. He's almost as good as he thinks he is."

"You wound me, Widdershins," Renard complained. "As you say, we are guests in this dear lady's establishment. I never steal from a host, Mademoiselle Marguilles. Bad for the social standing."

"Thief?" Genevieve tensed, as though she would bolt from the room. Widdershins passed her a goblet of wine, which the innkeep drained in one long swallow. "Is . . . ," she started, faltered, choking shallowly on her drink. "Is it really a good idea to be talking to him? I mean, after . . ."

Renard's smile faded. "I am indeed of the guild, Mademoiselle, but I can assure you that I strongly disagree with some small number of their more draconian policies—at least where my friends are concerned. Neither of you has aught to fear from me."

"That's true enough," Widdershins agreed blandly, refilling Genevieve's drink. "Since he knows I'd kill him three times if he tried anything." Then, despite herself, she grinned at the injured look on his face.

"Actually," she grudgingly acknowledged, "Renard's always done right by me. He was my assigned trainer when I joined the guild. Helped me assimilate, showed me the ropes."

"Since otherwise you were liable to get yourself hanged from one of them." Renard smiled.

"And he's got a serious hate for certain people who hate me, so I guess that puts him on my side. Whether I want him or not," she couldn't help but add.

Renard, classy and urbane Renard, stuck his tongue out at her.

"All of which," she concluded, "has taken us kind of away from the point. Which was, why *were* you skulking about in here?"

"I," Renard sniffed, "do not skulk. I sneak. I prowl. I have even, upon occasion and at need, been known to lurk. But I have never once—"

"—managed to keep silent for two minutes straight," Widdershins interrupted. "Would you shut up and answer the question?"

"Make up your mind. Which one?"

"Renard . . ."

"All right," he said, taking a seat at the table. "The truth is, I witnessed you guiding our lovely host over in this direction, and I snuck in before you got here. I need to talk to you, Widdershins, and I'd rather not have anyone else know of it."

"You snuck through my tavern?" Genevieve exclaimed, disbelief pushing her lingering fear to one side. "A tavern full of people? Dressed like *that*?!"

Renard smiled affably. "Indeed I did, my dear. As Widdershins has already so graciously testified, I am quite nearly as good as I think I am." His tone finally came over completely serious. "Widdershins, are you hurt?"

"A little banged up, but nothing serious. Brock and his cronies got the worst of it."

"Oooh, that's not good. He holds a grudge." Renard sighed. "Well, better that than the alternative, I suppose."

"Renard, *please* get to the point. Why is the guild angry at me?"

Another sigh. "I think we both know who ordered the attack on you, don't we, my dear?"

Widdershins nodded, but said nothing. It wouldn't do to mention names in front of an outsider, not even one she trusted.

But . . .

"Even she'd need an excuse, Renard. She doesn't have the authority to just decide to take out a member." *Not yet, anyway.*

"No, she doesn't. But the guild *is* cracking down on anyone who, um, *forgets* to pay their dues in full. They're gathering up all outstanding funds, since the plan is to suspend all major operations for the duration of the visit. Avoid any unpleasant attention, and all that."

Widdershins paused in the act of reaching for the decanter. "Visit? What visit?"

"You haven't heard?" Renard boggled, and even Genevieve stared in puzzlement. "You hang out in a tavern, you frequent the homes of the rich and powerful, and you haven't heard?"

"So I don't pay attention to the small talk. What are you on about?"

"Shins," Genevieve told her, "William de Laurent is coming to Davillon."

Widdershins's eyes looked as though they might pop from their sockets and career across the table like billiard balls. William de Laurent, archbishop of Chevareaux, was the greatest High Church official west of the Blackridge Mountains, inferior only to the twelve cardinals and the prelate himself. If he was coming here, important affairs of church and state were quite clearly afoot. Possibly even the appointment of a new bishop to Davillon, a position that had sat unoccupied since Bishop Fontaine had died of a fever a couple of years before.

All right, so that would obviously be important to the city, the aristocracy, and the devout masses. But, "Why does the *Finders' Guild* give a fig about that?"

"Because," Renard said, idly stroking his whiskers with a well-manicured finger, "if anything untoward happens during His Eminence's visit, the duchess and the Guard will come down on us so hard they'll be picking bits of us out from between the cracks in the cobblestones." His attention flickered to Genevieve, who somehow managed to look vaguely puzzled through an otherwise impenetrable mask of worry.

"Have you never wondered, my dear, why the city doesn't just smash us flat?"

"I'd sort of assumed," Genevieve offered hesitantly, "that someone else would just take your place. At least this way, they can keep an eye on you."

"Well . . ." Renard frowned, and Widdershins couldn't help but snicker. *So much for impressing the lady, Lambert.*

"Yes, that's true," he confessed. "But it's more than that. There've been times when they *wanted* to get rid of us, but the city's never declared war on the guild itself. It wouldn't be worth the bloodshed and financial repercussions, sure. Primarily, though, it's because of the Hallowed Pact."

The barkeep glanced at her friend. "He's not seriously trying to tell me that the *gods* want Davillon to leave its thieves alone."

Widdershins shrugged. "I'm not up on my theology, but yeah. The Shrouded God—"

"Our patron," Renard interjected with an oddly reverential tone.

"Yeah." Widdershins rolled her eyes so only Genevieve could see. "He's supposed to be one of the Pact, though I couldn't tell you which one. And since Davillon's patron is part of the Pact, and Demas of the Guard is part of the Pact . . ."

Genevieve understood. "So no wars between them. The Church forbids it."

"Precisely." Renard nodded, but his frown remained. "Still, the guild's nervous about making a nuisance of itself with a High Church official present. The archbishop just *might* have the authority to sanction an exception to laws forbidding an open conflict. Or he might not. Honestly, even our priests aren't entirely clear on the issue. In any case, we don't want to give him cause to consider it, or give the city cause to ask him. Better to lie low and sit this out. So the guild is snatching up what funds they can, and the Shrouded Lord—*Lord*, not *God*," he interjected as Genevieve's face grew puzzled once more. "—is allowing you-know-who to be as heavy-handed as she likes, in hopes of cowing the more rebellious elements into submission—"

He knew it was a mistake even as the words marched across his tongue, but he couldn't snap his teeth fast enough to trap them.

"Cow me into submission?" Both her friends could see the fog of an indignant huff settling around Widdershins.

"Perhaps a poor choice of words," Renard backtracked hastily.

Widdershins gave no indication of having heard him. "Who do those dried-up, incompetent, wrinkled, useless old half-wits think they are?!"

"Widdershins, such language!" Renard commented sarcastically. "Why, keep this up and you'll be calling them 'poop heads' within the hour, and *then* what will the children of Davillon think?"

Her glare bored into him, leaving scorch marks in his expensive finery. "I should teach the whole lot of you something—"

"Widdershins, please!" The dandy's tone finally broke through her mounting rant. "You and I both know that you've got a reputa-

tion for being, shall we say, precipitous—and not entirely unde-
served, at that. So you worry them. It's nothing personal, and you're
not the only one. Let it go."

"You're absolutely right, of course, Renard," Widdershins told
him with a gentle smile, her voice suddenly calm, even mild.

He squinted at her, not believing a word of it.

"In any event," he barged ahead, "as long as *she* thinks you're
holding out on your cut, that's all the excuse she needs."

"What are you telling me, Renard? That I better pay up, even
though I don't owe anything?" *Much.*

"If you have any emotional attachment to your kneecaps, yes. I'd
hate to see your legs broken, Widdershins. They're such *nice* legs."

"Fine," she sighed. With a grunt of disgust, she thrust her hand
deep into a pouch at her belt and scattered a large handful of coins
across the tabletop. "Start with this. I'll see what I can do about getting Li—uh, you-know-who the rest of her precious coins. *Before* his
Eminencialness shows up."

Renard nodded, scooped the marks into his own pouch, and
rose. "I imagine I can buy you a few days with this. Assuming," he
added with a twinkle in his eye, "that I don't decide to just go spend
them on a fabulous dinner and a bottle of good red." His smile faded
at the look on her face. "Uh, right. I'll let you know if you still have
reason to worry."

"I always have reason to worry, Renard."

"Of course. Widdershins, be careful," he said seriously. "Don't
do anything unwise."

"Who, me?"

"Hmph. Mademoiselle Genevieve, it was an exquisite pleasure
to meet you. Your establishment is lovely, though not nearly so
much as its owner." With another flamboyant bow, he swept from
the room like an arrogant wind.

"An interesting fellow," Genevieve commented blandly—*too*
blandly, Widdershins might have said—as the door shut behind

him. "Not at all what I expected from a thief. He was actually quite pleasant."

"Don't even think it, Gen. He's not safe to associate with."

"I associate with you, don't I?"

"Not *that* sort of association!"

"Ah." She looked up suddenly, accusing. "Shins, you told him you weren't holding back on the guild!"

"I'm not," the young woman insisted stubbornly, and then quailed beneath the barkeep's disapproving glower. "Well, no more than anyone else!" she protested somewhat less vehemently. "Really! It's expected of us, Gen! That's why the percentages are so high, because they know they won't get a full accounting!"

"Shins . . ."

"I'm doing them a favor! If I reported my take honestly, it would throw off their accounting system! They'd get too much from me. It would mess up their numbers, or they'd start expecting the same of *everybody*! It's my *duty* to hold back on them!"

Genevieve crossed her arms and began idly tapping a foot. It sounded like a small woodpecker, patiently chipping away at the floor.

Widdershins's face fell. "Who are they to tell me what to do anyway?" she mumbled petulantly.

"They're people who can get you in a whole mess of trouble if you don't do as they say, Shins." Genevieve frowned. "And from the looks of things, they're going to get *me* in trouble too."

"I'm sorry, Gen," the thief breathed. "You're right. I'll pay up. I promise."

"Good."

Genevieve said nothing more, but by the time Widdershins departed later that night, the worry still hadn't entirely faded from the barkeep's eyes.

✴

Lisette Suvagne, taskmaster of the Finders' Guild, second only to the
Shrouded Lord among Davillon's thieves, prostrated herself on the
worn carpets of the chapel. It was a posture, a reverence, an obedi-
ence she would offer to no man or woman—one that she loathed to
the depths of her soul. She was fire, was Lisette. From her blazing red
hair to her powder-keg temper to her burning ambitions, she was the
embodiment of flame. Only her outfit, all greens and blacks, failed
to promise a searing heat. Any mortal who had demanded such submission from her would have died in the asking.

But it was no mortal to whom she offered her devotion today.
Here at the center of the guild's complex, in the looming stone
shrine that smelled thickly of herbal incense, stood the city's only
known idol to the Shrouded God from which the leader of Davillon's
thieves took his own title. It loomed against the far wall, a stone icon
slightly taller than a man. Though tradition held that the Shrouded
God was one of the divinities of the Hallowed Pact, nobody in the
modern day—not even the eldest of the guild—remembered his
name. They called him simply by his title when they offered their
prayers of thanks for a particularly rich haul or a narrow escape from
the thief takers of the Guard.

The figure was clad simply, in sculpted images of soft boots, thick
pants, and snug tunic centuries out of fashion. A heavy hood of thick
black cloth—real, not hewn from the rock—covered the idol's head.
Guild tradition mandated that none but the Shrouded Lord might
ever look upon the face of their god—and even then only during the
ceremony that established him or her as the guild's new leader. Terrible curses both ancient and powerful were said to guard against blasphemy, ready to strike down any who would dare peer beneath that
hood; and though Lisette wasn't certain she believed in such curses,
her faith stayed her hand no matter how great her curiosity grew.

Faith in her god, who watched over her, and faith in herself that one day she would be permitted to look upon him properly, as she took her rightful place as the next Shrouded Lord.

There was, perhaps, no honor among thieves—but in the form of Lisette Suvagne, there was certainly fanaticism.

For long moments, she remained hunched, arms outstretched, until her muscles quivered and screamed for relief. Only then, her prayers and her penance complete, did she allow herself to rise lithely to her feet. A final bow to her one true lord, then she swept from the room to go and confront the man who—for now, only for now!—dared believe he held equal authority over her.

She stalked through several short corridors, finally stepping through an open archway into a chamber of haze. A steel portal slid shut behind her with ghostly silence, and Lisette bowed at the waist—the closest she would ever come to kneeling before any human—before her mortal liege, the sovereign of thieves across the length and breadth of Davillon.

The Shrouded Lord.

"Rise, Lisette."

She straightened and glared at the phantom before her.

No matter how often she saw it, the effect remained impressive. The chambers of the Shrouded Lord were thick with the musky smoke of several incense braziers that were never permitted to burn out and were larger by far than the one that perfumed the chapel. The great hood and ragged garb that was the uniform of the guild's leader blended perfectly with the haze, with the curtain before which he sat, with the cloths draped over his throne. It was impossible to tell where man left off and smoke or curtains began.

Brilliant. And also melodramatic almost to the level of cheap opera, but the thieves would have their traditions, no matter how theatrical. She wondered briefly, as she always did, which of her fellow Finders actually wore the hood. Nobody but the guild's own priests, who chose and oversaw the ascension of each Shrouded Lord, ever knew who spoke from behind that mantle.

"Report," he commanded in a bored tone.

Though she seethed internally, Lisette's voice was all business. "Laremy and Golvar have reported an average of a seven percent increase in dues since instituting our new policies. Assuming we can sustain this rate until the archbishop's arrival, we should have no difficulty maintaining standard expenses for the duration of his stay."

"And if not?" the Shrouded Lord asked.

Lisette shrugged. "Then we tap into emergency reserves for a few weeks. But I don't think the numbers *can* drop low enough from present levels to pose any real problems. In fact, I'd like to propose that we maintain these policies once de Laurent has departed. We—"

"Write it up and submit it. I'll consider it then."

Bastard. "Of course." She cleared her throat, irritated in part by the incense, as she gathered her thoughts. "In terms of specific payments—," she began, but again she was interrupted. The Shrouded Lord raised a hand, a phantasmal gesture amidst the smoke.

"What's this I hear about Brock attacking one of our people?"

Damn the man! How does he learn *these things so quickly?*

"I've had to sic several of our enforcers on a number of our members, my lord, as part of the fund-raising. Perhaps you might be more specific?"

The misty form leaned forward in his chair, or at least it seemed to. She couldn't entirely tell through the smoke. "Don't be dense, Taskmaster. We both know who I'm talking about."

Lisette frowned, absently fidgeting with the scabbard at her waist. "She was underreporting her take. I treated her no differently than anyone else!"

"Ah, Lisette. I believe, in fact, that Widdershins owes roughly a third as much as anyone else with whom Brock has 'talked.' You know I prefer to use him only as a last resort, since he tends to break things. And people. Are you truly still so angry with her after all this time?"

I spent a year *in planning the d'Arras job!* she wanted to scream at him. *It was a masterpiece, greater than anything the city had ever seen! It might even have made* me *the Shrouded Lord, and that little bitch comes along and—*

But it was a tirade the Shrouded Lord had heard a dozen times before—minus the bit about Lisette taking his mantle, of course—and he hadn't found it convincing then either. Perhaps new sins would build upon the old and finally tip the scales, but it hadn't happened yet.

When Lisette said nothing, the hooded form only nodded. "I see. I would hate, Taskmaster, to ever get the sense that you're abusing your position over a private vendetta. Our enforcers are to be used on guild business only, not personal. And Widdershins is to be treated like any other Finder. If she gives you a reason—a *real* reason—you may deal with her accordingly. Not until then."

"I understand, my lord." The words were more bitter than the smoke.

"Good. Write up the rest of your report, Lisette. I don't think I need to hear it just now."

Jaw clenched, Lisette bowed once more and backed from the room.

Still, by the time she'd reached her own quarters, her fury had cooled. All right, fine. She'd deal with Widdershins "like any other Finder." She would be very careful, very specific in her orders to Brock.

But then, she'd also remind Brock that if things got a little out of hand—well, it would be *her* job as taskmaster to see to his punishment. . . .

CHAPTER FIVE

"I'm not so sure about this, Pierre," Adrienne complained to the young man who all but dragged her along, his right hand clamped firmly on her left.

"When are you ever sure of anything anymore, Adrienne?" came the gruff response. "Now pick it up, would you? We'll be late if I have to haul you the whole way."

"Maybe we should be," the girl muttered, though she did, finally, allow herself to be rushed.

At thirteen now, give or take, Adrienne was beginning to shed the awkwardness of childhood. She was trim rather than scrawny, though meals remained a hit-or-miss proposition at best. Various escapes from angry "patrons" and Guardsmen had made her faster, more agile, even bestowed a bit of skill with the rapier that had hung at her side for the last two years. Though she'd snatched it with the firm intention of selling it—and had viciously berated herself for not doing just that, on many a cold and hungry night—she couldn't bear to part with it. If nothing else, it was something to impress the other street thieves with (even if she'd also had to use it to fight a few of them off, from time to time).

Something else had changed in recent days, as well: She'd met Pierre Lemarche.

Pierre had experienced both sides of life, and was deeply bitter to have been stuck with the bad. His parents were dead, his father having taken his own life as creditors confiscated the family's estates after one financial gamble too many, but not before putting a flint-lock ball through his wife's skull.

Pierre's soul was tightly wound around more than a little burning resentment. At the same time, he'd grown at least somewhat accustomed to his lower status, and he and his siblings had begun to make friends with others who shared their social and economic woes.

Something about Pierre, three years older than she, had won Adrienne over. Maybe it was the etiquette lingering from his days of wealth, an arsenal of charm into which he still dipped when the occasion warranted. Adrienne, accustomed to the crude advances of her peers, was rather taken by his flowery compliments and outrageous flattery. He could be kind, considerate, but also impatient, intolerant of others' failures, and filled with a burning need to somehow, someday, win back what the world had stripped from him. What he saw as his due.

Was she in love with the young man? Who could say? Love was at best an infrequent visitor to the circles in which Adrienne moved, and at her age, she scarcely had the experience to know. But she'd certainly grown quite fond of him, more so than any of the boys before. For a girl her age, it might as well have been love.

And that meant she had to deal with a whole slew of new emotions and experiences, not the least of which was worrying over him. Of late, Pierre had fallen in with . . . well, Adrienne couldn't say "a bad crowd," because that more or less defined everyone she'd ever known, but at least a "different crowd." She knew that she'd seen markedly less of him in recent weeks, and that he was constantly on about his new friends who would put him on the road "back to where I belong!" He often vanished for nights at a time and refused to speak of where he'd gone. Adrienne had finally demanded unequivocally that he take her to see what the hell he was doing.

She was more than a little startled when he agreed.

Dressed almost melodramatically in all black, he led her through the streets and alleyways of Davillon, quickly moving beyond her traditional stomping grounds. Adrienne was disturbed to see the rough stone façade of Davillon's outer wall looming between the squat buildings, illuminated at regular intervals by brightly burning lanterns. She'd never once set foot outside the walls of Davillon, and she wasn't certain that she wanted to start now.

Still she followed where Pierre led, eyes wide, ears alert for the slightest peep. The fallen aristocrat led her around a nearby structure—a warehouse, she guessed—and stopped at the back wall. It was an ungainly construction, squat in appearance even though it rose higher than the surrounding buildings. No windows marred the unbroken wooden walls, save a few tiny panes at the highest level, suggesting a foreman's suite. The alley's shadows, on this near-moonless night, draped the world in a heavy veil. It took Adrienne several moments to spot the door, high up on the wall between two of those windows, and the grill-work platform beneath it.

"There," Pierre whispered, pointing to a rickety metal stair that hauled itself up the side of the building, switching right to left and back again several times, panting and heaving all the way. "Manager's entrance."

"Are we going inside?" Adrienne asked dubiously, casting another glance at the wobbly ascent.

"Not exactly. Follow me." Pierre was already on the first of the steps.

Adrienne lingered a moment more, exceedingly unhappy and wishing that she'd never gotten involved in this . . . this . . . this whatever it was she'd gotten involved in!

Grumbling, she followed.

The stair held, though it trembled like a newborn fawn beneath their weight. Pierre stood waiting, smiling, as Adrienne reached the platform, her white knuckles clenched on the guardrail.

"It's perfectly safe, Adrienne," he said softly. "I've done this before."

"I'll bet," she snapped through clenched teeth.

"I'd never have let you come with me if it weren't safe, darling. I'd sooner open one of my own veins than risk allowing so much as a bruise to mar your beautiful—"

"Save it for later," she told him, though she couldn't quite keep a shallow smile from her face. "What's next?"

"Up." Pierre pointed a finger skyward.

"Up? Where up?" Adrienne blinked. "The roof?"

"The roof indeed." On cue, a rope snaked downward, dangling from the edge above.

"Are you sure about this?" she asked, once more strangely reluctant.

"Quite. If you want to turn back, sweetheart—"

That clinched it. "You just try and make me!" She was shimmying up the rope before Pierre could blink.

"Adrienne, wait! They're not—"

She scrambled over the edge of the roof, scarcely needing the rope at all, and looked up into a glittering array of blades.

"—expecting you," Pierre finished somewhat flaccidly, his head appearing over the precipice.

"My friends," he said, climbing to his feet atop the roof and dusting off his hands, "may I present to you Adrienne Satti? She'll be assisting us in the night's endeavors."

The blades withdrew with palpable reluctance, and Adrienne could only wonder yet again what Pierre had gotten her into.

CHAPTER SIX

In a rattling, bumping, shuddering, jostling carriage on the roads beyond Davillon, an elderly and normally distinguished voice complained for the umpteenth time, "Tell me again, Maurice, exactly what they've gotten me into."

Maurice—Brother Maurice, to be proper about it—smiled broadly. He leaned back in his insufficiently padded seat, his blond-tonsured head bobbing with the rocking of the heavy coach, and folded his hands inside the brown sleeves of his robe.

"Nothing at all, Your Eminence. There's absolutely nothing of any importance regarding your visit to Davillon. This is all just an elaborate scheme of the Church to force you into weeks of uncomfortable, rear-bruising travel in this abominable contraption, all for the amusement of your superiors and subordinates alike."

"Ah," the older passenger said. "Just as I suspected. Then why have you rebelled against this great Church conspiracy to inform me of it?"

"Well, after all, Your Eminence, I'm suffering too."

"The fickleness of youth," the high official lamented sadly. "Why, I remember the days when suffering for one's faith was considered noble."

"I believe that I'm sufficiently noble already, Your Eminence. I fear that if I spend too many more days with my backside being pounded into pulp by this carriage I shall be more noble than the king himself, and then I shall have to be executed for treason against the crown."

"I'm sure the Church will protect you, Maurice. You must have done *something* for her over the years."

The young monk of the Order of Saint Bertrand, dedicated entirely to attending the needs of High Church officials, could only laugh. The other man chuckled softly in turn and resumed gazing at the tree-bedecked countryside. He couldn't see much of it through the window of the ornate carriage that was, as Maurice complained, bruising its inhabitants to within an inch of their lives. Traveling in luxury, indeed!

William de Laurent, archbishop of Chevareaux, was getting on in years, despite his every effort to intimidate those years into keeping their distance. His hair was thin and gray, his face marred by more than its share of crevices and chasms, but his grip was strong, his gaze and his mind both sharp. His black robes of office draped him in a flowing aura, and the silver-forged Eternal Eye, supreme symbol of the High Church representing all 147 gods of the Hallowed Pact, hung about his neck. His shepherd's-crook staff of office leaned beside him.

He grimaced sourly as his limited view of the countryside was blocked by one of the outriders and began instead to contemplate his destination. The official purpose of his visit was a tour of Davillon, an inspection to identify any issues that needed correcting before a new bishop could be appointed, and to best determine which of the various candidates was most appropriate. That alone would have proved tedious enough; William looked ahead to the months of interaction with the city's aristocracy with, if not actual dread, then at least dread's distant cousin. The archbishop was a kindly old man, but he did not suffer fools—gladly or otherwise—and the nobility of Galice, he often felt, consisted of nothing but.

Essential a duty as it might be, though, it was also merely an excuse, a curtain behind which the Church might hide the true purpose of his visit.

The gods of the Pact smiled on their own, and the most faithful of Galice benefited from their divine influence. Oh, nothing the common man would recognize as "magic," none of the ancient sorceries of myth or fairy tale. But coincidence often placed them in the vicinity of momentous events. Fortune smiled upon them and frowned mightily upon those who opposed them. And sometimes, when the moon and the stars and the winds were right, they received warnings: dreams and omens, never clear but always urgent.

And William de Laurent had sensed . . . something. Something stirring in the dark, while the world slumbered in blissful ignorance. Something in Davillon.

William de Laurent unconsciously clenched his fists, stared out the window at the passing scenery, and prayed.

✸

"I'm tellin' you, she came this way!" The pockmarked fellow's voice was nasal, atonal, nearly as ugly as the face from which it emerged. The fact that his nose had recently been broken, and was likely to heal as crooked as a peg-legged usurer, probably had something to do with it.

"Sure." The other man, with the scar and the scraggly beard, idly (but *very* carefully) scratched at a bug bite on his neck with the edge of a curved blade. "She's just hiding behind the rats." He kicked a chunk of refuse, watched it bounce off the alleyway's nearest wall. It left a cluster of roaches where it hit, all of which swiftly darted off into the shadows.

"Damn it, she was here!"

Scarface shook his head. "You let me know what Brock says when you tell him we lost her."

"Me?! Why do I—?"

"Because you're the one who lost her."

"I didn't lose her!" The first thug scowled. "Look, she could still be here, right now. There's doorways—"

"Shallow. You see anyone hiding in 'em?"

"There's windows—"

"Boarded up."

"What about . . . ?" Pockmark gestured over and behind them. "Those steps?"

"Those rickety things?" They both turned, looking upward. "We'd have heard something if she'd been climbing those—"

And then they *did* hear something, all right: A few faint shrieks as bolts and wood separated, followed by a deafening clatter as the entire staircase broke away from the structure's walls. Boards and nails came crashing down from on high like a god's abandoned construction project, and Brock's two associates had just enough time to dread the pain that was coming their way before they found themselves bruised, battered, and buried.

✸

Widdershins peered over the lip of the building, blinking the dust from her eyes, chin leaning prettily on one fist. In the other, she clasped the rapier that had, with Olgun's assistance, served right nicely as a prybar to loosen the bolts of the ramshackle staircase. "Got 'em!" she crowed.

Then, her grin fading, "Well, no, I couldn't have collapsed the stairs without you. So, sure, I guess *we* got them, but . . ."

Another pause. "Yes, I *know* I couldn't have made the climb without them hearing me without your help either! What's your—? What? No, it *wasn't* 'you,' it was *we*. I was the one—*Oooh!*" Widdershins literally threw her hands in the air—managing through sheer luck to avoid sending her sword hurtling over the precipice—and stalked away from the edge. "You are *such* a glory hog! Just because I couldn't have done it without you does *not* mean you get the credit! What? I don't care! You're a god; *you* make it make sense!"

With astounding speed, she made her way down the building's

other side (despite the lack of anything resembling stairs) and out into the street, still muttering the entire way. But even as her mouth continued the argument, such as it was, her mind was already moving on to other concerns. Concerns like "If I hadn't spotted them, that could have gone a lot worse for me."

It was getting near time for Widdershins to make a few uncomfortable decisions.

＊

The days had slid past as though someone had greased them, blurring one into the next as the archbishop's arrival drew nigh. Streets, alleys, and courtyards—some of which had lain beneath such thick layers of refuse that nobody of the current generation had ever seen the cobblestones—were swept out and scrubbed clean, the better to glint with pristine dishonesty as de Laurent rode past. The homeless and destitute who normally dwelt along these lanes were encouraged to move on. A number were arrested "on suspicion," to be kept under lock and key—and out of sight—until the city gates clanged shut behind the departing backside of William de Laurent and his entourage, many weeks hence. Banners of House crests, guild icons, and a multitude of holy symbols dangled from walls and windows, or even bridged the gaps between buildings. Between the sundry colors spread throughout the streets and the untidy heaps of trash waiting to be carted away, Davillon was starting to resemble the playroom of a very large and very spoiled child.

Through it all crept Widdershins, her mind just as focused on the day of His Eminence's arrival, though for entirely different reasons. She performed a few small jobs in the interim, nothing spectacular, nothing to draw attention. The City Guard was on high alert; Lisette was looking for any excuse to have her drawn and quartered. (Pockmark and Scarface, as she'd thought of them since that day in the Flippant Witch, had only been the latest Finders she'd had to duck—though she hadn't felt the need to drop part of a building on any of the others.) It was, frankly, all she could do to gather sufficient funds to keep the damn guild off her back.

And off her friends'.

Despite her relatively light schedule, Widdershins hadn't found the time, in the week since the fight with Brock, to go back and visit Genevieve, to make sure she was all right.

No, that wasn't true. She'd not found the time because she hadn't looked. A part of her feared to go back, and it had taken her this long—and the recent encounter with Brock's cronies—to talk herself into it.

The crowds were heavy as always, the ambient sound thick enough to ladle into bowls and serve as a soup course, but Widdershins slipped gracefully through the temporary cracks in the wall of humanity. Making her way again through the colorful flag- and banner-strewn marketplace, which was slowly but surely beginning to resemble the leavings of a rainbow with digestive upset, she found herself once more on the steps of the Flippant Witch.

She'd awakened at the ungodly hour of noon, so the tavern wasn't open for patrons. On the other hand, she knew that Genevieve typically arrived early, to ensure that the place was suitable for human habitation when the doors opened for the ravening hordes of drunks and drunks-to-be.

On yet a third hand (she was starting to feel vaguely like an octopus), the fact that Genevieve was probably here didn't mean a blessed thing. Even assuming she wasn't deliberately avoiding Widdershins, she might well ignore *any* knocking at the door before business hours. Doubtless every day saw a few drunkards convinced that they were worthy of special consideration.

With a dismissive shrug—either the door would open or she'd pick the bloody lock—she rapped loudly on the heavy wood.

"We're closed!" came the immediate response. "Come back in about two hours!"

"Gen?" Widdershins called back. "Gen, it's me!"

A moment passed, then a moment more. Widdershins was just about to slink away in dejection when she heard the sound of a heavy lock—followed by a second, a third, and two deadbolts. The heavy portal swung ponderously inward.

"Hurry up before you're spotted!" Genevieve hissed. "If they see me letting someone in early, I'll *never* hear the end of it!"

Widdershins darted into the darkened room. The shutters stood firmly closed, the huge stone hearth bereft of flame. Only the lanterns burned merrily away, sucking greedily at their reservoirs of oil, but their light was sullen and cheerless, as though they, too, were drinking away their sorrows. In the maudlin illumination, even the white cross of Banin seemed gray and dour.

"Is it always this gloomy before you open?" Widdershins asked, her voice artificially light.

"It's usually worse, but I've sent the skulls and implements of torture out for cleaning."

Widdershins blinked. "You're feeling better," she observed, her tone almost accusatory.

Genevieve shrugged, and returned to stacking several bottles of her most popular spirits behind the bar, where they'd be well within easy reach come evening. "I suppose I am, at that," the proprietor admitted blandly as she worked. "Who'd have thought it?"

Widdershins stepped to the bar, watching her friend work for a few moments. At which point Genevieve slammed down one of the bottles—Widdershins jumped at the sound—and spun to face her.

"Why haven't you been back to see me, Shins?" No anger, there, only the vague seeds of hurt. "After what happened, I really needed a friend."

Widdershins swallowed, her throat suddenly tight as a noose. She looked down at the bar, shamefaced. "I thought you were upset at me," she admitted, suddenly a berated child rather than the adult she strove to appear. "I didn't think you'd *want* to see me."

She looked up at the touch of Genevieve's hand on her own, saw the blonde noblewoman smiling sadly. "Shins, I'm, um, not exactly an admirer of what you do. And the people you do it with scare the hell out of me. But you're still my best friend. Which," she added with a sudden smirk, "may say more about me, or about this damned city, than it does about you, but there you have it."

Widdershins forced herself to match her companion's own smile. "I'd say it just goes to prove how lucky you are."

Genevieve snorted, returning to the bottles. Widdershins continued to watch her work, her mind a playful kitten pouncing briefly upon a dozen different thoughts.

Then, "I am glad you're here, Shins," Genevieve said over her shoulder as she deftly stacked the glass carafes, "but I can't help wondering why."

"Do I have to have a reason?" the thief asked her, her attention dragged back to the issue at hand.

"You said you thought I was angry at you. Why pick today to come here and risk being smote by my great and terrible wrath?"

Widdershins sighed. "I ran into some of those guys again." Genevieve's widening eyes suggested that she needn't specify *which* guys she meant. "It's all right," she added swiftly. "It'll be at least a few days before they're up to causing any trouble. And they can't even pin it on me, not for sure."

"But they will anyway, you know."

"Yeah," the thief acknowledged. "They probably will. Anyway, it just made me think—about what happened, about what *could* happen. So . . ." A shallow shrug. "Here I am. Lucky you."

"Uh-huh." Genevieve reached out and poked her friend in the sternum. "Tell me another."

"It's true!" Widdershins protested. "Also, ouch."

"All right, it's true. But there's more. I'm a barkeep, Shins. I hear more half-truths every week than you've told in your life."

"Well, uh, there is one thing . . ."

"It's always 'one thing.'"

"I want you to come with me next week," Widdershins confessed.

The other woman blinked. "With you? Where?"

"The procession. I was planning to go and watch the archbishop arrive."

"Shins . . ."

"I'm not going to do anything! Honest, I'm not! I just want to see what all the fuss is about."

"I see. And this is in no way a means of thumbing your nose at the guild? Basically chanting 'I'm not touching him! I'm not touching him! Nyah, nyah!' and then running away like a little girl? Or maybe about seeing who's all gussied up in their finest to greet him, so you know who to rob after he's gone?"

Widdershins mumbled something unintelligible.

"I see," Gen told her. "What'd we *just* learn about me and half-truths, Shins?"

"I'm not asking you to do anything wrong, or dangerous," Widdershins insisted. "I just want some company."

"Half the city's going to be there."

Widdershins shrugged. "So all of a sudden you're uncomfortable with crowds? You own a tavern!"

"I prefer my crowds to be less . . . crowded."

"You," Widdershins said, rising, "don't get out enough. It makes perfect sense that you're my only friend. I'm a thief. I live in the shadows. I have no life. You, on the other hand, are a nobleman's daughter, even if he's not really all that noble, and you own a very popular tavern. So how come *you* don't have more friends?"

"I have lots of friends! There's Robin, for instance."

"She works for you."

"Well, how about Gerard?"

"Same as Robin. Employees don't count."

"Ertrand Recharl!" Genevieve announced smugly.

Widdershins scoffed. "Ertrand's not a friend! He's a drunk who keeps trying to get under your skirts!"

"All right. Well, there's that fellow who always sits at the corner table over there, the one with the beaver-skin cloak. He's always fun to talk to."

"If you don't know his name, Gen, you don't get to call him a friend. I'm pretty sure that's actually a rule, somewhere."

"So what's your point with all this, other than chopping down my self-esteem like a fir tree?"

"My point, Gen, is that you don't get out often enough, and that the celebration tomorrow is the perfect place to start."

Genevieve's eyelids lowered until they showed only thin crescents. "And you felt it necessary to point out that I should have more friends—besides you—as a way of convincing me to go to the celebration *with* you?"

The younger woman grinned widely. "You got it."

"Widdershins, you have absolutely lost your mind. I couldn't think of a less logical argument if I sat down and worked at it."

"Perfect! If it's not logical, you can't argue with it. I'll be at your place at noon."

The door slammed, and she was gone.

Genevieve shook her head, bemused. There was a great deal to be done before opening. And as for next week . . . Well, she hated to disappoint her friend, but there was no help for it. She was absolutely, positively, not going to that stupid parade. Not a chance. No way. Under no circumstances. No.

"Isn't this fun?" Widdershins shouted happily. "I told you you should get out!"

Genevieve gritted her teeth and tried to think about something other than throttling Widdershins with her bare hands.

She still wasn't sure precisely how this had even happened. One moment she was flopped out blissfully in bed, sleeping off a hectic but profitable night of drink-filling and food-slinging at the Flippant Witch, without a care in the world, snugly cocooned against the late autumn chill.

The next, Widdershins was in her bedroom, having picked the bloody lock, and practically dancing with excitement, shouting at Genevieve to hurry up and get dressed. It was barely after noon—the depth of night, as far as the tavern keep was concerned. This was absolutely outrageous behavior, even from a close friend, and Gen resolved to berate the thief soundly, just as soon as she had a moment to fully wake up, to regain her equilibrium, to . . .

They were outside and halfway through the marketplace before Genevieve reassembled her scrambled wits sufficiently to speak. And by then, of course, it was far too late. Genevieve smiled a tight, closed-mouth smile, wondered briefly how Widdershins had managed to get her dressed (with most of the laces tied properly, even!), and then grudgingly went along.

A decision she now bitterly regretted as the inexorable press of the gathering crowds hurled the pair this way and that, two floating bottles on the seas of Davillon's populace. The crowd was a living thing, moving and even breathing as one. The sensation was unpleasantly akin to that of being swept away by a very loud and sweaty tide.

Speech was very nearly impossible: lean over, shout at the top of your lungs in your friend's ear, scream your throat as raw as if you'd gargled with glass shavings, and it was still necessary to repeat yourself two or four times before the object of your comment (which probably wasn't all that important anyway) wandered out of view.

It was hot, too. Not the heat of the day—it wasn't all that long until winter—but the heat of thousands of bodies, each pressed uncomfortably close in a macabre parody of intimacy. The miasma of perspiration and perfume was enough to fell an ox at thirty paces.

Sweating in unladylike rivulets, jostled by strangers, bruised in uncountable tender areas by the morass of accidental blows, Genevieve hunched her shoulders against the storm of sound and fury and struggled to imagine a worse sort of hell.

Widdershins, of course, seemed perfectly happy, but Widdershins was weird.

※

"Hey, Olgun!" Widdershins whispered, confident he could hear no matter what. "Isn't this neat?"

The god's reply felt vaguely patronizing. She felt very much like she'd just been told, in all maternal seriousness, "Yes, dear, it's very nice. Why don't you go play over there for a while?"

"You don't think this is impressive?" she asked incredulously, drawing a curious stare from a nearby merchant who, through some fluke of acoustics, heard her clearly. The flabby, pasty-faced widower, flattered that a young woman might look his way, had opened his mouth to reply when it finally dawned on him that the girl was talking to herself, not to him.

Lunatic.

Olgun, during this time, had expressed to Widdershins, in no uncertain emotions, that nothing humans did impressed him— present company excluded, of course—and that a larger concentration of clowns might make them funnier, but generally not any more awe-inspiring.

"Oh, so we're clowns, are we? Just put here for your amusement? A little different than the way the creation myth tells it, yes?"

Widdershins's private deity smiled an amused smile, and refused to emote any further on the topic.

The obstinate thief wasn't about to let the subject drop, but as she opened her mouth to shout some witty rejoinder at her little pocket god, she felt Genevieve's fingers clenching on her arm.

THIEF'S COVENANT

"What is it?" she asked, hoping her expression would be enough
to carry her meaning, since the words almost certainly would not.

Genevieve, eyes wide with a contagious anticipation that she'd
tried her damnedest to elude, pointed over the heads of the crowd
toward the heavy, iron-bound gates that were Davillon's main
ingress. Huge pennants slowly rose and unfurled to wave majestically over the nearby buildings. The Eternal Eye stared down from
several banners, as though it could clearly see their every thought,
and didn't much approve of a one of them.

The crowd surged ahead, prevented from becoming a stampede
only by the lack of space to build momentum. Truth be told, it
would be more accurate to say that the crowd *shuffled* forward, a gla-
cier of clothes and flesh. Whispers, audible only because so many
people repeated them, scampered through the ranks of the waiting
masses.

"Did you see that?"

"The banners went up! He's here!"

"Here? He can't be here! It's but two hours past noon!"

"He's early! Did you hear? The archbishop's arriving early!"

And then the whispers were blown from the air like so much
skeet by the blast of two dozen trumpets, announcing the arrival of
His Eminence, the esteemed William de Laurent, archbishop of
Chevareaux.

Music blared, banners waved, and thousands of people shouted
their unbridled joy (even if most were celebrating not the archbishop's arrival—which meant little to them—but simply the
opportunity to celebrate). Only those who'd waited since the earliest
hours of the morning, ensuring that they got a street-side view or
high vantage, would actually see the pristine white carriage, flanked
by a dozen horsemen and followed by another seven or eight coaches
carrying the archbishop's staff. The rest of the crowd would see
nothing more exciting than the back of someone else's head.

One hand locked with bulldog determination on Genevieve's

wrist, Widdershins slipped, slid, twisted, squeezed, weaseled, pushed, shoved, elbowed, and otherwise forced her way through the living barricade isolating her from her goal. She even went so far, on occasion, as to call on Olgun: here a woman broke into a sneezing fit, forcing her to stagger aside and allowing Widdershins to slip through the gap; that fellow there felt his belt buckle give way, once more clearing a path as he fled, red-faced, holding his pants up with his hands. In a surprisingly brief span, the barkeep and the burglar forced their way street-side, gaining an unobstructed view of . . .

"A carriage," Genevieve muttered in her companion's ear, shaking her head. "All that, and you get to see a carriage. I hope you're happy, Shins. I know *I* haven't been this excited in *minutes*."

"It's not the carriage, Gen!" Widdershins announced gleefully, refusing to look away from the snowy stallions, the luxuriously curtained windows, the ponderous gilded wheels. "It's the passenger!"

"But you can't very well *see* the passenger, now, can you?" *Sometimes I just don't* understand *that girl!*

"No, but I know that he's—oh, figs."

Genevieve tensed. "What? 'Oh, figs' *what*?!"

"There." Widdershins pointed at one of the soldiers: not an outrider who'd ridden from Chevareaux, but one of the eight or so Davillon Guardsmen who'd fallen in with the ostentatious procession as an additional honor guard.

"That's Julien Bouniard," she whispered softly. "Right out in front."

Genevieve raised an eyebrow. "Oh, come on, Shins. It's not as though he's going to just pick you out of a crowd like this. The man's got more important things on his mind, don't you think?"

Widdershins chewed her lower lip and said nothing.

The young constable, whom she'd first watched from the rafters on that awful day two years ago, insisted on intertwining himself back into her life with all the persistence of a recurring dream. Now a major himself after a meteoric rise through the ranks, he was one of the city's best, his name cursed by many of Davillon's extralegal entrepreneurs. Good as she was, Widdershins had been arrested a handful of times over the years—and more often by Bouniard than anyone else. He always made her more than a little nervous, even though he couldn't possibly know that Widdershins was also Adrienne Satti.

But Genevieve was right. No matter how skilled, how experienced, how observant he was, he'd not likely single her out of a crowd of thousands. With a deep exhalation, Widdershins forced herself to relax and enjoy the parade.

✳

Julien Bouniard sat ramrod-straight, hands loosely clutching the reins. His tabard and uniform had been pressed and steamed, their lines crisp enough to shave with. The sterling fleur-de-lis and polished medallion of Demas glinted in the sun, and the feather in his flocked hat had been supplemented with the blue-and-green staring eye of a peacock plume.

Charlemagne, his gray-dappled steed, whickered in impatience at their plodding pace. He wanted to run, to prance ahead, at least to canter. Even a brisk walk would be nice. But no, here he was, trudging down the cobblestones, surrounded on all sides by other, inferior equines and the gargantuan wheeled contraptions, at roughly the pace of a mule with gout.

"Easy, Charles," Julien comforted him, laying a steady hand alongside the animal's neck. "I don't like it either."

The horse snorted once more, unimpressed.

Julien couldn't help but smile beneath his thick, walnut-brown mustache (an affectation he'd adopted along with his promotion to major, hoping it would make him look old enough for the part). He understood the beast's frustration—shared it, in fact. Ceremonial duties like this were enough to make him long for a fast-paced day of paperwork.

The Guardsman, ever alert for ambush, scowled as he spotted familiar features in the crowd. He knew, even without asking, that he'd never get permission to leave the procession. He was the ranking officer, and it was essential, or so it had been drummed into his head a million times over the past weeks, that the city make the best of all possible impressions on its revered guest.

So what sort of impression would it make on His Eminence if a street thief swiped his mantle off his shoulders, or used him as bait for some other, local catch? She wasn't the first known criminal he'd spotted in the crowd, and he'd deal with her as he had the others.

By taking no chances.

Pulling very subtly on the reins, Julien urged the warhorse to fall back a few paces, drawing even with the white-enameled carriage door. Leaning over, he rapped with leather-gloved knuckles on the rickety wooden portal.

The shade rose smoothly, the curtains drew back, and a kindly old face peered outward. "Is there a problem, Major?" William de Laurent asked curiously.

"Nothing serious, Your Eminence," Julien told him politely, bowing his head in a curt show of respect. "I've spotted a known criminal in the crowd, and—"

"Another one, Major? Had a bumper crop this year, did you?"

Julien frowned. He was walking a tightrope here, and he knew it, trying to balance the archbishop's safety on one hand, his impression of Davillon on the other.

"No more than any city's plagued with, Your Eminence. Crowds offer a lot of opportunities, though, so here they come."

"Of course. And you would like to dismiss a guard to run off and apprehend this criminal, as you did the last one?"

"Ah, perhaps two guards in this instance, Your Eminence."

The archbishop raised an eyebrow. "Is that necessary, Major? Might he not simply be here to enjoy the spectacle?"

"She, Your Eminence. And she very well might be, yes. On the other hand, I've experience with this particular thief. She's extremely resourceful, a ghost when she wants to be, and absolutely unencumbered by the weight of common sense. I'd feel better knowing that she was out of the way, and thus not planning to rob you blind— pardon me for saying so—for the duration of your visit. At the very least, I'd like to encourage her to move out of your general vicinity."

Julien was fully prepared to argue his case further, as politely as possible, but de Laurent simply smiled. "I believe you're worrying unnecessarily, Major. But I'm hardly qualified to tell you how to do your job. Dispatch your men if you think it best. I think I'll survive the hordes of assassins without them until they return."

Julien smiled broadly. "Thank you, Your Eminence."

William de Laurent nodded and closed the shade. Julien gestured to the nearest two guards, both of whom broke ranks and approached. As their horses plodded sluggishly forward, Julien growled his instructions.

*

When the two Guardsmen wheeled their horses around in her direction, Widdershins could no longer share Genevieve's confidence.

"Move!" she shouted, grabbing her friend by the hand and pulling her back through the crowd they'd battled moments earlier. "Gods, I don't believe this! What are the odds?"

"I'd have said pretty slim, but under the circumstances . . . ," Genevieve told her, eyes slightly glazed.

"There must be hundreds of known thieves in this crowd! Why is he singling *me* out?!"

"How many of those hundred thieves put themselves at the *front* of the crowd?"

"Well *now's* a fine time to point that out!"

Genevieve twisted, owl-like, glancing nervously behind her. The Guardsmen moved quickly, though there was insufficient room for their mounts. The crowd parted, shoved with swift-moving hands where the black-and-silver tabards weren't enough to clear the path.

With a sudden jerk, Genevieve yanked her hand from Widdershins's grip. "They're not after me, Shins!" she shouted, already separated from her friend by several layers of the milling assemblage. "I'll be fine! Run!"

"But—"

Genevieve pointed at the oncoming guards, moving through the throng far faster than she could match with her bad leg. "*Run!*"

Widdershins ran, first plowing through the crowd with all the grace of a runaway yak, then, once she'd calmed, more nimbly, dancing around people rather than knocking them aside. The Guardsmen gradually fell behind, and Widdershins burst from the mob and bolted for the nearest alley. All she needed was to get out of their sight for a handful of seconds and they'd never see her again.

Olgun screamed at her as she rounded the corner, but for once, even the great Widdershins's feline reflexes weren't fast enough. Something whistled from the shadows of the alleyway, crashing hard into her stomach. The thief doubled up, the agony a blade stabbing through her. She heard a strangled cry echoing from the darkened alleyway, and only faintly recognized the voice as her own. She found herself on her hands and knees in the garbage, violently retching up the contents of her stomach.

Vomit, she realized with a dull horror, mingled with blood.

A thoughtful look on his face, Brock materialized from the alley, his hammer swinging casually in a one-handed grip. "Oh, that doesn't look good for you, Widdershins," he commented, poking with one booted toe at the unpleasant mess she'd heaved up. "I think you may have ruptured something."

"Brock . . . ," Widdershins croaked through filth-encrusted lips, glaring with pain-deadened eyes.

"Are you upset, Widdershins? You're speaking in Chicken again." A look of rage twisted the enforcer's face just before he kicked his victim in the stomach, the force of the blow lifting her from the ground.

Widdershins screamed. Her stomach felt as though she'd swallowed a brimming mug of molten iron, and she spat up another mouthful of bile-tinged blood even as she landed, shoulder first, on the cobblestones. Unable to act, to think, she curled into a tight ball around the pain, gasping, lacking breath even to fuel the anguished sobs that racked her chest and throat.

"Hurts, doesn't it?" Brock continued conversationally, idly spinning the hammer. "A lot?" He smiled abruptly. "Maybe even more than being kicked—twice—in the pomegranates? More than having a damn staircase dropped on your head? Well, I'll do you a favor. I'll make the hurting stop."

"Can't . . ." Widdershins gulped several mouthfuls of air, trying to focus. "Can't . . . kill me . . ."

"Oh, can't I? Everyone knows your reputation for acting before you think, you stupid little bitch! No one'll doubt it when I say that you attacked me first."

"Olgun . . . ," she coughed, unable to whisper.

"Olgun?" Brock squinted. "Who the hell is Olgun? And why should I care if he believes me?"

"Help . . ." Another cough, another mouthful of brackish blood. Widdershins spit it out, nauseated at the metallic taste, the slimy feel as it oozed over her tongue and between her teeth. It splattered across the cobblestones in a thin red spray, dotting Brock's shoes.

"That was rude," he told her. "A guy might start to think you didn't care for him."

Widdershins wasn't listening. She lay huddled and shaking, and struggled to bite back a sob of relief as she felt the familiar tingling in the air around her, felt the deity's divine touch. The pain, a roaring blaze, dimmed to a low flame—still intense, still agonizing, but no longer crippling. She wouldn't be dancing any time soon, but at least she wasn't bleeding to death internally. Her stomach muscles spasmed as Olgun set to right several bits that had been ripped apart by Brock's brutal assault. She tried not to cringe at the feel of things shifting around inside her. Olgun had saved her . . . partially.

She'd have to finish the job herself.

"Brock . . . ," she croaked again.

"Yes?" the larger man asked pleasantly, stepping closer so he might hear. "Something you want to say before this is all over?"

"You're an idiot." Fighting past the agony that permeated her body, Widdershins punched upward, aiming at the same target that had worked so well the last time.

The blow landed between the man's legs with a loud clang. Widdershins bit her tongue to keep from crying out. Her fist throbbed, and one of her fingers had gone numb. The man was wearing a bloody codpiece under his pants!

Brock laughed, a vicious, ugly sound. "Anything else?" he asked.

Ignoring the tremor in her hands, Widdershins reached out with a strength Brock could never have expected, yanked the hammer from startled fingers, and let it fall heavily on his left foot.

Brock's high-pitched scream wasn't nearly enough to drown out the cracking of bone.

The huge enforcer collapsed, clutching at his shattered limb, even as Widdershins rose. She swayed, her stomach throbbing, as the adrenaline slowly faded from her limbs. Olgun had healed her as best he could, but without a few days of rest, she had nothing left to give.

Well, *almost* nothing. She had one last thing to take care of before she passed out, or collapsed, or whatever it was she was about to do. Widdershins was no murderer, never had been; but she couldn't let Brock come after her again, not knowing what he would do to her. Her arms trembling with the effort, sweat beading on her forehead, she raised the hammer in both hands. Her stomach heaved once more, and not just with the pain of her wound, but she ignored it as best she could, fully prepared to remove Brock from her life in the most final way imaginable.

"Don't move!"

Widdershins's fingers went slack, and the hammer fell to the street with a dull clatter. Her face pale, the thief stared over her shoulder.

Flintlocks drawn, the pursuing Guardsmen stepped into the alley. The first shifted to the side, bash-bang aimed unerringly at her chest, while the other yanked a pair of manacles from his belt.

"Widdershins," the second man, dark-haired and thick-bearded, intoned as he approached. "By order of Major Julien Bouniard, you are under arrest on suspicion of thievery." He glanced over at the fallen lump of quivering flesh that was Brock. "And assault," he added smugly.

Oh, no. No way. She wasn't about to go back to gaol. Not like this, not just because Bouniard was paranoid, and *certainly* not for defending herself against that towering slab of filth!

"Olgun," she began, focusing on the flintlocks. "I think that . . . that . . ."

The alley danced maniacally, the pain in her gut flared once more, and Widdershins collapsed, unconscious, to the cobblestones.

* * *

They watched, concealed in the shadows of a broken window above, as the two guards moved in, one kneeling by each of the fallen figures. Heavy manacles clattered shut around the thief's limbs. "Hey," the man at her side called to the other. "She's pretty bad off. I'm going to need your help carrying her so we don't make it worse."

"Who cares if we make it worse? She's just a—"

"You explain that to Major Bouniard."

A soft grumble. "What about this one?"

"He in any danger?"

"Doesn't look like it. Not with her gone, anyway. He'll be walking funny for a while, though."

"Then we'll send someone back to check on him after we get her squared away."

"All right."

With a level of care that at least somewhat belied his cavalier attitude, the second constable aided the first in lifting Widdershins, keeping her fairly level. Slowly, carefully, they made their way from the alley and back toward the horses they'd left behind.

A few minutes more, to make sure the Guardsmen were well and truly gone, that any incidental sounds would be lost to the dull roar of the crowded streets beyond. Only then, when they were certain, did Pockmark and Scarface emerge into the open—the former still limping, and both of them sporting bruises, unhealed abrasions, and stubborn splinters.

"We could've taken them," Pockmark insisted as they hurried to the knoll of quivering flesh that was their boss.

"Murdered two of the Guard? Without explicit orders from the taskmaster or the Shrouded Lord? I don't bloody think—"

"You're godsdamned right you don't!" Brock's voice was muffled by garbage and road dirt, tinged with hysteria. "You should've killed them! You should've killed *all* of them!"

"Are you all right, Brock?" Scarface asked as he knelt in an unconscious echo of the constable who had been here moments before.

In answer, Brock managed to push through the pain long enough to reach out and smack the other man across the face hard enough to make his beard stand on end. Then, once the fellow had managed to pick himself off the ground, "Help me up, you moron."

It actually required both men to heft the colossus, and even then it was a struggle that left all three puffing and panting, but once he was upright, Scarface alone was able to support him.

"You," Brock ordered through pale, clenched jaws. "Get out there and find those guards. They can't have gotten far carrying the little bitch."

"Uh . . . ," Pockmark began.

"I'm not telling you to attack them in the middle of the crowd, damn it! Just follow them, find out which prison they stick her in. Then meet us back at the guild, so we can do some planning." He was already turning away, practically dragging the man on whom he was leaning. "Widdershins isn't getting out of gaol alive."

CHAPTER SEVEN

The men and boys awaiting atop the roof were, to the last, disreputable—and given the sorts of people Adrienne was accustomed to dealing with, that was saying something. They were neither the fiercest nor the filthiest with whom Adrienne had ever dealt, not by any stretch, but something about them set warning bells to chiming in the back of her mind.

Perhaps the naked blades that had greeted her when she'd first clambered on the rooftop had something to do with it.

"Adrienne," Pierre continued his introductions, oblivious to her discomfort, "these are my friends. This is Joseph; that one's—"

Joseph, powerfully built, with a thick head of autumn-red hair, approached with unkind purpose. His black trousers and tunic— they *all*, Adrienne couldn't help but note, wore black trousers and tunic—hissed as he walked, conspiratorial whispers of cloth on cloth. At his side hung a curved knife that only barely failed to qualify as a sword (and probably resented it).

Adrienne flinched, but it was Pierre, not herself, on whom Joseph advanced. His fists clenched on Pierre's tunic and lifted him clear off his feet with only a modicum of strain. The young man's face paled and his boots kicked helplessly, inches from the roof.

"First off, you little turd," Joseph growled, "no names. Your little whore doesn't need to know who we are."

Adrienne bristled, her face flushing, but Pierre nodded his understanding as best he could. "Got it," he croaked. "Anything else?"

"Yes. Next time you want to bring someone in on one of our projects, *you ask first!*" Joseph shook him until his face purpled and his teeth clacked together like castanets.

The whisper of steel on leather heralded the touch of a rapier against Joseph's throat. Standing very still, his arms steady despite Pierre's dangling weight, Joseph turned his head as far as he could without tensing his neck against the blade.

"Let him go," Adrienne commanded, trying to infuse her voice with a confidence she didn't feel, and at the moment couldn't even remember. "I mean it. Put him down."

"You draw one drop of blood with that, girl, you and your boyfriend die on this roof. You know that, right?"

Adrienne had begun to sweat profusely—the pommel had already grown sticky with it—but she kept the fear from her voice. "You won't see it, though."

Joseph stared, and Adrienne stared back. No less steel-hard or razor-sharp than the rapier itself was the glare that bound them, one to the other.

Finally, without expression, Joseph dropped Pierre, with an audible thump and a whoosh of breath, to the roof. His own face a strange alloy of embarrassment and gratitude, Pierre struggled to his feet and scurried across the stone to stand beside her.

"Thank you," Adrienne breathed.

"You're welcome," Joseph replied formally, gingerly pushing the blade away from his throat with a forefinger. And then he laughed, hard, bent double with breath-stealing guffaws.

"Gods and demons, Pierre!" he exclaimed once he finally had the breath to do so. "You sure know how to pick them, don't you!" His laughter gradually depreciated into a faint chuckling, then faded into the night. "All right, you're both in. Let's do this."

"Wonderful!" Pierre exclaimed, all traces of injured pride vanished from his expression. "Thank you, Joseph. You won't be disappointed."

Adrienne's jaw fell slack.

"I better not be," Joseph warned. "All right, everyone gather round. I don't plan to say this more than once."

A dozen footsteps crunched across the rooftop, drowning out Pierre's gasp as something yanked on his sleeve, practically ripping it from his arm. He spun, hands rising to defend himself.

"Gods, Adrienne, you scared the—"

"What is *wrong* with you?!" she demanded in a strained, almost painful whisper. "After what he just did, we should be getting the hell out of here!"

Pierre shrugged, perplexed. "He was just a little upset, Adrienne. He's fine now."

"Upset?! Pierre, the man picked you up and shook you like a cat!"

"That's just his way. He doesn't mean anything by it."

"And they drew blades on me!"

"Well, you surprised them, that's all."

Fire blazed in the girl's features. "And he called me a whore!"

"But that was before he knew you, my sweet. Come, Adrienne, there's no call for this. Stop being unreasonable, and let's join the others before we miss what he's got to say."

And with that, Pierre strode across the roof, his companion's incredulous gaze following behind. Adrienne shook her head, sheathed her rapier, and gave more than a moment's thought to leaving the whole lot of them here to play while she went and found something less deranged to occupy her. Dodging runaway wagons, perhaps, or throwing horse droppings at City Guardsmen.

She'd do no such thing, of course, and heaved a heartfelt sigh when she *admitted* she'd do no such thing. Muttering darkly, her feet dragging, she shuffled over and took her place in the circle of conspirators.

"So desperately glad you could join us, Adrienne," Joseph snipped as she pushed between Pierre and the man beside him, an unwholesome fellow with brittle blond hair who bore a strong resemblance to a scarecrow.

"Stuff it sideways and clench, Joseph."

Pierre gaped, horrified, but the other thieves laughed uproari-
ously, Joseph louder than any. "Oh, I like her a *lot*," he told the
rooftop at large. "I may have to make you a regular on my jobs,
Adrienne."

"What say you tell us what *this* one is before you worry about
dragging me into the next, yes?"

"Fair enough." Joseph cleared his throat, taking in each and
every face that looked eagerly (or, in one case, not so eagerly) back at
him. "As some of you know, I've been cultivating friendships, and
spreading the occasional bribes, among the servants of certain—"

"Let's skip the foreplay," the scarecrow demanded in a voice
rather like a cheese grater running across gravel. "No disrespect or
nothing, but there's not any of us gives a rat's ass how you got the
information. What'd you find out?"

"You, Anton," Joseph rumbled, "are a boor."

"Long as you make me a rich boor, I can live with it. Spill."

"Well, since you asked so politely, it appears that Alexandre
Delacroix was unavoidably detained on a recent business trip to
Guillerne. Now, due to other business commitments here in
Davillon, he's rushed his trip back. You know, pushing the horses,
traveling into the night, that sort of thing."

"And?" Pierre asked, his voice excited—and, Adrienne couldn't
help but sneer, more than a touch sycophantic.

"And," Joseph continued, "according to the messengers who
came ahead, he should be arriving in town tonight. In about, oh, an
hour or so.

"Which gives us," he added to the silent circle around him, "just
enough time to get ourselves out of town and hit the carriage before
it comes within sight of the city wall."

Adrienne had obviously never met Alexandre Delacroix—
neither she nor anyone else on that roof, save perhaps Pierre when he
was much younger, would ever have been in any position to do so—

but few citizens of Davillon, regardless of social class, hadn't heard of him. Delacroix was an aristocrat's aristocrat, the sort of fellow whose horses and hounds were richer than most people. If his ilk ever mingled with Adrienne's type, it was only because Davillon didn't have enough streets to keep them from crossing each other's paths.

As she'd heard it, or at least as she vaguely *remembered* hearing it, House Delacroix was one of the city's oldest, with a rather storied history to boot. For some years, the House had lain in shambles, its fortunes shattered by a series of bad investments, and the whispers that it would soon be banished from the aristocracy had been so prevalent that even Adrienne had heard them. And then, scarcely more than a year ago, the Delacroix fortunes had turned just as swiftly as they'd gone bad, until Alexandre Delacroix was once again among the wealthiest of the city's nobles.

Unsurprisingly, given this history, the aristocrat made a habit of overseeing his House's businesses personally—it was just such a journey from which he was now returning—and would doubtless carry with him a great deal of coin. His guards would be worn out by the lengthy pilgrimage, exhausted by the rushed march home. And by striking beyond sight of the walls, the bandits could ensure that no detachment of the City Guard might come to his aid.

It was a solid plan, so far as it went, but it left one question unanswered, one Adrienne found herself reluctant to ask.

What was to happen to Delacroix and his retainers? Adrienne Satti had been a thief for much of her life, but while she'd shed blood on occasion when forced to defend herself, she had never *murdered* anyone.

But though her lips parted and the question hovered, tantalizing with a feather light touch upon the tip of her tongue, she never gave it breath. And as the band of thieves climbed down the rickety stairs and crept toward one of the many refuse hatches in the city walls, visions of gold marks consumed all other thoughts, filling her head until there was no room left for the question.

＊

They lurked, muscles tense and breath held, some in the leafy cover of the thick branches and obscuring foliage, some atop the paltry rises that bulged occasionally beside the roadway, and some lying flat beside that road, invisible in the night.

Adrienne sat at the highest vantage, clinging to the topmost branches of a towering tree. It was not a position she'd been asked to assume; no one came to her and said, "Hey, Adrienne, you're brand new and unproven, so why don't *you* be our lookout?" But as the lightest and most dexterous of the assembly, she could manage a perch where the others could not. So there she sat, greenery (well on its seasonal way to becoming orangery and brownery) tickling the back of her neck and her hands, sticks poking her in sensitive places. A gentle breeze, the soft breath of night, washed over her, danced a waltz with her hair, carried the scent of autumn's fallen leaves and the faintest hint of colder days to come.

And it carried, too, the indistinct but growing sound of hoofbeats, tired and unsteady, and the grinding rumble of heavy wheels.

She hissed down at the top of Pierre's head, his hair the only part of him visible in the moon's feeble glow. "Get ready!"

With a nod, he shimmied partway down the tree, passing the message along to the next in line.

Curiosity kept her up there a moment longer, peering intently as the small procession rounded the bend, their lanterns casting tiny moons against the night-dark road. Two men on horseback appeared first, each dressed in heavy leathers and thick cloaks, each carrying a rapier at his belt and a blunderbuss strapped to his saddle.

Four horses in harness clopped next into view, hauling the trundling carriage. Flanked by a second pair of guards, accoutered identically to the first, it made an impressive sight. The wood was stained a rich, dark hue, the doors and windows edged in silver that might or might not have been the real thing. It boasted no other decoration, save the family crest embossed in brass upon each door.

It was difficult to make out at this angle, but something about that crest nagged at her, like the refrain of a familiar tune that she couldn't quite place . . .

The carriage turned, following the curvature of the road, and Adrienne's heart sank. It was a familiar crest all right, though she'd seen it but once, and then only briefly.

A lion's head, mane flared, wearing a handheld domino mask.

Alexandre Delacroix was the man from whom she'd stolen the rapier that now hung accusingly at her side; the man who had stopped his servant from killing her, who had saved her life when any court in the city would have upheld his right to take it. And here she was, lurking atop a roadside tree, waiting for the right moment to attack him, to rob him, to . . .

To kill him, she admitted finally to herself as her sunken heart began to beat wildly about her chest. No, she wouldn't put sword through his gut or gun to his head, but she knew that it would happen. Joseph and his men would never reach the carriage so long as the guards lived, and they could never allow Delacroix to survive as a witness to the murder of the guards. The aristocrat had to die; and she'd gone along anyway, blinded at the thought of the riches to be won.

Would she have gone through with it, had the carriage conveyed anyone else? She didn't know; she never would. But it didn't, and she couldn't.

"Pierre!" she hissed as loudly as she dared, her voice barely rising above a whisper. "Pierre, we have to stop this! Pierre!" But he couldn't hear, having already dropped to the base of the tree so that he might take his position.

Adrienne slid as much as climbed her way to the ground. More than one splinter jabbed painfully into her palms and fingers before her feet touched soil, but she barely noticed. Her first instinct, nigh overwhelming, was to run as fast and as far as she could, to distance herself from the coming horror. Indeed, her feet pounded one after the other, carrying her at a dead sprint, dirt and leaves crunching underfoot.

Only when she smelled the horses, the wood, and the leather—when she glanced up and saw the road, and the first of the noble's guards looming before her—did it fully occur to her that she was *not* running away. In another second, two or three at most, she would be seen. She had exactly that long to make the most important decision of her life.

"Go back!" she called at the top of her lungs, her arms waving over her head. "Ambush! Bandits! Look out!" She didn't even know what she was shouting, really, only that she must warn them, must make them listen before it was too late.

She was certain, at first, that she'd failed, that she'd dashed headlong to her own grave, as the nearest guard slid his blunderbuss from the saddle and aimed it squarely at her. For a moment, she was back in the marketplace of Davillon two years ago, waiting in trembling helplessness for the lead to fly, to shatter her skull or her ribs or gods knew what else. This might even *be* the same man who'd almost shot her that day. In the dark of the moon, the face—with its red-brown goatee and mustache, and its cold, reptilian stare—certainly looked like the man she remembered.

But the weapon didn't fire. Even as the one guard covered her, unblinking, the others leapt into action. The remaining three guards—no, five, for a third pair of riders she'd never noticed were following behind—reined in their mounts, drawing into a tight circle around the carriage. They moved with practiced efficiency, so that the walls of the vehicle provided cover, so that their fields of fire overlapped, allowing no safe avenue of attack. The one who watched Adrienne slowly moved to his own station, motioning her forward, his barrel never once wavering. Uneasily, she followed.

❋

"What the hell is she doing?!" Joseph's voice was harsh, strangled, his throat clenched around the words as tightly as his fingers around his weapons. "She's ruining everything!"

"I—I don't understand!" Pierre stammered, his own features gone more than a little pale. "I—I don't—"

"Don't *what*?!" Joseph barked, raging. "This is your fault, you bastard! You brought the bitch along!"

"I—But she wasn't supposed to—"

"No, she wasn't!" Joseph drove his curved dagger through Pierre's ear, full to the hilt. Mouth agape in an eternal silent scream, the young man twitched and convulsed horribly, his feet dancing spastically across twig-littered earth. Only when Joseph yanked the weapon free, steel grinding hideously on bone, did Pierre finally collapse and lie still.

"We attack now," Joseph coldly informed the others.

"Joseph," Anton the scarecrow protested, glancing nervously at the bleeding corpse, then gesturing roughly toward the carriage with his crossbow, "you sure? They've been warned now, and I ain't exactly looking forward to—"

"I said we attack now, damn you! So what if they've been warned? We outnumber them four to one! *Move*!"

Anton sighed in resignation and, like the others, moved.

❋

In the glow of the lanterns that hung from the carriage, Adrienne could clearly see the face of the man who escorted her, and grew ever more convinced that he was indeed the same who had once tried to shoot her down. From his neck hung a pair of medallions, one bearing the masked-lion crest of House Delacroix, the other the same feline visage without the mask. She wondered what it meant.

"Bring her inside!" came the clipped, authoritative command
from the carriage. Adrienne jumped, startled at how familiar the
voice sounded, though she'd only ever heard it speak a handful of
words.

"Sir," the guard protested, "we don't know that she—"

"Now, Claude!"

Adrienne was shocked to see the servant blatantly roll his eyes
at his master's command, even as he acquiesced. "Yes, sir. May I at
least take her rapier from her first?"

"I think not."

"Very well. I'll say a nice prayer at your funeral." The carriage
door loomed open. Unable to see much within, Adrienne felt as
though she entered an abyss of endless darkness as she mounted the
single step.

"Sit down," the voice instructed.

She did, just as the attack began.

✳

Men charged, screaming, from the trees. Crossbows twanged and
firearms roared; bolts sliced through the air, lead balls and pellets
tumbling beside them in a hail of metal, punching cruelly through
flesh and bone.

It was a slaughter, but not the one Joseph and his thieves had
planned. The cover offered by the heavy wooden panels of the carriage—not to mention the sheets of iron installed within each, for
precisely this purpose—made the guards nigh impervious to any
attack that didn't come from directly before them. And any bandit
foolish enough to try to venture into that particular field was fired
upon in turn. Six blunderbuss fuses burned down, six flocks of lead
shot flew, and six flintlocks appeared from gods-knew-where. They,
too, discharged, before the smoke of the first volley faded.

Between Adrienne's defection, the execution of Pierre, and the opening fusillade, Joseph lost half his men before laying even one of the enemy low.

As the last of the loaded ammunition flew, rapiers, broadswords, and knives appeared with a sequence of leathery rasps, a horde of hissing serpents. Joseph charged, his men following on his heels, and the guards moved to meet them.

Without the advantage of cover, it seemed the greater number of the bandits might yet turn the tide. Joseph was the first to draw blood, his blade painting a gash of red across a dark-clad rider's leg. The other thieves flooded in behind him, massed too tightly for the mounted soldiers to take advantage of their horses' speed, pressing them back against the unmoving carriage.

But for all their numbers, all their desperation, even their lives of violence on the streets, these were not men trained for this sort of melee. Horses reared on command, hooves lashing out to shatter bone. The soldiers used their mounts' bulk to force their adversaries back, then set about them with a vicious array of cuts and thrusts, each carefully considered, each aimed at whatever flesh left itself exposed. Joseph's cry of triumph was cut abruptly short as the man whose leg he had slashed delivered a perfect riposte, the height of his horse providing devastating leverage. His blade plunged neatly into the soft spot at the base of Joseph's throat, and the large bandit died with his face forever locked in a parody of disbelief.

✸

The carriage rocked with the surrounding tumult, and Adrienne desperately wanted either to scream till her voice went raw or to dive for cover beneath the seat. Alexandre Delacroix did neither, however, so her pride allowed her no other option but to maintain her seat as chaos raged around her.

It ended mere moments after it had begun. Two of the defenders lay bloodied upon the ground—one who might be saved with proper attention, the other of whom had been opened from gut to groin and was clearly beyond help—alongside six or seven bandits. The few who survived, led by the gaunt and raggedy Anton, fled for the cover of the looming trees.

Everything was silence then—a moment between life and death when the hue and cry of battle faded away but the sounds of the night had not yet returned. The tentative peep of a mockingbird shattered the pall of quiet, followed by the buzzing chirp of crickets, and the night resumed its normal cacophony.

"It's over, Master Alexandre," the nearest guard called into the carriage. "All but a handful of the brigands are slain, and the rest have fled."

The old aristocrat surely made some reply to his man-at-arms, but Adrienne didn't hear it. Her blood hummed audibly in her ears, and sweat broke out fresh on her face.

All but a handful have been slain. . . .

"Pierre!" she shrieked, lunging at the carriage door. She flung it open, utterly unaware that she'd knocked the speaking bodyguard clear off his feet, and sprinted for the woods the moment her boots touched the road.

Adrienne never saw the blunderbuss, swung stock first. An abrupt fire blazed across the back of her head, and she fell unconscious to the roadway.

✸

The world was bouncing.

With a groan, Adrienne forced her eyelids open, staring at the carriage ceiling. It swayed back and forth, bounced up and down, made her dizzy, jarred her already throbbing head against the seat, and she knew that within a matter of seconds she would—

"Here," someone said, shoving a wooden bucket in her direction. She accepted it a bare instant before she would have emptied her stomach onto the floor. As it was, she very nearly upended the bucket—and its acrid, unpleasant contents—when she fell back with a gasp to lie once more upon the wooden bench.

"I think we'll just get rid of that," the same voice suggested. "Somehow, I think the cost of a new bucket is one I can absorb."

Adrienne continued to stare at the ceiling, even as she heard the sounds of the door opening and the bucket falling to the side of the road, where it would no doubt provide food for all sorts of desperate scavengers.

"That's a fine sword you've got," the carriage's other occupant continued conversationally. "Seems I've seen it somewhere before."

Though it hurt even to *think* about moving, Adrienne tilted her head just far enough to look at the man across from her. Alexandre Delacroix appeared much as he had at the market: hawk-nosed, sharp featured, practically bald . . . and smiling. Why in the name of all the gods was he smiling?

"Do . . ." Adrienne squeezed her eyes shut against a sudden wave of pain. "Do you . . . want it back?"

"I think, child, that it's a small price to pay for you saving my life back there."

"Just . . . just repaying a debt."

The carriage hit another rut, and Adrienne moaned. The older man's features clouded with concern. "I'm terribly sorry about this, child. You, uh, rather startled my guards, leaping from the carriage like that. I'm afraid that Martin hit you harder than he intended. You'll be all right, though. I'll have my best healers see to you personally.

"What did you mean," he continued a moment later, "about repaying a debt?"

"You . . . saved me from your man . . . in the market."

Delacroix's face twisted in puzzlement, then lit in comprehension. Softly, he chuckled. "I'm flattered you think so highly of me, child, but I fear you ascribe to me motives far more noble than I deserve. You were running smack dab through the middle of a crowded market, and the blunderbuss is not a precise weapon in even the most expert hands. The truth is, I was afraid that some of Claude's shot would strike bystanders in the crowd. If I could have been utterly certain of his accuracy, I'd have allowed him to fire."

Adrienne's mouth worked, but no sound emerged.

The aristocrat read her mind, or at least her expression. "What happened two years past is just that, child: past. You've saved my life tonight, and that wipes clean a great many sins. You are in no danger from me. After you've recovered, you'll be permitted to leave. Unharmed, I assure you."

That simple statement, far from bringing the reassurance Delacroix intended, served instead to dredge up the recollection of why she'd run in the first place.

"Pierre . . . ," she whispered, tears rolling down her cheeks.

Delacroix nodded slowly. "Pierre Lemarche? Yes, I recognized him. I knew his father, before the family's unfortunate decline. I fear he didn't survive the altercation. It looked as though one of the bandits killed him before the attack even began."

He looked on kindly, sitting silent as Adrienne wept.

Only when the girl had cried herself out did he continue. "I understand," he said, his tone sympathetic. "My wife passed nearly two years gone. Not long after you and I met, actually." Another pause. "What's your name, child?"

She sniffed once, trying to focus past the grief and the pounding agony in her skull, wanting nothing more than to drift off to sleep for a very long time. "Adrienne," she told him softly.

"Adrienne. Adrienne." He repeated the name, rolling it about his mouth, examining the taste just as he would a fine vintage wine. He seemed to be contemplating something, something beyond the simple presence of the girl before him, and through her pain, Adrienne grew afraid.

But for now, at least, there was little to be done. She couldn't run, couldn't even stand. And so she lay where she was, her head leaning back upon the bouncing bench, with its insufficient padding. And all she could do was pray that this strange aristocrat told the truth when he told her he meant no harm.

CHAPTER EIGHT

NOW:

Julian Bouniard strode past the ponderous door, rough with age but sturdy as the day it was hewn. He yanked the gauntlets from his hands as he walked, sticking them haphazardly through his belt. His nose wrinkled in distaste beneath the assault of the clinging mildew. Through ugly, claustrophobic corridors he passed, his path illuminated only by cheap lanterns suspended from the ceiling. The damn miserly city bookkeepers wouldn't even spring for decent lighting down here. The lamps were so poor that the light from one barely reached the circle of illumination from the next, and they smoked something awful, a constant irritant to the eyes and throat.

A second door, identical to the first, slowly materialized from the darkness before him. He fumbled at the keys on his belt, clanking them together softly, and unlatched the gargantuan lock with a resounding click.

The room beyond was cleaner than the hall, though this wasn't really much of an accomplishment, and was lit by modern lanterns far more efficient (and far less suffocating) than those in the cramped passage. A faded beige rug—or at least it was beige now, though Demas alone knew what color it might have been when new—covered the stone floor, and several old tapestries partially concealed the walls. An enormous desk occupied the room's far side, a series of cabinets stacked beside it, and yet a third door—not only locked, but barred with an iron-banded shaft as thick around as Julien's calf—lurked beyond.

The fellow behind that desk, garbed in a uniform that mirrored

Julien's own, glanced up from beneath an uneven black hairline. He recognized Bouniard, of course, but policy was policy. Instantly he aimed a pair of enormous crossbows, swivel-mounted to the desk, in the newcomer's direction.

"Today's password!" he demanded harshly.

"Holy water."

The other guard stood and saluted. "Major," he offered with far more courtesy.

"Jacques." Julien nodded. "Be seated." The constable sat, his chair digging furrows in the carpet, and the major was just opening his mouth to speak when his jaw fell ever so slightly agape. Shouts, muffled to the point of utter incomprehensibility, and the clattering of something beating on the bars, penetrated even the heavy door.

"Is there a problem in there, Constable?" Bouniard asked seriously, mustache wrinkling as he frowned.

"Not really, sir. The new tenant's making a racket. Doesn't feel she belongs here, arrested unfairly, all the usual hogwash—but, uh, louder. To be honest, Major, I've sort of drowned it out."

"I see. And she's been at it since she got here?" He sounded more than a little amazed.

"Well, after a fashion, sir. She's kept it up ever since she woke up, but that wasn't much more than two hours ago. I—"

"Woke up?" Julien leaned forward, hands on the desk. "Was she injured?" His damn ceremonial duties had kept him from hearing more than a perfunctory report on Widdershins's arrest.

"Again, Major, after a fashion. Way I hear tell, she was pretty bad off, but it wasn't our guys who did it. Seems they walked in on her and some big ox of a fellow having it out in the alley." He grinned. "Seems it was *his* life they saved, too, not hers."

Julien suppressed a grin of his own. *That* does *sound like her.* Aloud, he said, "I suppose I'd better go see to her, then. She's seen a healer?"

"Yes, sir. He felt that rest would be sufficient treatment."

"Well, she'll have plenty of time for that here." He paused. "The other man?"

"Sir?"

"The one she was fighting with."

"Ah. Couldn't say, sir. I understand he was long gone by the time any of our people got back there."

"I see. Be sure to get his description and pass it to the men, if it hasn't already been done. I'd like to have a word or two with him about fighting in the streets." *Especially with a girl.*

"I'll see it's done just as soon as I'm off shift, sir."

"Splendid, Constable. Which cell?"

"Twenty-three, sir. Put her in there alone, since she was hurt and all."

Jacques muscled the bar from its brackets, letting it thump heavily to the floor, and turned his key in a lock far more intricate than those on the previous doors. It swung open with a ghostly groan, a maw that opened into the depths of hell. With a shrug, Julien stepped through.

Another hallway, mildewed, smoky, and ill-lit with cheap lanterns, but this one was far from featureless. Every ten feet stood a door of heavy iron bars. And behind some of those gates stood, sat, or slept a rogue's gallery of Davillon's more unpleasant (or, in some cases, merely unfortunate) inhabitants. Catcalls, shouts, threats, and pleas rained down in a veritable blizzard as the major strode the hall. He made a clear show of ignoring them all.

Until he reached cell twenty-three, anyway. Widdershins, garbed in the drab brown that was Davillon's standard prisoner's wardrobe, her face marred by a few lingering trails of dried blood, shouted angrily and slammed her prison-issue ceramic mug—now cracking and crumbling into so much powder—into the bars.

"Those cost money, you know," Julien told her calmly.

Widdershins glowered at him. "You let me out of here, Bouniard! Right now!"

"What's with the hysterics?" he asked, arms crossed over his chest and standing well beyond arm's reach.

"I just wanted to get your bloody attention! Now let me *out*!"

"You know better than that, Widdershins," Julien told her, not entirely without sympathy.

The young woman sagged, her ruined cup falling from slackened fingers. "Bouniard, I didn't *do* anything!" *This time*, she added silently.

"Maybe, but I know you, Widdershins, and I can't risk assuming that your proximity to the archbishop—to say nothing of the city's rich and famous—was happy coincidence. Besides, I'm told you were fighting."

"Oh, self-defense is a crime, now, is it?" she barked. "He hit me with a *hammer*, Bouniard! Have you ever been hit with a hammer? It's not actually as funny as you'd think."

The major raised an eyebrow. "You look like hell, Widdershins, but I don't know that you look as bad as all *that*."

"I recover quickly, Bouniard. I—" The young woman shuddered once, and Julien saw her eyes roll back in her head. He lunged forward, arms reaching through the bars, catching her just before she would have collapsed in a jellified heap. Gently, he lowered her to the ground.

"Maybe not as quickly as you think," he told her softly. "You'll be safe here, and you'll have time to heal. Once the archbishop's gone, you'll be free to go."

Widdershins nodded weakly.

Julien rose and marched back toward the outer door. Was, in fact, reaching out to ring the bell that would alert Jacques he wanted out when he stopped, hand abruptly flying to his belt.

"Widdershins!" His face reddening, he pounded once more down the hallway, skidding to a stop before the young woman's cell. She'd moved back into the center of the room and now stared at him through a mask of pure, angelic innocence.

"Is there a problem, Bouniard?"

"You damn well know there is, Widdershins! Give them back!"

She blinked once. "Give what back?"

"My bloody keys!" Julien snarled, no longer in any mood to be accommodating. Imperiously, he gestured at the manacles that hung from the back wall of the cell. "Put those on, Widdershins," he ordered. "Now!"

"Wait a minute. I don't think——"

"Put them on, or I'll call a few constables in here and we'll put them on for you! And don't even try to leave them loose. I can tell!"

Muttering, Widdershins rose to her feet, staggered to the rear of the cell, and latched the heavy iron bands to her wrists.

At which point she looked straight at the fuming major and asked sweetly, "How are you going to open the cell door?"

An instant or two of silence, and then, as neighboring prisoners all burst out laughing, Julien cursed, face growing redder still, and left the corridor, returning moments later with a second set of keys.

The lock clicked, the bars swung inward, and the Guardsman stalked across the room, slamming to a halt directly before the young woman. "One last time, Widdershins. Give me my keys."

"I don't have your stupid keys, Bouniard!"

"Fine. I'll be as professional about this as I can." He began to search her, thoroughly. Prison garb didn't allow a plethora of hiding places, but Julien checked them all with an expert touch. Widdershins felt herself flush, but, true to his word, he remained professional, neither his eyes nor his hands lingering any longer than necessary.

As Bouniard neared the end of his search, Widdershins twisted her right wrist, just enough so the chain clanked audibly.

Bouniard instantly straightened, casting a suspicious glare first at that hand, and then at her face. "Don't move until I'm done," he ordered.

By then, of course, it was too late. In the instant he'd turned to her right, Widdershins's left hand had darted out, to the very end of the chain's slack, and snagged Bouniard's keys. She really *hadn't* stolen them when she'd collapsed against him at the bars. She'd simply moved them to the back of his belt, knowing he'd leap to conclusions when they weren't in their accustomed spot. This time, she swiped them properly, allowing them to rest inside the sleeve he'd already searched.

With a curse of disgust, Bouniard stood, graced her with another angry glower and a stern "Don't move," and unclasped the manacles, backing away swiftly as the iron clamps clicked open. Widdershins watched in mounting amusement as the major stormed from the cell. He slammed the gate with a resounding crash that echoed along the hall, apparently having taken up a formal patrol.

"Maybe you dropped them somewhere," she offered helpfully.

Bouniard's left cheek twitched twice, and then he was gone, leaving Widdershins once more alone in the dimly lit cell.

※

"After that," Widdershins continued earnestly over the rim of her goblet, brimming with a rich red that Genevieve had been saving for a special occasion, "it was just a matter of waiting long enough for the shift change. I just unlocked the cell door, went to the end of the hall, and rang the bell." She frowned briefly. "The other prisoners wanted me to let them out, too," she added thoughtfully. "But I just didn't think that would be right. I mean, I didn't want any *real* criminals to escape."

"Of course not," Gen agreed, hiding her smile behind her own goblet. "*Some* people *belong* in jail."

"Absolutely!" Widdershins assented, oblivious. "Anyway, the guard wasn't expecting the bell, since he knew none of his own people were in the prison hall, so he was pretty cautious. Probably should have sent for reinforcements first, but Olgun was sweet enough to encourage him to come and take a quick look before he disturbed the other constables. A gentle knock over the head, a quick rummage through the cabinets to get my stuff back, and here I am!" She spread her arms in a dramatic "taa-daa!" sloshing more than a few swallows-worth across the table.

"And I'm glad you *are* here, and safe," Gen told her seriously, though she eyed the wine-spattered tabletop with weary resignation. Careful not to spill a drop herself, she put down her own drink and leaned forward, expression somber. "Now let's try to *keep* you that way, shall we? Bouniard won't be happy about this, but if you lie low for a few months, I think the heat should—"

"I can't, Gen!" Widdershins insisted, shocked at such a profane suggestion. "I only have about four or six weeks before the archbishop leaves!"

A horrible suspicion crept up on Genevieve, tapping her urgently on the shoulder, but she refused to turn and acknowledge its presence. "What are you talking about?" she asked, almost sweetly.

Widdershins's face twisted into an ugly amalgamation of devious frustration. "Everyone's so sure they've got the right to walk all over me," she spat, fingers clenching on the table. "'Oh, Widdershins might get us into trouble while the archbishop's here, better beat her into jam so she can't hurt the guild!' 'Oh, Widdershins dared appear in the crowd to watch His Holiness arrive, better throw her in jail!' They have no *right*, Gen! None of them!"

"Well, no, they don't, but—"

The thief seemed not even to hear her. "So, fine. All right. If they're going to blame me anyway, I'm damned well going to do something to earn it."

That suspicion Genevieve had been ignoring turned into a shiver, running an icy, lecherous touch down her spine. "Shins . . . What are you talking about?"

"I'm going to rob the archbishop."

For long moments, no sound escaped Genevieve's throat, though her jaw worked furiously. No one, not even Widdershins, could be *that* crazy!

"It's not crazy!" the thief objected after her friend finally squeaked out a few syllables. Then, "Well, all right, maybe it is. But I have to do it anyway. I am *not* going to be pushed around like this, not for something I didn't even do! I'm going to rob the archbishop, and I'm not going to get caught, and nobody's going to be able to prove it was me, even though they're all going to know it! And they're all going to know that they're better off just leaving me the hell alone!"

"Shins—"

"No! I'm doing this, and damn the whole lot of them!"

"Shins!" Gen finally exploded. "*Think* a minute! All you'll accomplish is to bring them down on you harder than ever! So what if they can't *prove* it was you? You think either the Finders' Guild or the Guard is going to balk at leaping to conclusions?! You'll wind up arrested, or dead, or both! What is the *matter* with you?!"

What is *the matter with me?* Widdershins wondered, shaken more than she'd care to admit. Sure, she was a risk taker, always had been, and sure she was frustrated, angrier than she could ever remember. But she wasn't a moron—she knew that what she planned was not only crazy, it was nothing short of stupid.

But she knew, just as surely, that she would not, *could* not, back down. Nor, she realized with a gentle mental prod, would Olgun, who seemed just as anxious to see this done.

Could that be it? Was the god influencing her reactions, her emotions? Was Olgun prodding her into doing something from which she would normally have walked away? Did the tiny deity even *have* that much power over her?

No. Even if he could, why *would* he? This was nobody's decision but her own.

"I'm going," she said simply, voice steady, tone final. "I wish I could make you understand, Gen." *Then maybe you could explain it to me.* "But I *am* doing this. I'm sorry."

Genevieve cast her gaze downward, her fingers spinning the stem of her goblet.

"Who's de Laurent staying with first?" Widdershins asked softly.

Her friend refused to look up. "I can't stop you from getting yourself killed, Shins, but I'm certainly not going to help you!"

"You know I can find out elsewhere, Gen. I'd rather you be the one to tell me. Everyone else I ask adds that much more risk of word getting out. Please?"

The blonde barkeep's shoulders slumped. "The Marquis de Ducarte. He'll be there a week or so, and then he moves on to his next host."

"Thank you, Gen."

When she finally looked up, Genevieve's eyes brimmed with tears. "Shins, please come back alive!"

"I promise, Gen. If I come back, it'll be alive."

And then Widdershins was gone, before the fire that blazed suddenly in her friend's eyes could take root in any further word or deed.

✳

Pockmark—whose name was actually Eudes, not that it mattered much to anyone but himself—really, really didn't care for this idea. Constables of the Guard were the sort of men that one did well to avoid, and *certainly* he could have happily gone the rest of his life without ever seeing the inside (or even the outside) of one of the city's gaols.

But he had his orders, and he had access to the sorts of coin that made him think those orders came from somewhere a little higher than Brock, however unofficially. So he grumbled, and he fretted, and he worried. . . .

And he went.

In a deep doorway, he wore the shadows like a favorite outfit and waited, cursing his partner for every moment that passed. In truth, though, it wasn't long at all before a red-and-yellow flicker brightened the night, fingers of smoke rose to pluck the stars from the firmament. Doors and windows opened all along the block, and the nightmarish cry of "Fire!" shattered the stillness.

Men and women with buckets sprouted throughout the street, very much as though they grew wild, but it was a few moments more before a handful of constables appeared through the doors of the great granite hulk to join them.

Had to take time to make sure the cells were all secure, no doubt. But if the guards were worried at all, it was about folks breaking *out*. Not a one of them, whether outside wielding buckets or inside wielding blades, were watching for someone sneaking *in*.

Pockmark moved through the chaos and casually slipped between the massive wooden doors, shuddering at the weight of the stone and steel around him. Along the walls of a vast antechamber, well away from the clerk's desk, he made his way at a rapid crouch. His body still ached, mottled with bruises and partially healed lacerations; he walked with a slight limp, and every now and again he heard a faint ringing in his left ear. But none of it was enough to slow him down, especially with revenge so near he could smell it.

In one hand, he held a minuscule crossbow, a weapon far quieter than the flintlock with which he'd been more comfortable, aimed constantly at the man behind that desk. Thankfully, he didn't have to pull the trigger. The thick shadows and the distraction of the tumult outside were more than enough to divert the clerk's attention. In a matter of moments, Pockmark was through an inner door and into the lantern-lit hallways beyond.

He'd known it wouldn't actually be *that* difficult. The bulk of the Guard were on duty elsewhere, providing escort for His Eminence or working double shifts to keep the streets clean and quiet during the holy man's visit. The various Guard installations were staffed with a skeleton crew, and most of *those* weren't exactly the cream of Demas's crop. Three times only, as he crept his way toward his destination, did Pockmark encounter a constable he could not sneak past. And on two of those occasions, a heaping handful of coin was enough to buy their cooperation.

After all, it was just a prisoner he was after. What was the harm, really?

Had they known about the *third* constable, the uncooperative one, the one currently stuffed in a broom closet with a crossbow bolt in his throat, they might have reconsidered that cooperation.

Carefully he approached another door, reloaded crossbow in one tight fist, curved dagger in the other. He knew the layout of this next chamber from personal experience, knew of the desk-mounted crossbows trained on the entryway. He had to be ready to act, and faster than the constable beyond. Taking the dagger in his teeth, he carefully nudged the latch and then, returning the weapon to his fist, hit the door with his shoulder.

The heavy portal swung inward, impacting the wall with a dull thud. Pockmark had already dropped to one knee, crossbow trained on the desk—but there was nobody there. Indeed, the door across the room stood open, revealing the hall of cells, and the constable on duty lay slumped in that doorway.

Had someone else come to do the job?

Scowling, Pockmark crossed the room, glancing down at the dead man—no, just unconscious; he could see the fellow breathing—and continued on into the hall. Many of the prisoners began to shout as he passed, clamoring for release, but most fell back at the sight of him.

The more experienced crooks, at least, knew damn well that an armed stranger in the hall meant someone wasn't going to see tomorrow. Healthier not to attract his attention.

Frowning at the noise, the Finder thug studied each cell as he passed, looking, never finding. Some were empty, some packed with strangers, but none held his target. And then he came to one, just one, standing not only empty, but open.

And he knew.

Damn it!

It shouldn't have been possible, but not for a moment did he question. She'd bloody *escaped*! Ooh, Brock was *not* going to take this well . . .

Enough of the prisoners had fallen silent, now, that he heard the sudden gasp at the doorway. He spun, crossbow held steady, aimed right at the heart of the man who stood gaping down at the fallen constable.

Perfect. Just what I need.

Slowly, the guard looked up from his crumpled brother and met Pockmark's gaze. "I don't suppose," the man asked in a voice *almost* devoid of either surprise or fear, "that *you* know where my keys might have gone?"

The thug neither knew nor cared what the hell the lunatic was talking about. "Pistol and sword on the ground, guard. Now—and *slowly*."

Brass and leather scraped across the stone floor, the only sounds in a hall now grown deathly silent. Prisoners huddled in the cells, some with faces pressed to the bars so that they might see, others turned away to make it *damn* clear that they *didn't* see.

"Kick them away." More scraping on the stone.

"Get down on your knees." He was rewarded with a brief flicker of fear in the guard's face, but the man did as he was told.

Pockmark moved forward, tiny crossbow aimed squarely. Just a few steps closer, near enough to absolutely ensure a kill shot, not so close as to give the man a chance to grab at him. He had to get this done and get out before any of the constables returned from outside, or any of the men he'd bribed became aware that fellow guards had died tonight. He had to tell Brock, had to—

The thunder of a flintlock roared through the hall, echoes bounding almost playfully off the heavy walls. Pockmark staggered back, agony flaring through him, fire burning in his chest. He heard a distant *twang* as his own weapon discharged harmlessly into the

ceiling, then fell from disobedient fingers. His hands went to his
ribs, came away dripping.

But . . . but . . . Oh.

For just a moment, Pockmark's eyes focused on the bash-bang in
the guard's fist—not the one the man had when he came in, but the
one belonging to the unconscious constable beside whom he'd knelt.

"Well . . . Shit."

They were, as last words go, not terribly inspired. But Eudes
felt, before the floor rushed at him and the world went away, that
they were at least an accurate assessment.

A few seconds, long enough for the pounding of his heart to subside
at least a bit and his breath to come more easily to his lungs, and
Major Julien Bouniard rose to his feet. He even managed to be
almost steady at it. His own weapons once again firmly in his grasp,
he scanned the poorly lit hall, alert for any new attack, but it seemed
the man he'd just killed was alone.

Three steps, check the body—indeed, quite dead—and then a
sprint down the hall, ignoring the rising chorus of catcalls and questions from within the crowded cells. Only one door was ajar, only
one prisoner missing, and he couldn't even find it in himself to be
remotely surprised.

Julien wasn't certain precisely what had happened here—when
Widdershins had escaped, who the dead man might have been,
whether he'd come to free Widdershins or with a darker purpose in
mind—but one thing, at least, he knew.

The thieves and criminals of Davillon had brought their strug-
gles and their corruption into the house of Demas. And *that* was
simply unacceptable.

✳

Clarence Rittier, the Marquis de Ducarte and likely successor to the rule of Davillon should anything befall the duchess (gods keep her), was as much a bull of a man as the Baron d'Orreille had been a weasel. His features were squat and broad, as though he stared at life with his face pressed up against a window, and the rest of him followed suit. His coarse brown hair was currently masquerading behind a wig of longer brown curls, his cuffs were properly billowed, his coat and breeches were of the finest brown cloth—and despite the best efforts of his personal tailors, it all looked little shy of ludicrous on him. You can put a bull in formal wear, but he'll always be a bull.

The ballroom of his manor house churned with chatting, dancing, and aimlessly wandering aristocrats. So packed in were they, Rittier was quite certain he would soon see them hanging from the rafters, their finery flapping listlessly about them. The guest of honor himself, William de Laurent, hadn't made his appearance, probably would not for some hours, and most likely found the entire fiasco as arduous as the marquis did. But such was the price to be paid for power and privilege in Galicien culture.

Rittier turned, surveying the irritating creatures currently infesting his private domain, and nearly ran smack dab into one. A striking young woman with blue-green eyes, a wig of blonde tresses, and a velvet green dress cut distractingly low was drifting past as he pondered, and he scarcely pulled himself up short in time to keep from running her down.

Another social butterfly. "I beg your pardon, mademoiselle. How clumsy of me. Pray forgive me."

"Hmm? Oh!" The girl curtsied, her expression vaguely vacant. "No harm done, my lord."

"I'm so glad to hear it. Might I have the honor of your name?"

"Madeleine Valois, my lord," she told him. "This is a most excellent soiree, my lord, if I may say so."

Ninny. "A pleasure to meet you, Madeleine. I'm so glad you're enjoying my party."

"Me too," she breathed vapidly.

Fists and teeth clenched of their own accord. "Well, Mademoiselle Valois, I fear I have other guests I must see to. If you'll excuse me?"

She curtsied once again, giggling softly. Rittier fled the landing as rapidly as courtesy permitted.

*

Madeleine rolled her eyes at the marquis's back and swallowed a laugh. But while tormenting the nobility might be a hoot, it was growing near time for Madeleine to vanish for the night.

She regally climbed the broad and carpeted stairs, which opened onto an indoor balcony that offered a full view of the ballroom below. Once she was certain nobody watched her, Madeleine ducked beneath the balcony's guardrail, dropping out of sight of anyone on the lower floor. She darted swiftly to the nearest door, allowed herself (and Olgun) a brief moment to listen for any sounds behind it, and slipped inside.

It appeared to be a guest room, or so she guessed from the plain bed, dresser, and wardrobe she spotted before the door clicked shut. The chamber once more plunged into darkness, interrupted only by the twinkle of stars just barely visible through the tree overhanging the room's only window.

Within seconds, Widdershins had stripped off the velvet gown, rolling it into a careless parcel. The chill air of the room raised goose bumps across her flesh. More than a little uncomfortable standing around only partially clad, she slipped into the black-hued tunic and gloves she'd withdrawn from a large sack she'd kept well hidden beneath the folds of her dress. (She took a moment to thank the gods of the Pact that those stupid bell skirts were all the rage this year. She could probably have smuggled two backpacks, three extra outfits, and a trained mule under that thing. True, stuffing the gown into the sack meant breaking the hoops, and they wouldn't be cheap to replace, but you couldn't have *everything*, could you?) She shoved the bundled dress into the sack, followed by that abominable wig. Belt of tools and picks now strapped to her waist, rapier at her back, hair tied back with thick black yarn—she was ready to go.

"Madeleine Valois has left the party," she whispered softly. "She asked me to make her apologies."

Olgun chuckled.

"All right," she continued, voice low, "it doesn't much matter what we get, as long as there's no doubt who it belonged to." Widdershins padded back to the door as she spoke, soundless as the ghost of a cat. "As soon as we—"

Her right foot struck something limp and yielding, something that scraped across the carpet with a faint rustle, something she'd apparently stepped over and missed through sheer dumb luck when entering the darkened room.

Statue-still, Widdershins strained her senses. Sight was useless in the black; her ears detected no hint of noise save her own pounding heartbeat; her nose—wait! She did smell something, something with a familiar tang.

With agonizing slowness, Widdershins silently retrieved her flint-and-steel box with one hand, and what appeared to be a tiny iron cube with the other. It was, in fact, a miniature lantern, one she'd acquired at no little expense. The oil reservoir within was pathetic, allowing for a burn of less than five minutes. But it was easily concealed, and directional to boot. Widdershins lit it now, keeping the aperture at its narrowest, and directed the tiny beam at her feet.

One of the marquis's maids, if Widdershins could judge by the uniform. She lay haphazardly on the floor, one hand stretched over her head. It was that limp and lifeless limb Widdershins had kicked on her way toward the door. The poor woman's mouth was twisted in an eternal expression of crippling terror, and the front of her dress was drenched in blood.

There was something so utterly cold-blooded about the whole affair, it made Widdershins's head swim. The maid couldn't have been murdered here; there wasn't enough blood on the carpet. Someone had casually opened the woman's chest, and then tossed the body in here . . . Why? To hide it, obviously, at least for a short while.

Which meant, Widdershins realized with a sickened lurch, that the killer was assuredly still here. Unless someone bore this simple domestic servant one hell of a grudge, she wasn't the intended target. Most probably she'd stumbled on something she shouldn't have seen.

And if someone was to die here tonight, it didn't take a lot of detective work to identify the most likely victim.

"Oh, figs . . ." Good heaping helping of gods, her luck couldn't be *that* bad, could it? What were the odds that . . . ?

A moment's frantic thought—which actually took *two* moments, since first she had to fight down a moment's panic—and Widdershins realized that perhaps this wasn't nearly the coincidence she'd first thought. Rittier was, after all, the archbishop's first host in Davillon, and this, the first party he was scheduled to attend. That made tonight the first real opportunity to get at him—the distraction of the ball, combined with absolute knowledge that His Eminence would be present—and no assassin worth his salt would let such an opening pass him by. Indeed, that was why *she'd* chosen to act tonight, and she'd just wanted to lighten the man's purse!

"Would it be too much to ask that something go smoothly, just once?" she inquired of the room, the gods, and the universe at large. "Just for the novelty of it?"

Her only response was a swell of concern from Olgun.

"You're right. We have to get out of here, and quick!"

The god couldn't have agreed more.

"Then it's settled. We leave. Now."

Again, she felt Olgun's heartfelt assent. Yet she didn't move. Her feet seemed to have taken root in the carpet.

"The window would be best," she continued lifelessly. "The tree's right there. I can climb it to the ground, and we'll be gone with none the wiser."

She felt Olgun's growing impatience, a buzzing hornet biting at her neck and head. Still, she found herself most assuredly not moving.

The murdered maid stared at her accusingly, and Widdershins's shoulders slumped in defeat. She took a moment, her movements quite calm and methodical, to extinguish her miniature lantern and replace it in her pouch. She took a deep breath.

And then she was running, not to the window but out the door and into the hallway, careless of stealth now, speed her only priority. Olgun's startled squawk echoed in her mind as she pounded toward the stairs that would take her to the uppermost stories where she assumed—hoped—the guest of honor would be lodged.

"I know, I know!" she muttered between gasps and gritted teeth. "But we have to do this!"

The doubt washing over her was thick enough to drown in.

"Look, I just escaped gaol not two days ago. Who do you think they'll suspect if de Laurent winds up dead?"

Olgun wasn't particularly impressed with her argument. Which was just fine, since Widdershins wasn't taken with it either. Bouniard knew she hadn't a violent offense to her name, and wasn't likely to think she was starting now.

And yet she ran, taking the steps three at a time, driven by a need she couldn't explain to Olgun because she didn't understand it herself. Maybe later, when she found a few minutes to think—

Olgun shrieked even as her foot hit the top step, and something sliced from the shadows of the hall, something that gleamed in the flickering lantern-light of the top floor. Memories of Brock's brutal assault assailed her as she hurled herself violently aside.

The rapier etched a line of fire across her ribs, but the wound was shallow. It bled freely and it hurt like hell—particularly when added to the lingering traces of stomach pain that clung tenaciously, even after several days—but it wouldn't slow her down.

Her desperate evasion carried her clear over the banister, and the bottom dropped out of her stomach into the empty space beneath her. Throwing her legs out to the side, she spun completely over, like a roast turning on an invisible spit. For one heart-stopping instant, she was looking straight down at the floor almost forty feet below.

She lashed out, grabbing at the balcony's guardrail. Muscles screaming with the strain, aided by a swift boost from her guardian god, Widdershins yanked herself over the banister to land in a panting heap on solid floor.

Her side throbbed where the blade had cut her, her arms burned with the strain of her frantic acrobatics, and the pounding of her heart threatened to shatter her rib cage from the inside out. She wanted nothing more than to lie where she was, but she needed neither Olgun's warning nor the sound of running footsteps to know that her assailant hadn't abandoned his attack.

She did not rise, did not draw steel. She waited, favoring her injury, luring him closer.

The assassin lowered his rapier, echoing the lance of a charging knight of old, aimed unerringly at her bloodied rib cage. With a flex of her feet, the thief rolled at the last second, both palms planted firmly in the lush carpet. Even as the startled assassin stumbled past, braced for a thrust that never landed, Widdershins shifted the entirety of her weight to her already wearied arms and kicked back, mule-like, with both feet.

The assassin's grunt abruptly swelled into a crescendo of fear as he struck the guardrail and toppled over the balcony.

"Turnabout," Widdershins quoted to Olgun, "is fair—oh, son of a monkey!"

It was at that point, when the first screams wafted up from the ballroom below, that Widdershins pinpointed the flaw in her hastily conceived plan. Dropping assassins onto the heads of frolicking revelers did not, even by the most lax definition of the term, constitute stealth.

Despite his worry, Olgun couldn't help but snicker.

"Oh, shut up! I swear, one more comment from you, I'll have someone make me a new pair of god-skin boots!" She ran even as she spoke, one hand pressed tightly to her wounded side, and tried not to think about the fact that she'd probably just killed a man. She heard the commotion below rise to a fever pitch, detected the sound of footsteps on the stairs. Rittier's bodyguards, no doubt.

Lovely. Could this evening possibly get any better?

Fortune, however, hadn't abandoned her entirely. There were, Olgun indicated to her, only three living souls in the immediate vicinity, and only one shone to him with the light of true faith and divine favor. Without hesitation, fully aware that lots of men with pointy objects were liable to surge from the staircase at any moment like some metal tidal wave, Widdershins hurled herself at the door. It flew open, crashed resoundingly against the wall, and the thief, face caked with perspiration, left side with blood, stumbled into the chamber.

An old man in a black cassock rose from behind a sizable writing desk, gazing at her with a startling lack of alarm. One hand was held behind his back; the other rested with deceptive casualness on a staff of office more than thick enough to serve as an efficient head-breaker.

"Is there something I can do for you, young lady?" he asked disapprovingly, as though her ill-mannered entry was his only cause for concern.

"Have to get out!" she wheezed, panting for breath, wincing as the pain in her ribs flared anew. "You're . . . in danger! You—"

Shouts and racing footsteps sounded in the hall beyond the bedchamber, echoing from the stone walls.

"Rats!" the young intruder spat, with feeling. De Laurent raised an eyebrow.

And then she vanished through the window to the musical accompaniment of shattering glass, even as Rittier's personal guard, led by the red-faced marquis himself, burst through the door.

"Umm, Your Eminence . . ." Clarence Rittier, the powerful bull of a man, felt himself shrinking beneath the archbishop's unwavering stare. "Are you . . . are you all right?"

The old man responded not at all, didn't even blink. The Marquis de Ducarte, fully aware that this hideous breach of the dignitary's security would land squarely on his oversized shoulders, realized that he was in for a very unpleasant night.

✳

In the shadows at the corridor's far end, unseen by any of the so-called guards, Jean Luc—aristocrat, assassin, and guest at the marquis's ball—grimaced in thought. He didn't mourn the death of his companion; he'd never been all that fond of the man. The Apostle, however, would be ill-amused that Jean Luc hadn't fulfilled his commission. William de Laurent remained very much alive, and after the events of tonight, he would doubtless stay that way for a while. Rittier would be paranoid—almost certainly wouldn't leave the archbishop alone for an instant, probably not even long enough for de Laurent to fill his chamber pot with his own holy water. And while Jean Luc considered himself one of the best, he wasn't about to make an attempt on a man *that* well guarded.

No, the Apostle wouldn't be happy about this, but it didn't matter. Because Jean Luc had something else for him, a face he'd recognized as he hovered unnoticed in the dark of the hall.

For weeks, now, they'd searched for Madeleine Valois, and failed. It seemed as though the noblewoman simply didn't exist beyond the bounds of high-society parties—and now Jean Luc knew why.

All this time, they'd been looking for an aristocrat, when they should have been hunting a thief.

CHAPTER NINE

THREE YEARS AGO:

"Stop fidgeting, Cevora damn you! This would be long over if you'd just stand still and let the man get on with his business!"

"I can't help it!" Adrienne complained, glowering at Claude and shrinking from the tailor's hands as they pawed and prodded her. "He keeps poking me with those needles and—Ow!" She spun and smacked the harried old fellow across the face, raising a bright red blemish on his cheek.

Claude's lips twisted in a snarl, and he raised his own fist. "Don't you *ever* dare—"

"Claude!"

He and Adrienne froze as one, he ready to strike, she cringing from it, as Alexandre Delacroix entered the chamber.

"That will be quite enough, Claude."

"But sir, she struck—"

"And I shall speak to her about it. You, however, will *never* raise your fist to her. Is that clear?"

"Sir—"

"Yes or no will do, Claude."

"Yes, sir," the servant all but snarled, jaw clenched. Then, "May I go, sir? I've evening mass to prepare."

"By all means, go. And you," Alexandre continued as Claude stormed from the room. "Why you are hitting my servants?"

"Look!" Adrienne held up a finger, oozing a tiny trace of crimson.

Alexandre Delacroix raised an eyebrow at the tailor. "Are you hurting her, François?"

"Only because she'll not stand still, Master Alexandre." The man's voice was laden with a soul-deep weariness, his entire sentence one long sigh of exasperation.

Alexandre smiled gently, placing a hand on his tailor's shoulder. "I know you're doing your best." He reached his other hand down, helping the old clothier to his feet.

"Thank you, m'lord," was the grateful response, his knees popping in agreement as he rose.

Adrienne clutched the gown—or rather the half-formed accumulation of cloths, silks, and brocades that François swore would, at some point, mystically transform itself into a gown—and glared angrily at the tailor, at her benefactor, and, just for good measure, at the other Adrienne who stared back from the full-length mirror.

The room was laid out in elegant simplicity, something Adrienne had come to expect from the Delacroix mansion. Thickly upholstered chairs were placed throughout the room, as though ready to catch anyone who might collapse at any angle. A large wardrobe loomed beside the enormous mirror, a chest of drawers opposite, and the stool Adrienne currently occupied stood before them all. Once, before she'd passed away, this had been the Lady Delacroix's sewing room—a hobby she'd enjoyed despite the plethora of servants who might have done such jobs for her.

The door closed softly, and Adrienne could hear the aristocrat and his servant whispering out in the hall—about her, no doubt, and her singular lack of cooperation. She didn't give a damn.

No, that wasn't entirely true, was it? She didn't want to disappoint Alexandre.

Ten months ago, he had promised to let her leave once her wounds were tended. And indeed, she still could; it was just that neither particularly wanted her to go. They'd passed many hours in conversation as she convalesced, each learning about a sort of life they'd never imagined existed, and the weeks had passed almost without notice. Adrienne had found that she actually liked this old aristocrat—and, far more surprisingly, he seemed fond of her. For quite some time, even once she was hale and hearty, she'd never gotten around to leaving, and he'd never gotten around to asking her to.

No, she was no prisoner. She just knew that life within the walls of the Delacroix estates, while perhaps a bit dull, was far better than any life she'd known without.

Most people, including Adrienne herself, had quickly assumed the worst. An old widower, a young street girl with nowhere else to go . . . It took a mind far less cynical and worldly than Adrienne's to imagine that Alexandre's interests in her were more vulgar than virtuous.

But never once, in all that time, did Alexandre treat her with anything but the utmost care and—dare she think it?—respect. His behavior seemed less the lecherous advances of some dirty old man, more the courtesy due an honored guest or even long-lost relative. He'd taught her a great deal, not only about money and commerce, investments and business, but the ins and outs of high society. Under Alexandre's guidance, Adrienne had learned not only how to make substantial sums of money, but also how to behave among those who *controlled* that money.

In fairy tales, it was so common as to be almost cliché, but it never, *ever* happened in real life—and yet it was Adrienne's life all the same, no matter how certain she was that it couldn't be true.

Once, and once only, she'd worked up the nerve to ask him, "Are you ever going to make me leave?"

And Alexandre had only smiled, and said, "Why would I do that?"

Adrienne still didn't know exactly why she was here. What was she to Alexandre Delacroix? A charity case? An apprentice? A feeble replacement for his own offspring, stillborn several decades past? She truly had no idea—but as the months passed, she'd finally stopped worrying much about it.

Indeed, the only dark spots in life on the estate were the manservant and bodyguard Claude—who appeared to resent Adrienne's presence, and who seemed not to have a gentle bone in his body or a kind word in his head—and the interminable daily prayers to Cevora, the Delacroix patron god. It was, in fact, Claude who usually led those services, a fact that didn't help enamor Adrienne with that particular deity.

Well, perhaps not the *only* dark spots; there was also the occasional ball or party, to which she was never invited. Not even Alexandre could flout *every* social convention, and no matter how completely he'd taken her in, to the rest of the aristocracy she remained an outsider.

Frustrating? Absolutely. But weighed against starvation, exposure, and the violence of the streets, hardly intolerable.

And then, earlier that week, Alexandre had informed her that he'd soon be hosting another gala—and that she, finally, would be attending!

Her excitement and enthusiasm had lasted exactly as long as it took for Alexandre to arrange her first session with a tailor and hairdresser, at which point Adrienne lost patience with the entire process.

She glanced up, gaze smoldering, as Alexandre once more stepped into the room—alone. "I've given François the rest of the afternoon off," he told her as he lowered himself gracefully into the nearest chair. "We'll try this again tomorrow."

"Like hell we will!"

The aristocrat raised an eyebrow, a gesture that was starting to become instinctive around the girl. "You have a problem, Adrienne?"

"Me? A problem? Why would you think that?" She spread her arms melodramatically, the proto-gown crumpled into an uneven bundle and clutched in one hand. She wore only a heavy white chemise. "I've just spent three days standing around in my smallclothes, letting that decrepit snake stick me with needles and measure me in places that I could charge him for, and all for some stupid party where I'll be 'privileged' to stand around and hold riveting conversations about the state of the economy, and oh, dear, the market in beans has taken a dip, what shall we do, and what the hell is that third fork on the left for, anyway?" She finally stopped, face flushed, breathing deeply.

"Are you quite through?" Alexandre asked.

"I'll let you know."

"You do that. While you're thinking about that, start thinking about your behavior this evening." A frown of disapproval that cut Adrienne far more deeply than she'd admit settled on his face. "Have you listened to a word I've said over the past months?"

"Well, yes, but—"

"Then can you please tell me why you've found it necessary to embarrass me constantly this week?"

The red in her cheeks deepened abruptly, and she found herself staring down at her toes. "I'm sorry. I—"

"I invited you to this ball because I thought you were ready for it. If I was wrong, you'd best tell me now."

A fist of jagged ice closed around Adrienne's heart and squeezed. She finally looked up, stricken, unaware of the tears welling in her eyes.

Alexandre's own face softened. He dragged one of the other chairs over so it faced his own. "Adrienne," he said gently, "come sit." He leaned forward as she did so, cupping her hands in his.

"I know this is overwhelming. I'm sure it's been that way ever since you moved in. But that doesn't excuse this sort of behavior."

"I know," she whispered. "I'm sorry."

The aristocrat shook his head. "I'd planned to let this be a surprise," he continued, "but I think, perhaps, you don't need any more of those. This party is for you."

The girl looked up, puzzled. "What do you mean?"

"I mean that when it's done, you'll be one of us. One of the aristocracy. I don't think you'll be ready to go off on your own for some while, but at least you won't just be 'Delacroix's urchin' anymore."

"How . . . how can you do that? Why would anyone accept me?"

"Because Duchess Luchene is coming. I invited her, in your

name, and she's planning to attend. And if she recognizes you, even if only as a favor to me, the others will follow suit."

Adrienne sat stunned. Her hands shook, and the only response her dizzied mind could manage was an unsteady, "Oh, shit."

Alexandre's smile vanished once more. "What have I told you about profanity?"

The girl sighed, though she couldn't help but smile at the pedantic change of tone. "A true lady never curses," she parroted back at him.

"And do you know why?"

Adrienne blinked. He'd never gone into it, and she'd assumed it was another of the endlessly labyrinthine laws of etiquette. "Umm, because it's not ladylike?" she ventured.

"No. Because a true lady should have the wit and the imagination, or at the very least the restraint, to express herself without resorting to such base vocabulary.

"Now," he continued, releasing her hands and rising, oblivious to the strange expression his comment had inspired on his protégé's face, "I think it's time we see what Jeanette has for us for supper. Then I'll send word to François to be ready for another session bright and early tomorrow morning." He looked meaningfully at her. "Can I count on you to behave, Adrienne?"

The young woman sighed. "If he can keep from sticking any more needles in me, I promise to stand still."

"Good. Once he's done, I'll have Beatrice start work on your hair." He grinned evilly as he strode toward the exit. "You thought standing for the dress took patience . . ."

Adrienne slumped dejectedly in her chair. "Oh, fu—"

"Yes?" Alexandre asked, face gone stiff, frozen in the doorway with one hand on the latch. "Oh, *what?*"

"Figs."

"That's my girl." The door clicked shut.

CHAPTER TEN

"All right, all right! I'm coming, confound it all!" Through the living room of a small house, its interior neat and crisp as a military barracks awaiting inspection, the old man moved toward the front door. In one hand, he carried a small lantern, for he'd already doused the lights in preparation for bed. In the other, he carried a heavy bludgeon with which, even at his age, he was more than skilled enough to crack a skull or two. He wasn't expecting trouble, no, but neither was he expecting visitors—and one didn't reach an age to retire from the Guard of Davillon without knowing how to take precautions.

It took him an extra moment to work the lock and the latch on the door, what with both hands being full, but eventually he hauled the portal open a crack, just enough to see who waited on the other side.

"Well, I'll be . . . Come in, Major, come in!" The door swung wide in invitation.

"Thank you, Sergeant," Julien Bouniard told him as he stepped across the threshold, doffing his plumed hat.

"None of that, Major," Cristophe Chapelle told his former protégé with a smile far wider than any he'd offered during their years of working together. "No longer a sergeant, me. Unless you want me to call you 'Constable'?"

Julien smiled in turn. "There was a time the thought of calling you anything else would have terrified me out of a week's sleep."

"Well, I suppose you can go with 'sir' if it makes you comfortable." Then, still grinning, "Have a seat, Major. I fear I haven't anything prepared this late, but I could offer you a brandy."

It was a test, as much as an offer, and Chapelle saw in the younger man's face that he knew it. "Nothing for me, thank you," Julien demurred as he selected a chair.

"Not a social visit, then, is it?" The old soldier sat across from his guest. "Let me see. You obviously think of yourself on duty, but you're not precisely here in an official capacity. You need my advice on something, don't you?"

Julien couldn't help but chuckle. "You haven't lost a step, I see."

Chapelle harrumphed. "I could return to the job *tomorrow* if they wanted me." Then, more seriously, "Tell me about it, lad."

And that he did, from Widdershins's arrest to the bizarre incident at Rittier's manor, from the man he'd been forced to kill to the murdered guard they'd located only afterward.

"Monstrous!" Chapelle agreed, puffed up with enough indignant fury that he'd clearly forgotten he was no longer part of the Guard. "For them to come into one of *our* headquarters . . ."

Julien nodded. "I don't know what Widdershins is up to, or the rest of the Finders' Guild. I don't know if His Eminence is still in danger. But I do know that things are heating up, at a time where Davillon really can't afford them to. And I have no bloody idea what the Shrouded Lord could *possibly* be thinking, since he *should* be as anxious to avoid tumult during de Laurent's visit as the rest of us!"

Chapelle's turn to nod, but otherwise, he let the major continue uninterrupted.

"We can't let the guild think they can get away with something so brazen. But we can't afford an open war, either—not even if we could find some theological grounds to allow for it."

"And you want my advice, lad?"

"Ah—not exactly, sir. What I need is your *help*."

Again, Chapelle saw where Bouniard was hesitantly directing him. "You already *have* a plan, then. But it's not one that the Guard would let you carry out, so you need someone you can trust from the outside."

"That's about the size of it."

"I won't assist you in anything illegal, Major."

"I'd never dare expect you to, sir," Julien assured him. "It's not that the Guard would *disapprove*, exactly, so much as they'd probably find me unfit for duty, by reason of insanity, if they knew I was considering it."

Chapelle leaned back in his chair, suddenly wishing he'd gone for the brandy after all. "Oh, Demas, I'm not going to care for this at all, am I? All right, let's hear it. . . ."

※

The chamber seemed even darker than before, as though the shadows within had spawned, layering each new generation upon the foundations of the old. Jean Luc hated coming to this place even under the best of circumstances. Today, though he brought news to mitigate it, he would have to admit that he'd failed a commission.

The highborn assassin stood roughly at attention near the center of the room, equidistant from the heavy, black-hued doors and the "evil wall" across from them. In the torchlight, he could just make out the hideous visage staring from within the darkened stone. The dancing illumination created the nerve-racking illusion that the face was laughing at him.

The pall of silence was chipped away by the muttering of the other killers arrayed behind him, the crackling of the torches, and the steady footsteps of the Apostle, who once again paced before the graven image, pondering Jean Luc's report.

Finally, he halted directly before the embossed idol and faced the assembled assassins.

"The information you bring," he intoned, "is indeed valuable, more so than you know. I thank you for it.

"The fact remains, however, that you royally bollixed up a sensitive and equally vital task, one that fell squarely within your area of expertise. For this, you may find my thanks less palatable."

The leather-clad killer snarled, paring his nails with a long dagger. "How the hell were we supposed to know some damn thief'd show up and spoil it?"

"You weren't supposed to know that at all," the Apostle admitted, hands raised in a dramatic shrug. "Then again, six of you were assigned to this undertaking, but only two of you were actually in the house. That strikes me as poor resource management."

"We figured Jean Luc could handle it!" the assassin protested. "I mean, even the six of us together couldn't fight through the marquis's guards, and once it was just a matter of sneaking, we thought that a smaller group—"

"Had all of you been there, doing the job for which you were hired, Adrienne would never have won past you. Now, not only do I still have to track her down, I've got to find someone else to handle the archbishop."

"Someone else?!" The killer's voice was choked with rage, and the others behind him growled their agreement, all save Jean Luc, who was rapidly developing a sinking sensation in his gut. "You can't take us off this! You owe us—"

"For a job you failed to complete," their employer interjected, slicing off their protests like a gangrenous limb. "I'd say that makes us even.

"However," he continued more reasonably, before the argument could heat up, "I do have another task in mind for you. It doesn't pay as much as the archbishop would, but I think we can work something out."

The assassin looked far from happy, his face twisted in a scowl, dagger still clutched in his fist, but he wasn't entirely beyond the bounds of reason. "All right, let's hear it."

"In a moment, my impatient friend. I need to pray, seek guidance for my next step. I'll ask you all to bide just a few minutes. Except you." He pointed imperiously at Jean Luc. "You, come stand beside me."

The aristocratic killer blanched, though it went unnoticed in the cloak of shadows that draped the room, and reluctantly shuffled forward.

The Apostle turned to face the image and began to chant in a low, sonorous rumble, his lips, tongue, and throat twisting themselves around words that came from no language Jean Luc had ever heard. It sounded . . . "guttural" wasn't a strong enough term. Chthonic, perhaps, not just inhuman but inhumane.

A single horsefly circled the room once, buzzing softly, and then set down on the floor and spat up something tiny and unidentifiable, coated in blood. The insect convulsed as though suffering some sort of fit and then burst, adding its internal fluids to the tiny viscous pile already deposited.

A second horsefly appeared. It, too, vomited something strange into the minuscule but growing mass, and then ruptured. It was followed just as swiftly by a third, a fourth, a fifth, and then the chamber shook with the drone of a thousand horseflies, and even the dullest of the assassins knew that something was very wrong.

From every conceivable hiding place they came. From the corners of the room, the edges of the door, the folds and drapes of clothing, even the ears and nostrils and mouths of the horrified killers they flew, buzzing angrily, forever adding to the swelling *thing* upon the floor. The room filled with a nauseating, acrid odor, a miasma of rot and decay. The air blurred visibly with the heavy stench.

It wasn't until the leather-garbed assassin glanced down at his arm to see it shrivel and shrink, muscle and flesh disappearing from under the skin, that he knew what was happening.

And with that knowledge, so came pain. Suddenly, the men couldn't just see the horrific fate befalling them, they could *feel* it, now consciously aware of each and every fly-sized morsel that detached itself from their innards to be regurgitated across the room. Four mouths gaped open, to scream, to cry, perhaps to beg. Nothing emerged but an atrocious gurgle as various fluids mixed within their lungs. Blood and bile erupted from between cracked and drying lips; eyes collapsed as aqueous humors bubbled through punctured membranes and ran in monstrous tears down sunken cheeks. Limbs folded as bones and tendons liquefied beneath the unrelenting assault.

The shape on the floor began to pulse, palpitating in time with some unseen heart. With each beat, the mass shifted. Crests and ridges that formed with one pulse didn't quite subside with the next; hollows and cavities remained despite the press of fluids.

For long minutes the horror grew, and the helpless men writhed on the floor, deflated from within, until nothing remained save four sopping, gummy sets of clothing, each with a ring of teeth lying neatly nearby.

Jean Luc fell to his knees and retched, his stomach heaving long after it was empty of anything to purge. His expression thoughtful, the Apostle stood over him, watching the ongoing transformation.

The mass on the floor resolved itself into a clearly humanoid shape. It twitched once, twice, and rose to its feet. Even as it stood, a rough skin blossomed across its surface. Fingers flexed, testing muscles; eyes rolled up from within, sliding into formerly hollow sockets. Finally complete, it loomed above the watching mortals, death incarnate, and Jean Luc was certain that the abhorrent fate of his companions was nothing compared to what this monstrosity held in store for him. If Jean Luc could be grateful for one thing in this night of terrors, it was that the room's feeble lighting prevented him from seeing more details of the beast.

But then, he didn't have to look at it now. He'd seen it once before, two years ago . . .

"Do you know why you're alive, Jean Luc?" the Apostle demanded. "Do you know why you aren't currently a part of my pet here, like your companions?"

"I . . . I . . ."

"Get a grip, man! It was you who told me of Adrienne's illicit activities. That buys you some leeway. I also need your connections in the city's criminal element to track her down—and guide my little pet to her doorstep."

"Oh, gods, no! Please, you can't—"

"I can. My own people will accompany you. Both of you. Succeed, and all previous failures will be forgotten. Fail me again, though, Jean Luc . . ." He felt no need to complete the threat.

Jean Luc watched the demonic form collapse in on itself, flesh crumpling like old parchment before once more smoothing into a roughly human size. It couldn't be mistaken for mortal on close inspection, but seen briefly on the night-dimmed streets, it shouldn't draw attention.

And then, with a grin that wasn't *remotely* human, it bowed and gestured toward the door, allowing the weeping assassin to exit first.

※

"Again, Major, I would never presume to tell you how to do your job, but aren't you being just a wee bit excessive?"

Julien Bouniard glanced irritably at the black-frocked churchman—seated quite calmly, fingers steepled together before him, at the writing desk—and tried to blink back the first stirrings of what promised to be a right monster of a headache. The room was pristine, neat and organized; surprisingly so, considering that Bouniard's men had dug through it with rabid gusto last night, seeking any evidence the intruders might have left. Behind de Laurent, the young monk who had so meticulously straightened the room paced nervously, wringing his hands and muttering to himself. The three of them—as well as six guards in the hall outside, four standing on the grounds beneath the chamber's window, and two dozen more scattered throughout the house—awaited the archbishop's carriage, at which time the entire procession would head to the dignitary's next temporary domicile.

The Guardsman shook his head. "Excessive? No, Your Eminence, I don't think so. There's already been one attempt on your
life, one that the Marquis de Ducarte will never live down. I don't
think we want another."

De Laurent's expression turned wry. "For my sake, or for the sake
of whichever noble is next in line to be so dishonored?"

"Truthfully, Your Eminence, some of both. Look, your assistant
knows enough to be concerned. Why don't you?"

The archbishop craned his head. "Brother Maurice," he chided
gently, "you'll wear a hole through our kind host's carpeting."

"Good. Maybe you can use it as an escape route the next time
someone tries to kill you."

The high official smiled broadly. "There, you see?" he asked
Bouniard. "Maurice worries quite well enough for the both of us. For
me to fret would be redundant, and I so frown upon wasted effort.

"So," he continued swiftly, before the vague reddening of the
major's face boiled over into something unpleasant, "tell me about
this young lady we're so worked up about."

If de Laurent hoped to calm the incensed guard, he'd chosen his
topic poorly. Julien's lip curled under, and he fumed visibly. "There's
little to tell, Your Eminence. I'm going to find her, and wring her
scrawny neck with my bare hands." He waved dismissively, as if
shooing away an insect. "Everything past that is pretty much ancil-
lary detail."

"My, but we're taking this personally," the archbishop commented. "What do you have against this poor girl whom you're
planning to murder on my behalf?"

Julien's frown grew even deeper, a feat of true muscle contortion
that threatened to flip his entire face upside down on the front of his
head. He'd been exaggerating, of course. He had no true intention of
killing Widdershins, but the archbishop's quiet criticism was still a
slap in the face.

"Your Eminence, I've a burnt-out husk of a building, one dead

guard, another who'll be off work for a week until his head heals, and
I very nearly found myself winging off to meet the gods myself!"

"And you believe this girl responsible?"

"At the very least, she played me for a fool," the Guardsman
admitted after a few deep breaths. "I'm still not entirely certain how
she did it, but she played me, and managed, in doing so, to escape
from a prison with a seventeen-year vomit record."

"Vomit record?" de Laurent repeated cautiously.

"Escape," he clarified apologetically, flushing slightly. "When
someone escapes, we, umm, we usually refer to the prison as having
vomited them out. Thrown them up, as it were."

"I see. How droll."

"Yes. Ah, well, my point is that no one's escaped from that particular gaol in seventeen years, Your Eminence. But she did it, and
she used me to do it. That'd be enough to make me irritable even if
I didn't have the rest of it to deal with."

"I'd never have guessed," Maurice whispered as his pacing carried him past the archbishop's shoulder.

"Down, boy," de Laurent hissed, hiding a smile behind an
upraised hand. "Do continue," he said more loudly.

The Guardsman let the whispered exchange pass without comment. "I would have thought that her attempted assault on you
would have put you in a fouler mood than I, Your Eminence. Even
with the whole 'forgiveness doctrine' bit, you seem remarkably
unconcerned about this."

"'Forgiveness doctrine bit.' Oh, it warms my heart to see that
the Church's teachings are so happily embraced by the masses."

"I—"

"Major, I believe I have told you—more than once, in fact,
which is not a frequent experience for me unless I'm giving a classic
sermon—that this girl . . ." He frowned. "What was the bizarre
name you called her?"

"Widdershins. Most of Davillon's thieves have—"

"Widdershins, yes. I believe I've told you that Widdershins was not here last night to do me any harm."

"Your Eminence, with all due respect—"

"A statement," de Laurent noted to the young monk, "that is never followed by anything even remotely respectful."

"Disgraceful," Maurice confirmed.

"Indeed." The archbishop smiled once more. "If I may take a wild guess, Major? You were about to tell me, in the most respectful manner imaginable, that I'm a foolish old man who forgives far too easily, can't tell an assassin's dagger from a butter knife, and wouldn't know real danger if it came up and bit me on something that I cannot, as an official of the Church, admit to possessing. Is that about the size of it?"

Julien's jaw clamped shut tighter than a chastity belt.

"Major," he continued, leaning over his desk, all trace of good humor sliding from his face, "allow me to be absolutely, perfectly clear. I appreciate your concern for my well-being. I appreciate that you're trying to do your job to the best of your ability. And I will happily admit that I'm far less familiar with the bloodier aspects of life than you.

"At the same time, I am no stranger to violence. My life has been threatened more than once, and I have defended it more than once. I believe in the afterlife, and I even have the audacity to think that I'm headed to the more pleasant place when my time comes, but I'm in no rush to prove it. I am not an idiot, no matter what gossip you might hear, and I am not some ignorant old fool to be taken in by a pretty face.

"When this Widdershins burst into my chamber, she was wounded, and attempting to warn me of some coming danger. As you yourself informed me, she seems to have rather handily dispatched another disreputable fellow who was lurking about the house, one who most likely *did* intend me some amount of bodily harm. So tell me why I should be worried about this woman?"

"Your Eminence," Bouniard told him, fighting to keep his voice under control, "I'll acknowledge that she probably wasn't here to kill you. It's not her way. But she's *involved* with people of a much bloodier bent—and putting thoughts of murder aside, she was *definitely* here to rob you. I don't approve of that, even if you do. And *someone* wants to cause you harm. So either way, you're in danger. And either way, Widdershins is connected to it, and she's the only lead I've got.

"Now if you'll excuse me, I have to go see if your carriage is ready." Fists clenched so hard his leather gauntlets squeaked, the major rose, bowed stiffly, and swept from the room.

"That," Maurice noted as he moved to stand behind the archbishop's left shoulder, "is not a happy jasper."

"Indeed, no," William agreed.

"Maurice," he said suddenly, swiveling to face his young friend, "you'll not be traveling with me to our next residence. There's something I need you to do for me."

✸

"I'm a very busy woman, Jean Luc." Lisette Suvagne leaned, hawk-like, over the edge of the table, her face illuminated hellishly by the lamp blazing between her and her unexpected guests. "I have no work for you, and I certainly didn't summon you. So what the hell are you and your . . ."

She scowled irritably at the motley assortment. Jean Luc had always struck her as little more than a common dandy—he reminded her vaguely of Renard Lambert, come to think of it, even if he lacked the foppish thief's flamboyance—though she had to admit he was decent at his job. She didn't know the others: two, in their dueling vests and cheap rapiers, looked the part of common thugs. The last was tall, shrouded in a worn cloak, his hands and face bandaged as though to evoke the leprosy scares of old. Only the fact that Jean Luc had worked for the guild before, and swore he'd come on a matter of urgency, had won them admission past the guards. The red-haired taskmaster fully intended to have someone lashed if this didn't prove very, *very* important.

Or at least interesting. "You and your *friends* doing here?" she finally concluded, twisting a dagger between her fingers, scarring the heavy table with the blade. The sound of tiny splinters being gouged from the wood snuck through the chamber and went to go lurk in the corner, where it occasionally bounced back at them as an echo.

"That's not good for the steel, you know," Jean Luc said neutrally.

"Oh, thank you *so* much. I've never held a dagger before. They're sharp, aren't they?"

"I was just—"

"Just about to tell me why you're here, why I should talk to you when I frankly have no use for you, and why I shouldn't just have all your throats slit and your carcasses dumped in a deep hole with the rats." She grinned maliciously. "You don't necessarily have to answer to that last one, if it's too much of a strain."

Jean Luc returned her smile, obviously not cowed in the slightest. "I would very much like to know when the Finders' Guild was taken over by idiots and cretins."

Lisette rocked back in her seat. He couldn't *possibly* be talking about the attempt to kill Widdershins in gaol; not even the Shrouded Lord, let alone anyone *outside* the guild, could have linked her to it! And yet, what else could he . . . ? "Explain yourself— *quickly*," she hissed at him.

"What could possibly have possessed you," Jean Luc continued, ignoring the woman's posturing, "to authorize a job on the archbishop? That sort of attention's bad for *all* of us, not just your precious guild!"

The taskmaster's jaw snapped shut like a bear trap, allowing only the release of a strangled, "What?!"

"The archbishop," Jean Luc repeated slowly, as though explaining something to a child. "One of your thieves made an attempt on his belongings the night before last. My employer—"

"And that would be who, exactly?" she interrupted.

"You know full well that I can't tell you that, mademoiselle. But I'll say that it's someone who would make a very bad enemy." He fluttered his fingers in dismissal, as though shaking a clinging strand of cobweb from his gloves.

"I have plenty of enemies," Lisette told him stiffly, when it became clear he would offer no further answer. "One more doesn't scare me. But as it happens, we authorized no such operation. Perhaps you'd tell me more about it?"

"Really?" Jean Luc leaned back, thoughtfully rubbing his chin. "Not to doubt your word, but I find that hard to fathom. She was clearly a professional, mademoiselle."

"She?" Lisette's face lit up to shame the lantern. "Describe her," she all but cooed.

Jean Luc shrugged, and began. He'd scarcely gotten beyond eye and hair color before Lisette's own eyes blazed like a funeral pyre.

"Widdershins!" The woman's grin was somehow both wolfish and serpentine at once.

"Really. Don't any of you people have normal names, *Taskmaster?*"

Lisette ignored him. "The little scab was specifically ordered to keep *away* from de Laurent! I told them she'd be trouble, but no, have to give her the chance to hang herself first. Well, now she's done it, hasn't she?"

And made things much easier for Brock and me, for that matter.

Jean Luc rose to his feet and bowed politely to the woman sitting across from him. "I see this has become an internal guild matter, then. We'll leave you to your affairs, content in the knowledge that you can handle the situation. Good evening."

"Just a moment, Jean Luc," the taskmaster interrupted as he

rose, her voice oily as a well-greased hinge. "And what, precisely, were *you* doing at the Rittier household to witness little Widdershins's activities?"

The assassin ran a hand down his fine vest. "I was a guest," he said simply.

Lisette Suvagne was no fool; Jean Luc hailed from the aristocracy, yes, and he *could* have been innocently attending the party, but she didn't buy it for a moment. He'd been there on his own job, one that could have thrown the entire city into chaos if he'd meant to kill de Laurent himself. She was tempted to *demand* answers from him, even though she knew well she'd get none.

But there were always alternatives.

Lisette waved him away, waited until her guests had departed, then rose and strode from the room. She whispered instructions to the nearest guard, who nodded and darted off along the hall; then she moved in the other direction.

Widdershins had finally given Lisette cause to deal with her as she'd always wished. Not even the Shrouded Lord could object if she took action now, not without appearing weak. Lisette almost felt like skipping along the darkened halls, and many of her fellow Finders recoiled in fear from the gleeful malevolence in her grin.

✺

Huddled deep in a tattered cloak, good hand and bad both wrapped in a beggar's bandages, Henri Roubet waited in the shadows of a nearby alley. His companions had been inside a while, now, and the former Guardsman was growing ever more concerned that something had gone wrong—or that one of the guild sentries would decide he was more than the vagabond he seemed, and run him off. He'd give them a few more minutes, but then . . .

Then, thank the gods, Jean Luc and the others emerged, apparently unharmed. They looked this way and that, as though getting their bearings, but for a split second the assassin met his eyes and nodded. All right, they had what they needed. Now it was his turn.

Jean Luc and the others disappeared down a side street, followed a moment later—as they'd known they would be—by several guild thieves, determined to learn whom they served. Roubet let them go; they weren't his concern.

The second group, however, led by the large, limping man with the hammer, were *definitely* his concern. Sticking close to the shadows, Roubet flitted after them.

✹

"I see that you're not the only crazy man out and about tonight, Major."

"Of course not," Julien Bouniard said as he carefully slid both rapier and scabbard from the frog at his belt. "You're here with me, sir."

"Amusing, lad. But that's not what I meant." Chapelle reached out and grabbed the guard by the shoulders, physically turning him so that he would have to gaze down over the lip of the roof on which they stood. From above, the pair of them watched as multiple groups departed the structure across the lane.

Julien's eyes narrowed at the sight of the second group. "That big fellow there may be the man who was fighting with Widdershins," he noted.

"Good. Go chase him. It's by far the saner activity."

"You agreed this had to be done, sir."

"I did no such thing. I agreed to help you do it, because I'd feel guilty if you went off and got yourself killed and I could've done something. That doesn't remotely alter the fact that I think you're mad as a syphilitic hatter."

The younger man's eyes widened just a bit, and Chapelle muttered something about his years out of uniform having made him too lax about watching his tongue.

And then there was nothing to be done but for the old former sergeant to watch as his companion—his friend—moved down the rickety stairs and made his way, unarmed, toward the heart of organized crime in Davillon.

✴

Julien struggled to keep his breathing even and his shoulders straight as he neared the doorway, but there was nothing he could do about the sweat gathering on his palms, or the hairs rising on the nape of his neck. The Finders' Guild had lasted this long, in part, by staying smart—they weren't going to murder a member of the guard without cause. Then again, the incident in the gaol suggested that their attitudes might've changed recently, and even if they had not, the *guild* acting smart didn't mean everyone *in* the guild had a brain to call their own.

A faint breeze gusted along the roadway, hauling the scents of woods and meats and smokes on its back, setting Julien's cloak to rustling. He was certain he was being watched, that the guild must have eyes trained on the street, but damned if he could spot any of them. With a fist that wasn't shaking at all—and he was rather proud of himself for that—Julien pounded on the door.

A sliding panel, so cunningly concealed in the woodwork that Julien hadn't the vaguest suspicion it was there, slid open with a loud clack. He couldn't see much of the person behind it, just barely enough to guess that it was a woman. Her voice confirmed that guess when she barked out, "We're closed for business at this hour, and we're not looking for new clients at any rate."

"I want to see the Shrouded Lord."

It was, at the least, unexpected enough to stay her hand before she could slide the aperture shut once more. "*What?*"

"You heard me. Let's not waste either of our time pretending that this place is something it's not. I need to speak to the Shrouded Lord. Immediately."

"You . . ." The woman clearly hadn't the slightest idea how to respond. "You're mad!"

"Getting there," Julien told her. "Nearer every moment we stand here arguing, in fact. I'm unarmed. I'm planning no tricks. Now be a good little thief and let me in." Then, at the narrowing of her eyes, "And don't even think it. I'm not alone."

He waved, and at that prearranged signal, a lantern blazed from atop the roof, then just as swiftly vanished. Julien knew that Chapelle was already moving to a new vantage point, in case any of the thieves chose to converge on the source of the light. But it was enough to prove that Julien was being watched by eyes from *both* sides of the law.

"So," the major continued, "your options are exactly these. You can refuse to let me in, and risk the possibility that what I've to say to your master is something he'd wish to hear. You can kill me, of course, but then you've committed the cold-blooded murder of a Guardsman—with a witness, no less—right outside your headquarters, and I'll just bet that *that* wouldn't make you popular with your boss, either. Or you can let me in, and allow me to speak with him, and let *him* decide what's to be done with me and the news I bring."

Almost a full minute passed as the thief on guard duty struggled with a conundrum for which she obviously wasn't remotely prepared. And then, finally, Julien heard the clank of a heavy deadbolt. The door swung slowly open before him, and with a nervous swallow, a frantic prayer to Demas, and a sudden deluge of second thoughts for which it was already far too late, Major Julien Bouniard stepped across the threshold into the headquarters of the Finders' Guild.

✳

Lisette wound her way along darkened corridors, hollow worms that twisted through the depths of the Finders' Guild. It was nothing but a modest and mildly dilapidated building on the surface, but the sprawling complex beneath was nearly as large and convoluted as the palace of Galice's king. Any poor soul who didn't know what he was doing could easily find himself lost for days on end down here—assuming one of the guards didn't end his visit prematurely.

Lisette's journey finally carried her into the gargantuan stone shrine roughly at the center of the complex. She settled to her knees atop a long, plush cushion that some thoughtful soul had placed before the idol, and offered up to her patron her heartfelt thanks.

Her reverie was interrupted perhaps fifteen minutes later by the gentle swish of a chapel door.

Gracefully, her gaze remaining locked on the god of Davillon's thieves, Lisette stood, a rising serpent. Only then did she look away from the stone deity, turning toward the newcomer and nodding her head in acknowledgment.

"He wants to see you," the thief told her. He didn't say, and she didn't ask, who "he" was. Head high and haughty, she made her way to the smoke-filled chamber.

"I understand we've had visitors," the Shrouded Lord announced without preamble.

"We have indeed," she confirmed.

"Tell me."

For long moments Lisette spoke, the triumph in her voice marred only by the occasional cough as the fumes in the chamber tickled her throat. Still longer moments passed in silence when she was done, as the Shrouded Lord sat immobile, considering her words.

The taskmaster grinned again, nothing but teeth. "I told you she would hand us enough rope to hang herself. It's time to tie us a noose."

"I . . ." Was it her imagination, or was the Shrouded Lord *hesitating*? "Yes, I suppose we—"

Whatever he might have said was lost in a loud tapping at his chamber door. "Enter!"

One of the Finders—the same who had fetched Lisette from the shrine—stuck his head through the doorway. "You've got a visitor."

"Can't you see that we're busy?" Lisette snapped at him, furious that her moment of triumph had been interrupted.

"I—yes, Taskmaster, but I think you two *really* need to see him." Only then did Lisette recognize the underlying sense of astonishment beneath the man's words.

"Our little clubhouse seems popular tonight," the Shrouded Lord observed before his lieutenant could speak further. "All right, escort him in."

She wasn't certain what she was expecting, but a man clad in full uniform, sporting the fleur-de-lis of the Davillon Guard, was absolutely not on the list. Lisette couldn't help sucking her breath through her teeth in shock, and even the Shrouded Lord, obscured by the smoke and his ragged garb, seemed to twitch in surprise.

"He's been searched," the thief behind the door announced. "Three times, at least. He's unarmed."

"Go," the Shrouded Lord said simply, and the thief vanished, pulling the portal shut behind him. "You're a brave man, Constable . . . ?"

"Or a stupid one," Lisette muttered, not entirely under her breath.

"Major," the other man corrected. "And with your indulgence, I believe I'd like to forgo names for the time being."

Lisette opened her mouth to object, thought better of it. *Best see where this leads. . . .*

"Very well, *Major*," the mouth growled from behind the shroud. "If we're forgoing the pleasantries, what the hell are you thinking?"

"I'm thinking that neither of us wants open bloodshed in the streets of Davillon, so with all due respect, perhaps you should tell me what the hell *you* were thinking?"

Lisette struggled to hide a smirk—partly because she enjoyed seeing someone else speaking to the Shrouded Lord without sim-

pering to him, mostly because she was pretty sure she knew what was
coming. If the Guard was just as furious at Widdershins's actions
against the archbishop, was prepared to hold them against the guild,
it was just that much more impetus to hunt her down and—

"Sending an assassin into a city gaol, 'my lord'? Murdering
Guardsmen? Are you *trying* to start a war?"

Oh, shit . . .

"Because I'll tell you, 'my lord,' if we have to petition de
Laurent to find us a way around the ban on conflict within the Pact,
we're fully prepared to—"

"Major, shut up."

The Guardsman's mouth clacked shut.

"Are you going to tolerate this from him?" Lisette demanded,
desperate to get the man out of the chamber. "We should—"

"Taskmaster? Kindly follow the major's example and *be silent*!"

Her face nearly as red as her hair, burning with an almost
painful fury, she obeyed.

"Wonderful. Now . . ." The Shrouded Lord leaned forward,
seeming almost to drift closer within the smoke. "Tell me, Major,
exactly what happened."

"What makes you so certain," he asked when the tale was concluded,
"that this has anything to do with the Finders' Guild?"

"It was well organized," the major told him. "He had partners
to set the fire, distract the guards. It was well funded, considering
how much he was able to offer in bribes. And this all happened in
front of a hall full of convicts. It took some doing, but I found a few
willing to identify the fellow as one of yours."

"I see. And you feel certain that he was there for Widdershins?"

"I am."

Lisette seethed, but there was precious little she could do.

"Hers was the only door open; she was the only one missing," the Guardsman continued. "I can't say if he was there to free her or to kill her, but either way, a Guardsman is dead because of it. If you're going to start coming into our house, we cannot justify allowing—"

"Major, I respect the risk you took in coming here. And while I know you didn't do it for our sake, an open war would indeed be as bad for us as for you—perhaps worse. So let me assure you, I did *not* authorize any operation within your gaol, either to free or to kill one of your prisoners."

"I see. But I can't just accept that on faith and forget that it ever—"

"Nor am I asking you to. Taskmaster?"

"What?" she asked, voice sullen.

"You will spread this announcement for me. Whoever is responsible for this act has one day to come forward. If he does so, he will be turned over to the Guard for punishment."

"That's hardly a convincing—"

"If he does *not*, and I later learn who he is, it will be *I* doling out punishments."

"Oh."

The major looked as though he wanted to object, then thought better of it.

"Further," the Shrouded Lord added, turning his gaze toward the Guardsman once more, "should you succeed in identifying the rest of the conspirators before we do—assuming you have *real* proof, Major—nobody in the guild will lift a finger to shelter them from you, nor to take vengeance for their arrest and sentencing.

"I should think that this—in addition to your being allowed to leave here unharmed—should be more than sufficient to avert any additional conflict that might arise from this unfortunate misunderstanding?"

"I should think so," the Guardsman agreed, unable to keep a touch of relief from his voice.

"Excellent." The Shrouded Lord pulled a small rope all but

hidden in the smoke, and the door opened once more. "Show this fellow out," he ordered. "Politely."

"Ah, of course," the thief acknowledged. And then he was gone, the major trailing behind.

"I assume you had no prior knowledge of this, Taskmaster?"

"Of course not," she offered, her tone sullen.

"I'm so glad."

"This doesn't change what Widdershins did. We still have to—"

"No."

Lisette's jaw dropped.

"I am gravely disappointed in Widdershins's actions," the Shrouded Lord told her, his sepulchral tones weighted down with a light frosting of regret. "But even *if* Jean Luc's accusations are true—"

"We've no reason to assume they're not, my lord," Lisette insisted, panicked as she felt her long-awaited victory slipping through her fingers. "It fits her pattern. Underreporting her takes, refusing to pay us our due . . . There's no reason to think that she wouldn't—"

"I will hear it from her. The assassin has been useful in the past, but he's not one of us. I will hear her confession, or her denial, from her own mouth, as I would any other of my thieves. More to the point and *as I was saying*," he continued, trampling the objections forming on Lisette's lips, "*even* if the assassin's told us the truth, Widdershins is also clearly mixed up in something larger, something that seems to involve rogue elements within my own guild. And I won't have that sort of thing in my house, Taskmaster. So listen and listen well, Suvagne. I want her brought in *alive*."

Though these were his chambers, and it was his custom to dismiss visitors from his presence when their audience was concluded, the Shrouded Lord rose to his feet with those words. Two steps backward and he'd vanished into the smoke-hued curtains, leaving Lisette to fret and fume in the thick haze.

✳

"How'd it go, lad?" Chapelle asked, falling into step behind the stiff-legged major.

"I'm alive," Julien said, holding out an open hand. "So I guess as well as I had any right to expect."

The old sergeant placed the younger man's rapier into the waiting palm, waited for him to strap it on, then handed over his bash-bang as well.

"I *think* I learned something important," Julien said finally. "The Finders aren't behind what happened. They don't want a war any more than we do, and they're worried de Laurent might just authorize one."

"Assuming," Chapelle noted, "that you can believe a word they said to you."

"Assuming that, yes." The rest of the walk was silence, broken only by their heavy footsteps.

CHAPTER ELEVEN

STILL NOW:

"Ouch!"

"Oh, stop fidgeting, Shins. This would all be over if you'd just stand still for a damn minute!"

"I can't help it," the thief complained with a vague sense of déjà vu, shrinking from her friend's skillful, but not terribly gentle, touch. "You're hurting me!"

"Oh, in Banin's name, Shins! You're such a whiner!" Genevieve retorted, pressing a strip of cloth over the wound, trying for the third time to sop up the excess blood. "It'll hurt a lot more if I have to keep reapplying this stupid thing, so stop dancing like some drunk floozy and let me get this done! And it wouldn't be feverish if you'd just come to me straightaway, you know."

Widdershins gritted her teeth, partially against the pain, primarily to avoid saying something thoughtless. It's never a wise prospect to annoy the person currently poking and prodding at one's seeping wounds.

After her dramatic dive from the archbishop's window to the grounds of Rittier's estate, she'd made a beeline through the alleyways of Davillon toward one of her many bolt-holes, hiding out for almost a full day before she was convinced that neither the City Guard nor any Finder enforcers had followed her from the estate. Only then had she, limping and reluctant, found her way to the Flippant Witch. She'd nowhere else to go, though she wouldn't have blamed the barkeep for sending her away at the door.

Genevieve had, of course, done no such thing. Tired as she was from a busy night at the tavern, Gen took her friend in her arms and led Shins back inside to sprawl out on one of the tables. Only after Gen had relit the lamps, gathered supplies, offered Shins a stiff drink to dull the pain, and begun to tend to the embarrassed thief's injury did she set in on the lecture.

Widdershins didn't hear most of it. She was too busy having a silent argument with her ever-present partner.

"Tell me again," she hissed at him, "why you can't just fix this up like you did the last time?"

She knew the answer, of course, even before she felt Olgun's irritated sigh. She'd been injured enough times to know that there was only so much healing the god could provide—and only so much a mortal body could take.

In other words: suck it up and deal like any other human being. It's not that bad.

"Easy for you to say!" she growled in response to his exasperation. "You're not the one with notches on your ribs! I—ouch!"

Which pretty much brought the conversation full circle.

"All right," Gen finally announced, straightening up and arching her back with several loud pops. "I think I've got most of the, um, leakage taken care of. I just need to clean the wound one last time, slap a few new bandages on it, and you should be fine."

Widdershins opened her mouth to ask some question or other, only to find a tumbler of spirits pressed to her lips. Startled, she drank, and very nearly coughed up a vital organ. Her chest heaved, tears ran down her face, and her throat threatened to crawl from her mouth and quit the whole situation in protest.

"Wha . . . ?" she croaked eloquently.

"I thought it might take the edge off," Gen told her, the bottle held in one hand, several loose bandages fluttering from the other.

"Off of what?" Widdershins gasped.

"This," Genevieve said, and proceeded to pour a double serving of the powerful beverage over the open wound. The resulting scream was something akin to a banshee who'd stubbed her toe.

"Wow," Genevieve exclaimed, putting the bottle down so as to free up a finger, which she used to prod carefully at her ringing ears. "I didn't know a human being could *make* a sound like that."

Widdershins, now curled up so tightly in a fetal ball she could have pulled her boots on with her teeth, whimpered something largely unintelligible, but distinctly ending with the words ". . . kill you with fire."

"Come on, Shins," Gen said tenderly. "You're going to set it to bleeding again if you keep pulling against it, and I still have to apply the bandages." A task she completed swiftly and surely, wrapping the wound so tightly that Widdershins felt her rib cage might just pop out through her head and shoulders, like someone squeezing a lump of soap.

"Well," Widdershins breathed as she forced herself to sit upright atop the unyielding (and bloodstained) table, "it certainly wasn't the most pleasant experience I've ever had, but—"

The front door of the Flippant Witch gave a series of loud clicks and swung inward. Renard Lambert, his blue-and-purple finery resembling a plum in the twitching lanterns, practically hurled himself through the open doorway.

"Widdershins!" he called loudly, cape flowing behind him, "I—gaaack!" He ducked, barely in time to avoid the carafe that shattered loudly against the wall just behind his head. The tinkling of broken glass, a dangerous entry chime indeed, sounded around him.

"Oh," Genevieve said, her tone only vaguely contrite. "It's just your friend. Sorry, Renard."

"Sorry? *Sorry?!* What the hell were you—ah. Um, hello, ah, Widdershins."

Widdershins, who had lurched to her feet as the door opened, was suddenly and forcibly reminded by Renard's stunned stare that Genevieve had disrobed her in order to get at the rapier wound. Blushing as furiously as a nun in a brothel, she ducked behind her blonde-haired friend and groped desperately for her shirt.

"Didn't mean to take your head off, Renard," Genevieve said, mainly to distract him. "But you rather startled us."

"Quite understandable," the popinjay responded absently, his eyes flickering madly as he fought to locate some safe place to put them.

"Were you here for any particular reason?" Genevieve asked icily. "Or did you just come by to ogle my friend?"

"There bloody well *better* be a reason!" Widdershins chimed in from behind Genevieve, her voice muffled by the tunic she was currently pulling over her head. "Assuming," she continued, stepping once more into view, fully clad if somewhat rumpled, "he wants to leave here with all the parts he carried when he entered."

Renard straightened. "I most assuredly did have a higher purpose in coming here, dear ladies, though if I were to grow crass enough at my age to make a habit of 'ogling,' I could only hope to find two subjects as lovely as—"

"Get on with it!" they snapped in unison.

"Right." Renard's expression fell. "Widdershins," he said seriously, "the guild's coming for you. Soon."

"Tell me something I don't know, Renard."

"They've already murdered one Guardsman to do it."

Pain and blood loss could no longer account for her pallor. "What?"

The flamboyant thief offered an abbreviated recounting of the tale that was making the rounds throughout Davillon's underbelly, concluding with "You're lucky you got out before he arrived."

"Well, yes, but that's Brock holding a grudge. I don't—"

"Not anymore. Maybe it's just been a personal vendetta so far, but now the guild itself is involved. The next time they come for you, it'll be fully authorized, with the word of the Shrouded Lord behind it."

"Why?" It came out as a child's whine.

"It seems that someone's been spreading stories about you making some foolish attempt to rob the archbishop."

"Oh, Shins," Genevieve lamented, sinking down into the nearest chair.

"It can't be! Renard, that's not possible! No one saw me there except the archbishop himself!" She seemed oblivious to the fact that she'd just confirmed to Renard that the story was true. "Except . . ."

"Yes?"

Widdershins, too, fell into a chair. "De Laurent must have described me to Julien Bouniard. That, or the assassin could have had an accomplice who spotted me warning the archbishop."

Renard blinked. "Assassin?"

"Uh, yeah. Long story. I'll tell you later."

"But—"

"Long. Story. Tell. Later."

"Um, right. Whatever the case, Shins," Renard told her, "you need to get out of here. I can't be much more than an hour ahead of them. Right now, their orders are to take you alive and relatively unharmed, but you know how unpredictable these things get. Especially since Brock's leading one of the packs."

"All right, let's go." Stiffly, Widdershins rose once more, wincing as she bent to retrieve her rapier and tools from the floor. "Gen, you're coming with me."

"What? I—"

"Look, Gen. Normally, you being my friend wouldn't be sufficient cause for the guild to bother you. It's bad for business to pester the merchants when they haven't done anything wrong. But right now, they just might be angry enough to take it out on you. So you're coming with me. You can come back later, during business hours, when it's safe."

"But—"

"Now."

Genevieve sighed, but she knew better than to argue. The oddly matched trio were out the door almost instantly, leaving nothing but bloodied cloths and a newly stained table behind.

*

Jean Luc and Henri Roubet met in a small outdoor café, illuminated only by candles on the tables, where a group of friends would draw no attention, and nobody on the street could see them well enough to make out a face. The Apostle's two thugs sat nearby, the bandage-wrapped figure looming behind them.

". . . sound very happy," Roubet was reporting. "Seems she never showed the first night, and when they set up to watch the place *tonight*, they found the tavern empty. They don't have enough people to keep an eye on it every minute of the day, but they'll be back there eventually. They seem pretty sure she'll appear there sooner or later, and right now, Brock's willing to watch and wait."

"And does this tavern have a name?" Jean Luc asked, sipping at a small cup of tea, pinky finger pointing skyward.

"The Flippant Witch."

"Show me."

Both men looked up as the otherworldly thing spoke behind its mask of bandages, its voice causing the table to tremble, the candle flame to dance.

"Of course. Do you mind if we just finish—?"

"Show me *now*."

Technically, Jean Luc was in charge. That didn't stop him and Roubet both from rising instantly to their feet, unwilling to argue.

For just a moment, as they took to the streets once more, Roubet wondered what had happened to the thieves assigned to follow Jean Luc and his demoniac ally. And just as swiftly he decided that he really, *really* didn't want to know.

*

"This is stupid, Shins!" Genevieve hissed for roughly the sixth time as the fugitive trio slunk through yet another filthy, trash-strewn alleyway. The aromas of rotting garbage, alcohol, vomit, and human offal intertwined to form a vulgar scent that caressed the dank streets with all the false affection of a diseased trollop. It even kept the rats at bay. Things squelched underfoot as they walked, each spurt of unidentifiable ooze adding a new and poignant layer to the near-poisonous miasma.

"I'm inclined to agree with Mademoiselle Marguilles," Renard added, pausing long enough to lift up one boot and sadly examine the encrusted sole. "Even leaving aside the danger to our well-being—which is, I feel constrained to point out, quite substantial—there are other, no less immediate concerns. This outfit, I fear, is quite unsalvageable. I shall perforce be required to burn it."

Widdershins, gliding silently through the alley ahead of them, drew to a halt, her shoulders rising in a sigh. "All right, that's enough, both of you! This is important, so hush up and let's keep moving. The faster we get there . . ."

". . . the sooner we can leave," the barkeep and the thief parroted in unison. "So you keep telling us," Genevieve added. "But that's only if you survive, Shins."

"Look!" Widdershins turned, wincing as the motion tugged disagreeably at her bandages. "We've got to hide, yes? Maybe for quite a while. Therefore, ergo, and to wit, we need money. Where am I losing you two?"

Renard cleared his throat, a fist hovering just before his face. "I believe, Widdershins, that it would be at the part where you decide to go back home and gather up your stash of coin, even though the people hunting you may well know where you live."

The young woman idly kicked a clump of something from the road before her. It hit the left wall of the alley with a moist plop, and stuck. "I've told you, I don't live here. It's one of several rooms I keep around the city. Under fake names," she added as Genevieve drew breath to speak, only to come over vaguely green as the atmosphere of the alley flooded her lungs. "I've got funds stashed in each.

Enough to keep us going for a while, if need be. And it's perfectly safe!" she insisted in the face of their continuing glare. "It's not humanly possible for anyone to know about this place. There's no way to trace it to me. None!

"If it'll make you feel better," she continued, "the two of you can wait here while I run up and gather the marks." She pointed at a dilap-idated building, four ugly stories in height. There were more holes in the wall than there were bricks. The wooden staircase—running up the side of the building and sagging like a dying vine—leaned several feet from the wall at multiple points, and pretty much looked to be about as sturdy and well designed as a glass battering ram.

"You know," Genevieve replied dubiously, "that might be for the best."

Widdershins smiled despite herself. "I'll just be a minute or three, I promise. There's nothing to worry about."

"Worry?" Genevieve asked Renard as their mutual friend faded into the shadows. "Why would we possibly be worried?"

"I'm sure I can't imagine."

For long moments they stood, trying their damnedest not to breathe for fear their lungs would rebel and physically fight their way free of the alley. Until, eventually, Genevieve turned, her gaze meeting Renard's squarely for perhaps the first time.

"She doesn't know, does she?"

"I beg your pardon, my dear? Who doesn't know what?"

"Widdershins. She doesn't know about you."

Renard's eyes widened briefly, then narrowed. "I'm sure I have no idea what you're—"

"Oh, please. You're a professional thief, you're a member in good standing of the guild, and you're risking your life and your position just *being* here. I love Widdershins to death, Renard, but she can be a real idiot on occasion. I assure you, though, that *I* am not."

The fop just about deflated; even the garish colors of his outfit seemed to go suddenly dull (though to be fair, that might simply have been the miasma of the alley eating away at the dyes). "You won't say anything, will you?" he all but begged.

"Why won't you?" Gen asked, not unkindly.

"Look at me, mademoiselle. I am many things, and I make no apologies for most of them—but do you believe me to be a man Widdershins could ever take seriously?"

"You might be surprised," she told him. "But no, I won't tell her. It's not my place."

"Thank you."

And there seemed, at that, to be nothing more for them to say.

✸

Widdershins's unshakable confidence lasted almost precisely to the midpoint of the first flight of stairs, which was, not coincidentally, the exact same point at which the entire structure emitted a mighty groan and shifted several inches to the left. She froze, hand clasped so tightly to the guardrail that the rotting wood began to disintegrate in her fist.

"Olgun?" she croaked. "Olgun, can . . . umm, that is, you *can* make sure this thing doesn't fall out from under me, can't you?"

There was no reply save another faint shift of the rickety stair. Dust cascaded from above, sifting into Widdershins's hair, tickling her nose. Only several heavy gasps prevented a sneeze that might have brought down the entire contraption.

"Olgun?" Little more than a whisper, this time, for fear that even so tiny a sound might have deadly repercussions.

Then, accompanied by a burst of silent laughter, Widdershins sensed the familiar pins-and-needles in the air, felt the decaying wood shore up beneath her feet and her ever-tightening grip.

"Oh, *very* funny, Olgun!" she growled, face inflamed at the laughter that sounded around her soul. "Hysterical, even."

The mischievous deity continued to chortle.

"When you're through entertaining yourself," Widdershins told him haughtily, "we can just be on our way."

It took a moment more for the god to get a hold of himself—a long moment during which Widdershins stared irritably upward at the constellations not washed out by the light of the moon or hidden by long streaks of cloud. *We'll probably have rain by morning*, she noted absently.

Finally, Olgun decided the joke was over, and they continued up the now steady stairs.

Widdershins halted at the top floor, not beside the door but at the right-most edge of the tiny landing. Fingers expertly found the cracks and crevices in the wall, feet sliding easily into the gaps that were, to her, as good as carved steps. Scuttling sideways, sure-footed as a spider, she passed over several windows, stopping finally at the fourth. She flipped a well-concealed catch on the pane, lifted the window, and slipped inside, all as silently as the moonlight pooling thickly on the floor.

"All right," she commented, though whether to herself, to Olgun, or to the empty room at large was debatable. "That was easy enough." Unhindered by the darkness, she made her way around the room, gathering her supplies. Within moments, she'd stopped by the cheap wardrobe in the corner. The gold lay hidden in a tiny hollow low in the wall behind it. She knelt, preparing to shove it aside to get at the prize beyond. "Let's get this done and get out of here."

"I couldn't agree more."

It was a hard voice, guttural, rumbling, a mastiff speaking through a mouthful of gravel and broken glass. Widdershins rolled backward and came instantly to her feet, rapier in hand. It was too dark in the chamber for her to see her opponent, though she was certain there had been no one present a moment before. Who was it? How did he get in?

More importantly, why had Olgun not warned her about him?

And *most* importantly, how the happy horses had they *found* her?!

"It's not possible!" she whispered as she braced for an attack, unaware she'd spoken aloud.

"Actually, what I believe you told your companions waiting outside in that filthy little alley was that it wasn't *humanly* possible," the voice grated at her. "And in that, you're entirely correct."

Widdershins lunged, blade aimed unerringly at the horrible sound, and connected with nothing at all.

"Who do you intend to stab with that needle, little girl?" The question came from off to her right. In that horrible voice, Widdershins sensed nothing human, nothing but contempt.

"You, if you've the courage to show yourself!" Fine, so it was mostly bluster, but she needed to see who she faced.

"As you wish." A shadow moved, a darker blot in the night-cloaked room, and a shape appeared in the sickly moonlight.

"Is this more to your liking?"

Widdershins couldn't speak, could barely even breathe. Nothing save a primal whimper of hopelessness emerged from between her lips.

It was tall, bent low to avoid the ceiling overhead. All four limbs were hideously long and slender, as though some demented sorcerer had taken a normal man and stretched him like taffy to half again his starting height. Its flesh was the decomposing brown of poorly tanned leather, its jagged talons rusted iron, its head a misshapen amalgamation of man and boar. Thin patagia fluttered between its arms and distended rib cage, and a thrashing, serpentine appendage protruded obscenely from between its legs, complete with jagged fangs and forked tongue.

And it smelled, incongruously, hideously, of honey.

But it was neither horror nor fear that had drawn such a primitive, despairing sound from Widdershins. It was recognition.

"Hello, Adrienne," the hell-spawned beast purred, thoughtfully stroking its twisted chin with claw-tipped fingers. Widdershins felt the space around her grow darker, heavier, as though the creature's very shadow were a palpable presence. "Or would you prefer Widdershins now? I would so hate to offend you, after so many years apart."

It lunged, its enormous stride taking it across the room in a single step, and Widdershins had nowhere, nowhere at all, to run.

CHAPTER TWELVE

TWO YEARS AGO:

Adrienne allowed the rhythm of the music, the ebb and flow of the dance, to sweep her through the hall of whirling couples and spinning bodies. The musicians were magnificent, the strings and winds weaving a tapestry of pure emotion. Dresses and gowns of the finest cloths, formal coats with silver buttons—all flashed past as her feet carried her the length of Alexandre Delacroix's massive ballroom. Her every move as graceful as those who were born to this life, Adrienne found herself smiling with a foreign sentiment she only scarcely recognized as contentment.

And if she had more difficulty in finding a dance partner than other women; if she danced alone more often than not; if some of the aristocrats fell back as she drew near, lips curled in a moue of arrogant disdain . . . well, it was their loss, as Alexandre had told her again and again, in the long nights when their disrespect had sent her sobbing or raging to her chambers. Some of Davillon's nobility had indeed learned to welcome this strange addition with open arms. Those who didn't, didn't matter.

The waltz wound to a close, the minstrels taking a much-deserved break before launching into their next piece, and Adrienne breathlessly worked her way through the milling throng. Her gown was modest, a deep lavender with tight sleeves of rich blue, a gift her mentor had insisted upon giving even though Adrienne could easily afford such things on her own, now. It was just that sort of behavior that kept the rumors of their nonexistent romance alive. For two years she'd lived in Delacroix's manor. Today, she could afford a place of her own as easily as she could the gown.

She loved the old man, true enough—as family, not as the gossips suggested—but this wasn't why she stayed.

Adrienne was afraid—afraid that without Alexandre at her side, her hard-won acceptance in Davillon's upper echelons would blow away like so much dandelion fuzz. She feared that, once she grew only a few years older, custom and propriety would force her to hire servants of her own, to throw her own parties, to play her own politics—all elements of high society she could happily do without.

But most of all, she feared that stepping out that door would bring her old life rushing back. She'd pushed it down, crushed it beneath the weight of stubborn determination, but still it haunted her at night, when such terrors shamble from their dens to torment innocent insomniacs. The sting of hunger and the itch of matted filth were never far from her thoughts. She'd never shaken the notion that this was all some majestic dream or fantasy, and she clung unconsciously to the childish notion that it was Alexandre himself who kept that fate at bay. As long as he remained in her life, the dream would continue.

These, however, were darker thoughts for other nights. Tonight was for music, for dancing, for . . .

"Watch where you're stepping, damn it!"

Adrienne spun aside just as the trailing end of a heavy banner flopped down where she'd been standing. She glanced up into Claude's angry eyes. He stood atop a ladder, struggling to straighten a hanging that had come loose. The image was the lion's head—not the masked crest of House Delacroix, but the unadorned feline face that was the symbol of Cevora.

But of course it was. Claude would hardly have cared enough to fix any of the *other* banners, would he?

"Don't you have a psalm to go sing?" Adrienne snapped at him, then spun off into the crowd before the angry retort in his eyes could reach his tongue.

All right, so maybe some dark thoughts are *appropriate for tonight.*

"Would it be presumptuous of me, Mademoiselle Satti, to say that you are easily the most radiant, most enchanting, and most wonderful sight present in this house tonight?"

And then again . . .

The young woman teasingly rolled her eyes heavenward, though her smile grew wide. "Presumptuous, Monsieur Lemarche? Not at all. Rather silly, though."

Darien Lemarche, current patriarch of the Lemarche family, younger brother of the late and lamented Pierre, bowed gallantly and took a seat beside her.

He was very much like his brother, though he lacked, or at least appeared to lack, Pierre's selfish streak. Some eight or nine months after Alexandre took Adrienne in, the Lemarche family had—in an almost perfect echo of Alexandre's own social and economic recovery—reversed their fortunes once again and reentered the aristocracy without a trace of their old patriarch's stigma. Darien had recognized Adrienne by name when they'd first met. If he blamed her in any way for the death of his older brother, or even knew that she'd been involved in Pierre's final scheme, he never showed it, treating her with exquisite courtesy. She, in turn, considered Darien one of the few friends she'd made among the nobility, who were, by and large, more amiable in groups than as individuals.

Tonight, Darien was dressed in a magnificent overcoat of deepest burgundy, atop a pair of white hose and a black ruffled shirt. He'd chosen to forgo a wig, and his dark hair was swept immaculately back. He was, at least where Adrienne was concerned, more than a little stunning.

"Seriously," he said, taking the time to nod a friendly greeting to another passing acquaintance, "how are you?"

The young woman was taken aback, not by the question, but its tone. "I'm just fine, Darien. Why?"

"I don't know. You just seem . . . I'm sorry." He shook his head, jolting several curls out of alignment. "It's not my place."

"Oh, please." Adrienne smiled. "We've both been around enough to know where you can stick your 'place.'" Darien blinked. "Tell me," she insisted.

The young patriarch sighed. "As you wish, Adrienne. You just haven't seemed content of late, that's all." He leaned forward, close enough to draw a few scandalized stares. "Haven't you felt at all, well, incomplete?"

She couldn't help but smile once more. "You sound like you're selling something. I'm quite happy here, Darien."

"But it's not enough, is it?"

Adrienne frowned, her earlier thoughts circling through her mind once more.

"Adrienne," he told her, fingers idly stroking the smooth arm of the chair, "I have something I'd like to show you." He smiled. "Considering your—if you'll please pardon the unflattering cliché—'rags-to-riches' story, it's very possible he's been calling to you anyway. He may even have had a hand in your success."

"He? He who? Who's he? What are you talking about?"

"The one who restored my family's fortunes, Adrienne." Darien rose to his feet, extended a hand to the young lady. "Let's find someplace we can talk," he told her softly. "You'll find it worth your while, I promise."

✸

They found their spot upon one of the manor's balconies, overlooking the intricate rose garden. Other couples, seeking privacy of their own, wandered below them, following the twists and turns of the almost-but-not-quite-maze of blossoms. The moonlight illuminated this jewel or that bauble, reflected from this woman's hair, from that gentleman's bald pate. A faint breeze, perfumed by the roses below, wafted across the open landing, ruffling Adrienne's gown as though she had some other small creature in there with her.

Darien's expression was sincere, imploring. Hers was, to put it mildly, incredulous.

"You're joking," she finally said.

The young man's face fell, but he refused to give in. "Not at all, Adrienne."

"A god."

"A god," he repeated. "His name is Olgun."

"I've never heard of him."

"I'd be shocked if you had. He's not one of the gods of the Pact; I don't think the High Church has even *heard* of him, let alone thought about recognizing him. We only know him because our founder discovered his last shrine on a trading expedition to the northlands. There was one man there—Olgun's last priest, we think, but he spoke no civilized language, and died mere hours after they found him. We think Olgun was a major northman deity once, long, long ago."

"And he put your family back on its feet," she said doubtfully. "And you think he was responsible for my good fortune as well? Come on, Darien."

"Adrienne, why do you think the Houses and guilds and governments *have* patron deities? How many icons to Cevora have you seen around Alexandre's home? For that matter, how do you think he recovered his family fortunes, if not with divine aid?"

She shrugged. "Luck? Skill? Random chance? I'm sorry, Darien. I believe in the gods, I just—well, they've certainly never done anything for *me*."

"Haven't they?" Darien said cryptically. Then, at the look on her face, "Adrienne, you needn't take my word for it. There's over twenty of us, now. All aristocracy, all wealthy, and all of us have known a tremendous amount of good fortune since we joined. We're Olgun's only worshippers. It's not like the gods of the Pact, who have hundreds, thousands, maybe even millions calling on them at any given time. Olgun can concentrate on us alone, and he's not bound by the strictures of the Pact gods. With him at our side, we never risk losing what we have. No disgrace will ever befall my family again, I promise you."

"Even if it's true, Darien," Adrienne told him, her tone suggesting it was anything but, "what would I need Olgun for? I have all I need." *And besides, if Cevora was responsible for Alexandre's recovery, did she want to risk insulting him?*

"Except," the young man argued, "the freedom to do what you want with it."

Adrienne's jaw clenched.

"Come with me to one service," he implored. "Just one. Olgun's not an evil god, or cruel. If you don't wish to join us, there won't be any repercussions. You have my word."

"Why?"

"Because," Darien said softly, "I would . . . very much like for you to be a greater part of my life. And I would have you see what fortune I have to share."

She looked at the garden below, grateful that the pale moonlight hid the flush in her cheeks.

"Please, Adrienne. What have you got to lose?"

✳

One evening the following week, while Alexandre was out on business of his own, Darien arrived at Delacroix Manor. Adrienne, clad formally in a red gown and a bodice of black suede, met him at the door. The servants would probably gossip, but somehow, Adrienne was pretty sure that an illicit religious rite was not among the activities on which their speculations would land.

They rode in style through the streets of Davillon, seated in a small carriage as fancy as Alexandre's own, and markedly more comfortable. The benches were well padded, upholstered in the finest velvet and cushioned with goose feathers. Horses and driver clearly knew the route, for there was a confidence in their step, a familiarity in the monotonous clop-clop of hooves on cobblestone. Idyllic, really, or it would have been had Darien not kept the windows shuttered and refused outright to tell Adrienne where they were going.

The young man's reticence, his dour expression and solemn mien, were amusing—initially. Adrienne couldn't help but chuckle, so out of character was the cheerful, happy-go-lucky aristocrat. After a half hour passed, however, and he'd said no more than three contiguous words, when she still had no idea where they were headed, when she'd attempted surreptitiously to lift the window shade and discovered it bolted down . . . then, finally, she began to grow just a bit miffed.

"Darien," she growled, "you are going to tell me where we're going, right now, or I am going to get up and leave this carriage, right now."

"Not a good idea, Adrienne. We're moving."

"Not quickly, we're not. I'll take my chances."

"The door's locked," he pointed out.

The young woman's expression turned to ice. "I'm sorry, I didn't quite hear you. I thought you said the door was locked."

Darien nodded.

"Lemarche, you let me out of this carriage this instant!"

"I can't do that, Adrienne. You're not allowed to know where our shrine is until after you've been accepted."

"Darien—"

"Adrienne, no harm will come to you, I swear it. Trust me."

"Oh, because you're making it so easy, aren't you?"

But Darien subsided again into a solemn silence, one that Adrienne, for all her threats and demands, could not penetrate. Finally, worn out, angry, and growing ever more anxious, she, too, fell petulantly silent, save for occasional grumbles about how much Darien was coming to resemble his older brother.

Another twenty minutes passed, and for all Adrienne knew, they could be halfway across town, or only three doors from where they had started. When the coach finally trundled to a halt, Darien attempted to hand the young woman a blindfold, opening his mouth to explain that it was required, that it wasn't really up to him.

He quailed beneath her withering glare and put it away without uttering a word.

Despite her anger and mounting trepidation, Adrienne couldn't help but smirk contemptuously as her companion unfolded a bundle of gray cloth from beneath his seat and pulled it over his head. Unknown gods, hidden cult gatherings, and now a plain hooded cloak. This was starting to look less like a secret sect and more like the opening act of a bad melodrama.

"Well?" she asked, when Darien reached over to knock on the carriage door. "Don't I get one, too?"

The young man shook his head, the gesture strangely twisted by the hood. "No. It's traditional that the entire sect be permitted to look upon new petitioners as they determine their suitability to join."

"I'm not petitioning, I'm observing. One service, remember, to judge for myself? So far," she added bitterly, "I'm not terribly impressed."

The door swung open, pulled aside by several figures that were, as Adrienne expected, similarly hooded and cloaked. A brief spate of whispers and mutters erupted as they took in Adrienne's unveiled face, and one of the small band glowered at Darien.

"She's supposed to be blindfolded!" he hissed in a stage whisper.

She left Darien to explain her lack of ocular wrappings as best he could, directing her attention instead to the building. It wasn't impressive, just a nondescript structure, ungainly and ugly. It didn't quite seem to be a warehouse, nor a storefront, nor a tavern, nor a tenement. Tucked away on a cluttered street, it was so unremarkable, so actively unimportant, that she doubted anyone gave it a first glance, let alone a second.

Not a bad place for a clandestine sect, actually. Her respect for

Darien's people rose a bit—still below scalp lice, but now higher in her estimation than the thin film that covered the floor around a public privy.

The cloaked fellow who'd barked at Darien stormed toward her, clearly unhappy with the results of his conversation. Despite the hood, Adrienne had already seen enough of his jawline that, combined with his not-quite-whisper, she could identify the man from more than a few parties.

"Do you swear, Adrienne Satti," he asked in a feigned rasp, "to remain silent regarding what you see here tonight, to reveal nothing of your activities this evening, and to expose the power of our god and our faith to no outsider, upon your very soul?"

"Yeah, sure, Tim. Whatever you say."

Timothy Pardeau, patriarch and owner of a horse- and livestock-trading empire, uttered a strangled gasp and retreated several steps, glaring fire from beneath his cowl. Abruptly he spun, grabbing Darien by the collar with both hands. "This is your fault," he seethed at the young Lemarche patriarch. "If this goes badly, I'll see to it personally that you catch the brunt of it! I—"

"If you're through threatening your fellow true believer," Adrienne said, idly tapping a foot, "I thought there was supposed to be a floor show tonight."

Timothy shouted something garbled and incoherent at her, then shoved past and practically flew into the building. With a shrug— and a second, larger shrug in response to Darien's whispered "Are you *trying* to ruin it?"—Adrienne followed the cloaked cultists inside.

✳

Though she'd have scoffed if anyone had suggested it beforehand, Adrienne Satti's life changed forever in the following hour.

She'd rolled her eyes at the winding staircase that led to the underground shrine, formerly a basement. She'd shaken her head at the mass of gray-robed worshippers staring at her, good little sheep lined up between the door and the center of the domed chamber (which still sported rafters and platforms from recent reconstruction). She yawned through the sermon, some claptrap about health and fortune, delivered with gusto by an obviously enraptured Timothy. She snickered as they tugged on the hidden lever, engaging a series of heavy gears and pulleys that raised Olgun's likeness up into the center of the room, and she laughed aloud at the horned, bearded visage that hove into view. She was all but ready to tell Darien and his friends to stick their deity and his divine favor someplace very, very cramped when Timothy finished his benediction with "Speak to us, your faithful, mighty Olgun. Reveal to us your favor!"

In the single biggest shock of Adrienne's life, the god replied!

Not with deep-voiced words, thundering from on high, nor with obscure omens or a rain of frogs, but with what Adrienne could describe only as a gentle wave of emotion. It flowed through the chamber in a cleansing stream—kind, tender, washing them clean of their worries and cares. Adrienne tried to remain skeptical, even in the face of that outpouring of peace and tranquility, to convince herself that it was an illusion, some magic spell, perhaps even a drug in the smoke of the dancing torches.

And then Olgun touched her soul personally. Adrienne never knew if he'd communicated individually with anyone else that night, or if only she was so honored. And what he sent to her was not some empty sense of his own magnificence, not some haughty attempt to convince her of what she should or should not accept. No, the emotion that washed over Adrienne had been, as best she could translate into words:

"Pretty silly, isn't it?"

From that day onward, Adrienne never missed even one of their weekly gatherings. She accepted Olgun, and his worshippers, and they, in turn, accepted her as their newest acolyte, though some were more eager to take her in than others. Even here there were those who felt that Adrienne was attempting to rise above her station, that her recent fortune didn't make up for the cardinal sin of a common birth. As the weeks passed, however, germinating slowly into months, even the hard-liners were forced to accept that Olgun himself had chosen Adrienne as one of his own. Haughty and convinced of their own superiority they might be, but they weren't prepared to challenge the judgment of their god himself.

Olgun rarely spoke to her personally after that first night, though she experienced his touch each week, as he reached out to his worshippers en masse. His signs of favor were obvious, though, to those who knew to look. Alexandre had instructed Adrienne well, and she'd proven herself an apt student; but following her discovery of Olgun—or perhaps Olgun's discovery of her—the riches she'd accumulated in two years practically doubled in two *months*. Every endeavor seemed blessed with a bit of extra luck, never dramatically, just enough to nudge things in her favor. The silkworms of the east ceased production early that year, only after she'd stockpiled her own stores; a sudden rain kept a competitor's goods off the market while hers were bought and sold.

Adrienne's luck turned in other areas as well, and she found herself in Darien's company on as many social occasions as religious ones. And that, too, seemed to open further the doors of high society, to smooth the rough edges with which the aristocracy treated her.

And then, one night, he appeared beside her as Olgun's services came to an end, and the small crowd began to disperse.

"We should get a move on, love," she said to him with a smile. "Don't get me wrong, I prefer listening to cats mate than going to opera, but if you don't want to be late . . ."

"Actually," he said, his face strangely serious, "we're not going to the theater tonight. There's someone you need to talk to."

Adrienne frowned, but followed as Darien led her across the room, his boots reverberating on the heavy stone. Finally, they stood before another gray-robed figure, his deep hood obscuring his face. She'd seen him earlier, standing near the back of the service, and had wondered who he was, but had forgotten all about it during the service.

He reached up, slowly—were his hands trembling?—to draw back his hood. Adrienne's eyes grew wide, and a surge of joy wrestled with a vague sense of betrayal deep in her gut.

"Hello, Adrienne," said Alexandre Delacroix.

For long minutes they walked, side by side, along the streets of one of Davillon's higher-rent districts—away from either the shrine or the estate, but also far from anywhere they might feel unsafe.

"Why?" she finally asked. She could have meant any one of a dozen questions.

Alexandre sighed. "I've wrestled with this since the day we met, Adrienne."

"Stop wrestling and start explaining."

He couldn't help but chuckle. "Olgun turned my fortunes around, Adrienne. House Delacroix was destined for poverty, for disgrace, for social exile. I was desperate for a way to save the House—to save myself—and Olgun offered it."

"And Cevora?"

The aristocrat's face fell. "Cevora has been patron of my House for generations beyond counting, and he's been good to us in our time. But either he chose to withhold his favors recently, or they proved insufficient for the tasks at hand. Either way, I shall never fail to honor Cevora for all he's done, for so many years of watching over us. I worship him still. But I grant my faith to Olgun as well, and he has honored me in return. It's why I've allowed Claude to take over most of the religious duties of the household. I revere Cevora, but it didn't feel right for me to be leading the services, you see?"

Alexandre smiled shallowly. "Just as well, really. From the day I hired him, Claude took to the worship of Cevora as though he were born to it. I think he's more devout than I ever was."

"All very nice," Adrienne said, face turning briefly jaundiced as they passed beneath a streetlight in dire need of a good cleaning. "But that's not really what I meant, you know."

"Yes, I know." Alexandre stopped and turned, putting his hands on her shoulders. "Adrienne, I believe Olgun willed us to meet that night."

"I'm sorry, what?"

"By the evening we met, I'd been attending Olgun's services for slightly more than a year," Alexandre explained. "And it was everything I could do to keep it a secret—from my own servants, especially. You can just imagine how well Claude took it when I missed evening mass once every week or two."

Adrienne snickered.

"I'd just decided, while on my journey, that I'd have to attend less often—or perhaps find someone who could attend in my stead. But of course, there was nobody I could possibly trust enough to do so. Don't you see, Adrienne? I'd *just* begun contemplating that, and suddenly there you were! It couldn't be a coincidence!"

"Is that the only reason you took me in?" she asked quietly.

"At first," he admitted. "But only at first, Adrienne. I swear it."

"All right," she said, pretending that the streetlight wasn't blurring behind unshed tears, "but you never *told* me about Olgun! If I was supposed to be your—your . . ." She waved her hands helplessly.

"Proxy?" Alexandre provided.

"Yeah, that."

"At first, because I had to be sure I could trust you. And then because I was afraid you'd feel used, that I'd taken you in with ulterior motives—which, of course, I had. But I discovered I was more worried of you leaving than I was about being found out.

"And finally, though I was attending less and less often, my fortunes didn't fall. And I realized that Olgun must still be happy with me. That maybe he'd brought you to me for an entirely different reason—because you needed me."

Adrienne's cheeks glistened, for she wept openly now. With a soft cry, she threw herself into the old man's arms. And she pretended, as he held her close, not to notice his own tears shining in the lamplight.

"Of course," he said, clearing his throat and stepping back, "when young Lord Lemarche asked permission to induct you, I could hardly say no, could I? Best of both worlds and all that." Alexandre looked down at her with a sudden gleam in his eye that had nothing to do with tears. "You could do worse, you know."

Adrienne flushed and elbowed him in the ribs, but she laughed as she did it, and she felt as light as a feather as they began the long walk back home.

✳

"Excited, love?"

Adrienne smiled, standing on tiptoes to kiss Darien's cheek. "Maybe a little," she admitted, fluttering a coquettish smile swiftly hidden beneath her acolyte-white hood. "I've waited months for this." Hands clasped, they wound their way together down the spiraling stair.

This would be her last service as a probationary member of the sect. Tonight, she would replace her white robe with the darker gray worn by the others. She could participate directly in services, rather than parroting back the congregational replies. She could speak without waiting for an older member to acknowledge her.

Fairly prosaic benefits, at best, but a sense of anticipation clung to her throughout the service like a second skin. Her only regret, though she fully understood, was that Alexandre's other, more public duties kept him away from this special gathering.

Just like that, it was done. The hour passed, Timothy uttered his closing benediction, and the service concluded with a cheerful announcement that today they welcomed a new sister in Olgun. Congratulations were offered (most of which were even sincere); the hidden lever was pulled; the horned idol sank slowly and majestically into the floor.

And the door to the cult's underground sanctum flew open with a deafening crash. Through it roared an apparition so terrible that several of Olgun's more weak-willed worshippers went quite literally mad at the sight of it.

It was accompanied by several human compatriots, but Adrienne never got a good look at them. Her gaze locked in fascinated horror on the demonic entity that even now ripped jagged, iron claws through poor Timothy's ample girth. It lifted him by his innards, his feet kicking spastically as blood poured across his killer in some twisted baptism. Before the merchant finished twitching, the creature dropped him, driving the claw on its left thumb through the screaming face of Marie Richelieu. Her terrified cries rose in a brief crescendo of agony, ending in a hideous rattle as her skull broke apart.

With each second, another of Adrienne's friends died horribly, organs and limbs ripped from their housing and strewn about the room like so many children's toys. Blood sprayed across the chamber, a red-tinged geyser that soaked Adrienne and the others down to the skin. Some of Olgun's rapidly shrinking congregation scattered in panic, only to find their exit blocked by the demon's human allies. Several chose that route anyway, preferring a clean death on assassins' blades to dismemberment by the long-limbed monstrosity. Still others, like Adrienne herself, stood rooted in place. She couldn't move enough even to blink away her tears when Darien's left shoulder vanished completely into the creature's gaping maw, disintegrating between those inhuman jaws.

Adrienne might have stood with the rest, paralyzed, until death took her in its own sweet time, but something pulled her from her stricken trance: a single stab of terrible, almost childlike fear. It came not from the screams of her dying companions, nor from the depths of her own mind, but with the unmistakable "voice" of Olgun himself.

The god, Adrienne realized with a lurch that nearly stopped her heart, was frightened. *"We're Olgun's only worshippers, Adrienne,"* Darien had told her. *So what happened to a god when his worshippers, all his worshippers, were gone?*

That thought spurred her into motion where fear for her own life and limb had not. As the others fell around her, reduced to so much bloody chaff, Adrienne found her hands and feet moving of their own accord. Skills that had lain dormant for years flared to life; fingers and toes grasped at cracks and crevices in the wall. In two blinks of an eye, she was up among the rafters, invisible in the depths of shadow.

And she watched, helpless, as the world turned red beneath her. . . .

CHAPTER THIRTEEN

NOW:

It wasn't that Olgun had *chosen* to remain silent.

No, the tiny deity hadn't warned Widdershins of the hideous presence seeping into the room because he had failed utterly to *notice* it. It was only Widdershins's own reactions, the wave of unadulterated terror and helpless panic flowing suddenly through her that alerted Olgun that something was wrong.

And he froze.

Confronted by something completely beyond his experience, the god found himself paralyzed. It shouldn't have been possible! Nothing, *nothing* should have been able to slip by him! And yet, his last disciple was threatened by something that he just *couldn't see*. The forgotten god knew fear, and still he hesitated, his mind struggling to cope with the shock.

Though the creature remained undetectable to Olgun's divine senses, the signs of its passage were visible, written across the fabric of reality in a script only a god could read. The shift of floorboards beneath its weight, the play of dust around it as it moved, even the currents in the air—all signaled the presence of something otherwise unseen.

And there was so little he could do! Even when she called upon him, channeling his resolve through the conduit of her faith, his abilities were feeble indeed. Only the simplest magics remained within his purview, and that was with Widdershins's focus guiding his own, her will and conviction providing Olgun tools with which to work. Without her consciously calling on him, without her motivation to channel his own, he was very nearly helpless.

Nearly, but not entirely. The *impossible* was beyond his reach; the *improbable* might yet be feasible.

With an act of will unlike any he'd attempted in a thousand years, Olgun focused what little power he retained. Widdershins didn't even notice the tingle in the air as the creature lunged, jaws agape and claws outstretched to rend her limb from bloody, twitching limb. Its clawed foot landed hard as it loomed over her, the shadow of death itself.

Olgun's power reached its peak, and the floor, weakened by years of neglect in this poverty-stricken tenement, eaten away by dampness and rot, gave out.

✴

With a startled cry, the hellish creature tumbled through the splitting floorboards, unable in the cramped space available to spread its patagia and slow its fall. The creature's momentum was more than enough, even without Olgun's continued prodding, to send it through the third floor as well, and the second, and the first. The beast finally slammed to a halt in the earthen floor of the cellar, covered in dust and splinters and very, *very* angry.

People screamed on the stories above, the entire building swayed like a ship at sea, but the structure held.

Stairs fell away beneath its feet as the creature pounded upward. It burst through the doorway atop the staircase, door dangling loosely from one clenched fist, to find the room empty.

That was all right, though. It could find her again.

The creature sniffed, inhuman eyes narrowing in aggravation. The scent was gone! The spiritual trail, the unique tang of Widdershins's soul that it had followed all the way from the Flippant Witch, had vanished.

The midget deity must have blocked the scent, much as the demonic beast had used the power of its own divine patron to hide from Olgun. Irritating, but merely inconvenient. It had other ways to track its quarry down.

※

"Everyone getting you settled in all right, Your Eminence?"

De Laurent glanced up from the desk that was the only salient feature of his current office, provided by the second of what was to be an interminable number of hosts. "Good evening, Major. Yes, everything is satisfactory, thank you for asking."

"No further problems?" Julien asked, still standing in the doorway.

"Would your men not have told you if there were?"

"They would. Still . . ."

"Yes, still. No, nothing untoward. Won't you come in for a moment?"

"I can't, Your Eminence. Too much to do. I just wanted to make sure you were well, and to apologize that I haven't been around much personally these past few nights."

"Quite all right, Major. Your men have been more than satisfactory. They—"

"Excellent. Good night, then, Your Eminence. I'll check in again tomorrow."

Brother Maurice appeared in the doorway even as Major Bouniard, looking back over his shoulder, passed through it. "He's looking a bit ill, don't you think?" the young monk asked.

But the archbishop, his face pensive, shook his head. No, not ill. The major was beginning to look exhausted.

And perhaps more than a little frightened.

※

"Widdershins," Renard whispered, voice muffled behind his scented kerchief, "were you able to get—gods above!"

Genevieve raced forward, grabbing her best friend by the shoulders as the young thief staggered. "Shins, what happened?!"

Widdershins bled from a dozen scrapes and splinters inflicted by the collapsing floor, perspired freely from her flight down the rickety stairs and her terror at her worst nightmare returned from the Pit.

Her vision swam. The grimy, filth-encrusted alley twisted and warped beneath a second, transparent image of her friends and fellow congregants spread in oozing chunks across the floor of Olgun's shrine. It wasn't enough that the Finders' Guild wanted her dead. It wasn't even enough that they'd summoned some fiend from the deepest dark to hunt her down. But now, to learn that they were responsible for the worst chapter in her life, that it was they who had forced Adrienne Satti to vanish with the stain of murder and worse than murder besmirching her name, ignited a fire in Widdershins's soul.

"I am tired," she told Genevieve, voice colder than winter, "of running." Her hard stare flickered to Renard, who mumbled something under his breath and looked away. "You'll see she has a safe place to stay until the tavern opens, yes?"

"I'm not sure you should—"

"Please, Renard. I need you to do this for me."

"Of course," he said softly.

Widdershins took several steps before Genevieve's hand closed on her shoulder. The thief peered at it as though not entirely certain what it was.

"Shins, wait! You can't go running off by yourself! You're—"

"Going to the guild, Genevieve," Widdershins whispered.

The barkeep blanched visibly. "What?"

"They're sending demons after me now, Gen. This has to stop."

"Demons? Shins, you're crazy!"

That brought a brief bob of a head and the flutter of deep auburn hair. "Quite possibly," the thief admitted. "I'm serious about the demon, though. And I'm serious about taking this back to the guild." For an instant, her face softened, her façade cracked. "Gen, I don't want to die. And I don't want you to get hurt. I *have* to find out what this is about, and I have to do something about it, and I have to do it now. I'm sorry."

Gently, she raised her left hand to her right shoulder, lifted Genevieve's pale and trembling fingers from her tunic, and vanished once more into the clustering shadows.

✳

Widdershins crouched on a rooftop across from the Finders' Guild hall—the same rooftop, in fact, that Bouniard and Chapelle had chosen as their own vantage point, though of course she had no way of knowing that. In all official records and upon any casual inspection, the building on which she'd locked her gaze was simply a large office for a company—relatively unsuccessful, at that—specialized in pawn-brokering, money-lending, and insurance policies on long-distance caravans.

Few people on either side of Davillon's law-and-order divide remained ignorant of the place's true nature. But everyone who attempted to infiltrate the place was murdered in some brutal fashion, and even if the City Guard had possessed the manpower and the cannon to take the place by main force, the Hallowed Pact forbade open war between two organizations with patron deities. So the Guard pretended they didn't know about the place and left it well alone; it was the only sane thing to do.

Tonight, Widdershins was ever so slightly south of sane, and she wasn't about to let anything as insignificant as near-certain death come between her and the answers she so desperately needed.

She'd made a quick stopover after parting company with Gen and Renard, darting briefly into an apothecary's shop that the proprietor foolishly thought was closed for the evening. Her own knowledge of herbs and medicines would have fit on an arrowhead, while still leaving room for a jaunty sonnet. Olgun, however, was more than able to fill in the gaps in Widdershins's knowledge. In a matter of moments, she'd gathered what she needed and flitted from the shop.

Now she took a last look around, drew in a long, deep breath. "All right, Olgun," she exhaled. "You ready?"

There was no mistaking the god's nervous response for anything but a heartfelt no.

"Ah, buck up, Olgun. It'll be fun, yes?"

She got no response to that at all. With an unconcerned shrug, she slipped away from the edge of the roof.

✳

There was, Hubert lamented silently as he shifted foot to foot in the sickly moonlight, absolutely no justice in this world. Normally, that was a good thing, what with him being a thief and all. But tonight, as the air grew pregnant with the weight of coming rain and he shivered in his "unobtrusive" clothes, he felt more than a little bitter.

And why was he stuck out here, on this gods-forsaken night, while most of his companions were either inside enjoying dice and spiced wine, or out relieving citizens of their encumbering coins? Why was he garbed as a beggar when he preferred the newest styles of the aristocracy?

It was because he, Hubert Juste, member in good standing of the Finders' Guild and loyal servant of the Shrouded Lord, had proven himself trustworthy enough for guard duty. It was, he'd been told repeatedly, an honor. This was a Good Thing. It meant that he'd been noticed by the people above, people who mattered. He was on his way to big things with the guild, no doubt about it, big things indeed!

Hubert huddled closer inside his beggarly disguise, winced as the first corpse-cold drops of an icy drizzle pelted him in the face, and cursed the whole bloody lot of them.

If this is what comes of proving one's worth, let's just see how well I do on my next job, damn them all to—

"Excuse me."

Keeping to his beggar routine, Hubert coughed, forcing a moist, phlegmy sound through his throat, and lurched forward with a slight stumble. Inside his coat, he dropped a hand toward his thin-bladed dirk, and the alarm whistle that hung at his side. Between this and the visitors of a few nights ago, this place was getting downright popular. "Some'at I kin do fer ya, missy?" he wheezed.

"Actually, yes," she simpered softly, her tone seductive, one arm slinking out as though she intended to embrace or caress the filthy miscreant. "My name is Widdershins," she told him. "I'm Taskmaster Lisette's most wanted. I intend to drug you, and force you to be my guide."

Hubert blinked, startled. "What—?"

Widdershins opened her palm, now directly beneath the bewildered guard's face, and blew. The powder, clenched tight in her fist to prevent the rain from transforming it into so much paste, billowed out in a thick cloud. Hubert gasped, backpedaling, but it was far too late.

He staggered, all but slapping himself as he grabbed for both his whistle and his blade. The former fell back to his chest unsounded, swinging pendulously on its lanyard as he collapsed in a torrential choking fit. His dagger clattered to the cobblestones, the tip bent and the blade notched by the impact. Hubert fell to his knees, ripping even more holes in his patchwork pants.

✳

Widdershins glanced around furtively, brushing hair and rainwater from her eyes. Once she was satisfied nobody had seen them, she reached out and helped the dazed fellow to his feet. The air sparked with a surge of Olgun's power, enhancing even further the effects of the drug on the sentry's system.

"What's your name?" Widdershins asked softly, shivering as a rill of rainwater cascaded down her back.

"Hubert Juste," he answered dreamily.

"Hubert, how are you feeling?"

"Funny," he admitted, punctuating the sentiment with an almost girlish giggle.

Widdershins couldn't help but grin in response. "It *is* funny," she admitted, watching him nod vigorously in agreement. "Hubert," she said, voice dropping into a conspiratorial whisper, "I need you to help me with something. Can you do that?"

"I can help!" he insisted, still nodding. Widdershins worried that his head might fly off and go bouncing down the street, gibbering softly.

"I don't know," she hemmed. "This is pretty tough. . . ."

"I can do it! I'm good at shtuf—stuff!"

"Maybe you are, at that," she conceded. "All right, Hubert, I need you to guide me through the Finders' Guild. You see, I've only ever been in the upper levels, and the lower floors have all sorts of bloodthirsty guards, and tricky passages, and I'd *so* hate to get hurt down there. You wouldn't want that, would you?"

"Oh, no!" he insisted, nodding his head yes.

"Good. Then lead the way, my friend." She followed his unsteady but determined tread through the main doors, pausing only to retrieve his abandoned dagger from the street. There was nothing she could do to prevent the thieves from discovering their sentry had vanished, but she could at least remove any evidence that something untoward had happened. Let them wonder.

They'd barely passed the front door when she learned that it wasn't to be that easy.

"Hey! Hubert!"

From a platform above the door, a slender young woman, built much like Widdershins herself, dropped to the floor. She was garbed in tight red hose, brown boots, and a blue tunic cut so low that

Widdershins actually started to blush. Her hands clasped a small crossbow—presumably, or so Widdershins guessed, because it'd do less harm to the walls than a flintlock if she had to fire it indoors. The weapon was sufficient indication that, despite her wardrobe, she meant business.

"What the hell do you think you're doing?" she demanded, getting right up in Hubert's face and staring up at him. "You know damn well you're not to leave your post for *any* reason, certainly not for some doxy off the streets!"

"Especially when he can just walk through the doors and have his pick of any doxy from inside, right?" Widdershins asked mildly.

The other thief spun angrily, straight into a brutal right hook. She staggered, her eyes rolling so far back in her head that she could probably have counted the wrinkles in her gray matter, and fell with a dull thud.

Widdershins shook her aching fist and considered. She really didn't want to have to kill anybody here. On top of any moral compunctions, she'd be in enough trouble over this as it was. With no other option, she stashed the senseless brigand in a nearby coat closet, tying her hands and feet with the woman's own boot-laces, and gagging her with the tiny scrap of fabric she'd apparently mistaken for a shirt. Hubert, his confused expression betraying no understanding of the situation, resumed his guided tour. The passages grew dim as they continued, lit only by the occasional lantern or torch. Widdershins pulled one burning brand from the wall to carry with her as she walked.

As they moved into the heart of the guild, deeper than she'd ever gone before—save once, when her initiation had required her to swear certain oaths at the feet of the Shrouded God—Widdershins found herself stunned at the magnitude of the task she'd so blithely undertaken. The complex was enormous, easily the size of a large palace. The halls were so twisted and confusing that "labyrinthine" scarcely did them justice. She imagined that the architects had dropped an enormous handful of string, or perhaps some sort of noodle, and designed their floor plan on the resulting patterns. Thieves stood guard at random intervals, in scattered intersections. Thankfully, none of them seemed to recognize her on sight— unsurprising, given the size of the guild's roster—but still, without Hubert's presence to justify her own, Widdershins was pretty sure she'd have been stopped for more than polite questioning. Without the presence of her drug-confounded escort, Widdershins knew that all her precious skills would have availed her naught. She'd have been hopelessly lost, and quite probably dead, and neither her own abilities nor Olgun's guidance could have saved her. As it was, she walked in fear that one of the sentries would know that her guide was supposed to be outside, rather than in, and stop them anyway.

On they walked, forever onward, footsteps echoing forlornly through darkened halls. Some of the passageways showed signs of regular usage: The dust on the floor was thin; torches occupied the sconces along the walls. Others appeared to have survived untouched for decades. Guards grew scarce; cobwebs hung thick; the air stank of mold; sconces were empty or sprouted only rotted wood that could no longer hold a flame. Obviously her drugged guide wasn't exactly taking the most direct route through the place—not that Widdershins had any destination in mind more specific than "where the important rooms are"—and she could only hope they'd indeed wind up somewhere worthwhile. Well, not her *only* hope. She prayed that Olgun could retrace the path they'd taken, should circumstances demand a hasty withdrawal.

But it seemed, finally, that they might just be getting someplace. Signs of regular passage and the echoes of distant voices grew more common with each subsequent hallway, until it became clear that they traveled through a major hub of the complex. Widdershins tensed, alert to the slightest sign that they might no longer be alone.

They encountered no one at all. Widdershins didn't know if most of the thieves were engaged in other pursuits, or whether it was sheer dumb luck, but it made her as nervous as it did relieved. Hubert, his pace slackening and his eyes beginning to glaze like a pastry, jerked to an unsteady halt before a heavy iron door. "Center," he murmured, his voice thick, his tongue dry.

"The center?" Widdershins repeated. "Of the complex?"

"Yeah . . ."

"What is it?"

"Chapel." Hubert giggled again, a flaccid sound. "We should go pray."

Widdershins barely caught him before he slumped, unconscious, to the floor.

Ah, well. I suppose he lasted as long as I needed him to.

Widdershins put her ear to the metallic portal. She heard nothing beyond, but then, it was a hefty door. When Olgun's own divine senses confirmed her observations, however, Widdershins confidently gave the door a heavy shove—rather shocked at the ease and silence with which it opened—and dragged the slumbering sentry inside with her.

The chamber sparked the vaguest of memories. She'd been here only once, over a year ago, and then only for a few moments. It held a number of softly gleaming lanterns that pressed the shadows up to the ceiling where they hung, a thin, dark awning. Wormy tendrils of smoke reached sinuously from those tiny lights, intertwining at the ceiling and flowing through numerous concealed holes.

The young woman's attention was drawn to the towering stone statue at the front of the room. Her curiosity piqued, she glided, ghostlike, up the dais and around the podium.

Other than its prodigious size, the carving could have represented an ordinary man. His garb was loose, a style popular many generations back. The only other oddity was the statue's head, covered by a thick, heavy cloth of darkest jet.

She thought she remembered it being a lot more impressive.

"The Shrouded God," Widdershins intoned melodramatically. "Beware his terribly wrathful terrible wrath."

Olgun chuckled disdainfully.

"You know," she said, reaching upward, "I've always wondered . . ."

Her fingertips had brushed against the roughly woven hood before Olgun screamed in her mind, a shriek the likes of which she'd never heard. She stumbled away from the idol, palms pressed to her ears.

"Ow! Purple steaming hell, Olgun! What was *that* for?"

The god continued to shout his warning at her—more calmly and far more softly, at least.

"Oh, come on," she scoffed. "It's not like there's *really* some spooky ancient curse on whoever looks at the stupid thing."

Her eyes widened at the sense of absolute certainty that washed over her soul.

"There *is*? What does it do?"

No answer. Either Olgun didn't know, or he didn't want to tell her. Widdershins cast a final glance at the statue and decided to let the issue drop.

"All right, all right. Look, the Shrouded Lord's office has to be close to the chapel, right? So let's head out there and find him, and maybe we can get this damn thing resolved before—"

"You!" There was enough venom in that single word not merely to knock a person dead, but to sicken the worms and beetles who would feast upon the corpse.

"Or," Widdershins muttered, "we can let someone find us dilly-dallying about here." She spun, one hand clasping the hilt of the rapier, and stared into the face she'd grown to hate with every fiber of her being.

Lisette Suvagne, her fiery mane radiating about her head like a corona, stepped over the insensate body of Hubert Juste. Her eyes all but glowed from within.

"I don't know how you got in here, you little scab, but I'm glad you did!" The taskmaster stopped halfway through the chapel. With a low, eager sound, her rapier slid obscenely from its scabbard, her dagger appearing as swiftly in her left hand. The blades glinted dully in the lantern light. "It's so much more satisfying this way."

Widdershins's own blade whipped over her back, cut fine lines in the air before her. "Hello, Lisette. You're looking stressed, did you know that? Are you taking proper care of yourself?"

The redhead smiled. "I'm going to feel a lot better in a few minutes, Widdershins." Cautiously, she took several steps; Widdershins did not walk, but leapt from the side of the idol to meet her. They stood only feet apart now, close enough for the tips of the rapiers to kiss one another with a metallic chime.

"So what happened, Lisette? I haven't seen you this upset since d'Arras Tower." She smiled sweetly. "You're not still miffed about *that*, are you?"

The taskmaster lunged with a bestial snarl. Widdershins parried casually, contemptuously smacking the blade aside, retreating rather than taking the obvious riposte. Lisette flailed briefly, scrambling to retain her balance with an undignified whirling of limbs.

"I'll see you dead, bitch!"

"Only if the ceiling falls on me, Lisette."

The room echoed, as though a rain of nails had suddenly fallen from the night-blackened skies. Over and over, the taskmaster's rapier lashed at the black-clad intruder. Her dagger was the flickering sting of a scorpion, seeking any opening the rapier might leave.

Nothing connected. Widdershins pivoted impossibly fast, twisting to face any direction from which Lisette could attack. Her arm flashed up, out, to either side; her wrist turned at impossible angles, whipping the thin steel into the path of the taskmaster's weapons.

They moved swiftly across the chamber, Widdershins deliberately falling back before Lisette's furious assault, concentrating entirely on defense, refusing to take so much as a single stab at the foe. Though gilded in a veneer of style and civility, trained into her during her years as the ward of a nobleman, Widdershins's swordplay was, at its core, brutal, direct—not fencing but street fighting. Nothing in her experience should have allowed her to turn away blow after blow as she was, yet she kept her lone blade constantly interposed between both Lisette's weapons.

The taskmaster was good, very good. But Lisette, for all her faith, didn't have a god watching over her shoulder and guiding her blades. And slowly, slowly, she began to tire. She found herself flinching from counterattacks that never came, her eyes drifting dangerously to follow Widdershins's footwork when they should remain focused elsewhere.

And then, as their path took them past the towering idol of the Shrouded God, Widdershins lashed out with the tip of her blade and scored a thin line straight down the stone deity's crotch.

Lisette froze, shocked to the core of her being, more horrified at Widdershins's blasphemy than she could ever have been at merely mortal suffering. And in that instant of paralysis, when Lisette's jaw and fingers had both fallen slack, Widdershins stepped in and slammed her rapier down on the taskmaster's sword, knocking it from her fist to skip and skitter across the carpeted floor. Even as Lisette turned, cognizant once more of the danger, Widdershins grabbed the taskmaster's left wrist with her own free hand and, with only a modicum of exertion, drove Lisette's own dagger deep into the woman's upper thigh.

"If we're through playing now," Widdershins told the woman, now lying curled around a growing pool of blood, "I'd really like to ask you a few questions before you bleed to death."

"Go to hell!" Lisette gasped around broken sobs. She tried to crane her head, to look up with some last show of dignity; but her leggings, already plastered to her skin by the torrent of blood, pulled rudely at the gaping wound, and she couldn't so much as shift her weight for the pain. "Killing me won't stop them! They'll come after you, no matter what!"

"I don't know, Lisette," Widdershins said thoughtfully. "I think

I'd be doing them a favor by popping whatever sack of contagion you have for a heart. I'm sure there are quite a few here who would send me flowers. Maybe a nice fruit basket."

"Even if that's true," the taskmaster wheezed, "the Shrouded Lord doesn't take kindly to being disobeyed."

"I didn't disobey anything until you'd already punished me for it," Widdershins protested. "And it's certainly a bit of overkill to throw a blooming *demon* at me, don't you think?"

Lisette laughed aloud, the sound changing to a gurgle of pain as the movement jostled her injured leg. "I'll tell Brock you think so highly of him," she gasped.

Maybe it was her tone, but the young thief didn't doubt the woman for a moment. Lisette really didn't know what Widdershins was talking about. Someone *else* was trying to kill her, someone outside the guild—the same someone who had slaughtered Olgun's cult! She was after the wrong people!

Sheathing her blade, she delivered a swift and brutal kick to Lisette's injured leg. Then, as the taskmaster's scream drowned out all other sound, she slid open the door behind her and slipped out the winding corridors. Long before Lisette's cries could attract attention in the largely empty halls, Widdershins was already gone, lost in the labyrinthine corridors, leaving only the fading echo of her footsteps to prove she'd been present at all.

CHAPTER FOURTEEN

ALMOST TWO YEARS AGO:

Even in darkest night, life continued in Davillon's central market. Though stalls and shops were long since closed, windows shuttered and doors thoroughly locked, the marketplace offered other attractions. Illicit deals and unlawful exchanges occupied shadowed culs-de-sac, dimly lit offices, corner booths in smoke-filled taverns—anywhere the participants could place at least one wall at their back. And for each audible voice lurked another individual whose mouth remained firmly shut, ready to cut the strings of a purse or the flesh of a throat. The nighttime market, without the scents of fruits and perfumes and sweetmeats, was redolent of sweat and drying horse manure.

Tonight, Adrienne smelled none of it. She didn't hear the muted whispers circling the market like carrion crows. She didn't taste the charged excitement that spiced the air, or feel the sodden sense of fear that brushed across her skin.

No, tonight Adrienne saw only the hideous sea of red through which she'd waded; smelled and tasted only the iron pungency of blood and the bitter stench of death; felt nothing save the clammy embrace of her gore-soaked gown.

In the back of her mind, Olgun yammered away in his own peculiar fashion, a barrage of emotions that Adrienne lacked the practice and the presence of mind to interpret. In later years, she would look back on this moment and realize that her divine companion, too, had been scared witless. It was one thing she never, in all her days, teased him about.

Adrienne flitted from alley to roadway and back again, keeping herself cloaked in the ambient darkness as she swept through the muted heart of Davillon. City Guard patrols passed her on the street, couples foolishly out for a late-night stroll meandered by, yet she remained unseen.

The claustrophobic confines of the city's center faded away, slowly metamorphosing into the well-kept and far more spacious properties of Davillon's better districts. Through this, too, she drifted, until finally she found herself before the high walls of the most prosperous, if not necessarily the largest or most pretentious, of the lot.

It occurred to Adrienne, through her exhausted fugue, that she might do better to avoid the guard at the front gate. Andre, like all the servants—except Claude—had never treated her with anything but kindness. But somehow, she couldn't see even easygoing Andre taking her current condition with aplomb, and she wanted to avoid a ruckus until she'd spoken to Alexandre, made sure he was safe and asked him what the hell she should do.

Eventually, without ever really remembering how she got there, she found herself clinging to a tree branch outside Alexandre's sitting room, listening in growing horror to the conversation within.

On the other side of the window, a small fire crackled in the hearth, popping in cheerful counterpoint to the low susurration of voices around it. The room was lined on two sides with floor-to-ceiling bookcases. The other two walls sported trophies of their master's more adventurous past. An old rapier hung above the fireplace, crossed by a primitive arquebus. A lion's head roared silently from above the door, stuffed and mounted to perfectly match the face of Cevora, its gaze locked with that of the small albino rhinoceros that stared just as ferociously from above the mounted weapons.

A quartet of richly upholstered chairs faced one another, a small tea table set between them. Alexandre Delacroix, clad in rumpled nightclothes, sat directly opposite the window; Claude, fully dressed, loomed over his master's shoulder. The other three chairs were occupied by Guardsmen. On the right was the young constable, Bouniard, and the commander himself sat nearest the window.

". . . be some mistake," Alexandre was insisting when Adrienne pressed her ear to the glass, his jaw incredulously slack. "Or else a jest in unbelievably poor taste! Whatever your game, Major Chapelle, I can't say I find it amusing."

"I'd hardly expect you to find it so, my lord," the old Guardsman said respectfully. "And I assure you, I couldn't be more serious. I think the murder of twenty-six individuals, and most especially these particular individuals, falls well outside the bounds of humor."

Alexandre shook his head, fists clenched. "Major, I don't for one moment doubt you when you tell me what happened. Gods, those poor . . . I *know* most of these people! So if I'm a bit distraught, I trust you'll forgive me."

Over the top of the chair, Adrienne saw Chapelle's head dip in a brisk nod.

"But to come here," the master of the house continued, "and tell me that you think Adrienne, of all people . . . Good gods, man, it's insane! I've raised her as my own daughter for years! Even assuming any human being were capable of the sort of carnage you've described, there's no way my Adrienne could be involved. She's not that person, no matter what gossip you've been listening to!"

Adrienne almost gasped in relief. He still believed in her. . . .

"Monsieur Delacroix," Chapelle said calmly, "I can only begin to imagine how hard this must be to hear. If the situation were any different, I would have preferred to do this slowly, more gently. But we simply haven't that sort of time, so I must be blunt. You've asked my forgiveness for your emotional state. I now ask yours for following the dictates of my job.

"What we found, monsieur, was a religious cult, devoted to no god of the Hallowed Pact. Until we learn more about this god, we've no idea what the cult might have been about, or what aims it might have pursued. More to the immediate point, however, is the fact that we located, at the scene, a log of sect membership."

"The sect kept names?" Alexandre asked, incredulously—and perhaps just a tad fearfully.

"Names, no. But numbers." Chapelle seemed to completely miss the aristocrat's faint shudder of relief. "And that is sufficient for us to note that one or two members of the sect were not present amidst the dead.

"The bloodshed was atrocious," the constable continued relentlessly, driving his arguments home with a cold efficiency, "yet there were no bodies but those of the cultists themselves. Either they failed to kill even a single one of their attackers, or all other bodies were removed. In either case, that suggests an overwhelming force, and to me, that also suggests collusion. For a large group to even *find* the hidden shrine, let alone enter it without being detected in time to allow for some sort of escape or defense, would have all but *required* inside help."

Alexandre nodded softly. "I can certainly see how that could be, Major. But I fail to see what my Adrienne has to do with it all."

"One of the dead was Lord Darien Lemarche. I've heard enough 'gossip,' as you say, to know that he's rarely alone these days—and to know with whom he keeps his company."

Alexandre's face twisted. "I see."

"We *must* find Adrienne Satti, monsieur, preferably before anyone else. She is a suspect, yes. But the Guard, at least, will offer her the chance to defend herself. You know well that when the Houses hear of this, they may well decide she's guilty without benefit of investigation or trial. She must be questioned, and we must know what happened. So please, for all our sakes, including her own, where is she?"

For a very long while, Alexandre Delacroix gazed into the

capering flames, his fingers restively twisting a goblet of untouched wine. The light played across his face, his hair, the glass in his hands, creating a mottled, shifting pattern. He seemed a phantasm out of a half-forgotten dream. Claude, in a moment of what was, for him, shocking tenderness, placed a hand on the old man's shoulder and squeezed.

Adrienne realized that she'd been holding her breath, forced herself to take a desperate gasp of air to clear the tightness in her chest and the will-o'-the-wisps that danced before her eyes.

And then, the master of the manor shook his head sadly, his expression utterly defeated.

"I can't tell you where Adrienne might be, Major. I honestly don't know. She slipped out earlier in the evening. Her life is, after all, her own. . . ." He trailed off. "If I knew," he finished, his voice steadier if no less saddened, "I would tell you, Major. I'm sorry."

Adrienne sobbed aloud, just once. None heard her through the window. Between their own voices and the crackling of the fire— and, just perhaps, the subtle efforts of a traumatized god—they remained oblivious.

". . . constables to search her room," she heard Major Chapelle say when she focused, once again, on the voices beyond the window. "They'll be respectful of your property, of course, monsieur, but I'm afraid I must insist. And I'll need to leave a few behind to guard the chamber for a day or two, in case she should return."

Alexandre nodded shallowly. "Of course," he conceded in a low monotone. "Claude will show your men where to go."

"Then," the major concluded, rising respectfully to his feet and gesturing for his Guardsmen to do the same, "I'll take up no more of your time. My constables should be here in less than an hour." He paused, and his expression softened ever so slightly. "For what it's worth, Monsieur Delacroix," he said, his gruff tone almost gentle, "I'm sorry."

Claude showed them out, leaving Alexandre to stare at the door that shut behind them. And then he hurled his wine goblet to shatter across the room, buried his face in his hands, and wept until his entire body shook.

Almost blinded by her own tears, Adrienne shimmied down the tree and scaled the back wall of the manor, near the window to her chambers. She paused a moment to wipe her eyes, shoving despair to the back of her mind.

She couldn't do it, couldn't go to him, though her heart screamed his name and her entire body quivered. Even if he trusted in her, even if he would help her—and she believed, to the depths of her soul, that he would—she couldn't ask it. He had too much to lose if he was caught.

In the dark, without the proper tools, it took her an unacceptably long time to jimmy the latch. The window creaked as it swung open, though not so loudly as the frantic pounding of her heart. She slithered inside, leaving flakes of dried blood across the sill.

She had only minutes before the constables would arrive to search the chamber, yet she couldn't bring herself to leave without first stripping the gore-spattered gown from her body, replacing it with the first dark-hued tunic and hose she could find. She wished she had the time to wash, to cleanse the blood from her hair, her hands, her skin . . . but the quick change of outfits would have to suffice.

Adrienne laid out everything she could carry that might come in handy. A blanket swept from the bed and tied shut at the corners made a passable bag. Five hundred gold marks kept on hand for emergencies, and twice that value again in various jewelry and baubles, landed haphazardly on the blanket, followed by a set of brushes and toiletries, and anything in her wardrobe that didn't blatantly scream "nobility." And then, without really thinking about it, Adrienne swept up the rapier that leaned against the wall. The ornate basket of silver and brass somehow managed to glint in the dark confines of the bedroom.

The weapon dropped from her slackened fingers, bouncing first from the blanket and then from the bed. Sheer luck prevented it from slamming into the bedposts, where the clatter would assuredly have roused the whole household. Adrienne found herself on her knees, hands clutching her stomach as her entire body was wrenched by deep, soul-racking sobs.

"I *can't*! Oh, gods, I can't be alone again! Please . . ."

Her tear-filled gaze fell again upon the fallen rapier. For a heart-wrenching instant, she seriously considered aiming the tip toward her own breast, ending her anguish in a single, final flash of pain.

Softly, tenderly, she felt a touch on the side of her face. An invisible hand cupped her chin and gently turned her tear-reddened face away from the blade glittering seductively before her. The air came alive, and she felt Olgun's mind brush against her own.

There was no trace, now, of the panic the deity had suffered earlier, no fear or uncertainty in his thoughts. There was only the gentle, calming tide she'd felt before, secure in the confines of his shrine.

And there was need, as well. Olgun—a startlingly weak god, now, but a god nonetheless—needed her. Cared for her. Would never leave her.

She wasn't alone.

Adrienne rose to her feet, drove the rapier into its scabbard without looking, and laid it across the blanket with everything else. She tied her makeshift sack, hefted it from the bed. Within, everything she needed to survive, and nothing but that blade to connect her to the noblewoman she'd been for years. The noblewoman she now left behind.

CHAPTER FIFTEEN

NOW:

Two years might change a person, but rarely a city. As Widdershins slipped through the darkened alleyways that flowed into Davillon's central marketplace, she couldn't help but remember that hellish night. The sights and sounds and scents were the same. People still shouted their arguments or whispered their black-market deals, and footpads still waylaid lone wanderers through the nighttime streets, taking money and lives.

And demons, Widdershins reminded herself with a shiver, still lurked in the shadows.

She'd escaped the confines of the Finders' Guild with ease—troubling ease, when she thought about it. True, Olgun had indeed remembered their route, guided her through the maze of passages. Still, she'd been certain there would be armed guards waiting at the exit, or skulking in ambush along the way.

But she'd met few Finders, and those she encountered allowed her to pass without incident, either having seen her moments ago with Hubert, or simply assuming that anyone this deep into the guild's headquarters must *belong* there. And it only got easier still. Near the front door, Widdershins encountered no sign of life, save the pained moans of the woman she'd dumped unceremoniously in the closet. It was just one more worry to add to her growing collection.

She lurked now across the street from the Flippant Witch, and wondered again if she'd been right to come here. Olgun swore he could hide her trail from the creature hunting her, at least for a while. But she knew there were other ways to find her, and she feared she might be putting Genevieve in terrible danger.

All the same, Widdershins felt a desperate need to know that her friend was all right.

"This is stupid," she berated herself, as she abandoned her hiding spot, flickering across the street in a blur of motion. "I told her to find someplace safe until opening time; she's probably not even in there. Just Robin and the other servants . . ." Her hand closed on the door's tarnished latch.

"Pardon me, mademoiselle. I wonder if I might impose for a moment of your—"

Considering the evening's prior events, it's perhaps understandable that Widdershins reacted as she did. With a closed fist, she backhanded the speaker across the jaw before he could finish, knocking him from the steps. He landed hard, looking up to find her already standing over him, blade drawn.

". . . time," the young man finished with an audible swallow, his voice rising several octaves, one hand clutched to his bleeding lip.

Widdershins frowned. This gangly, brown-robed youth didn't look much like either a guild assassin or demon conjurer. Nevertheless, she kept her rapier rock-steady against his neck.

"Of course," he continued nervously, "if that's too much to ask, I'm more than willing to negotiate."

"Who are you?" Widdershins barked at him. "What do you want?"

"Oh. That is, my name is Brother Maurice. And as far as what I want, well, I imagine that the first priority would be to have your sword just a bit farther from my throat."

She stepped back, moving the blade away from Maurice's jugular. "Stand up."

He did so, and it was only then that she finally noticed the tonsure shaved into the top of his head.

Maurice brushed the worst of the dirt from his chest, attempting to salvage some modicum of dignity. He carefully smoothed the front of his robe and met Widdershins eye-to-eye, though he couldn't entirely hide the fear lurking behind his own. Widdershins reluctantly lowered the rapier.

"I wouldn't dream of speaking for you," the young monk told her, "but I find this arrangement substantially more comfortable."

"Did you want something, Brother Maurice?" she asked bluntly, eyes darting in all directions. This felt too much like a deliberate distraction.

"My instructions," he said, taking refuge in duty and orders, "are to deliver to you an invitation. That is, assuming you *are* the thie—ah, lady called Widdershins?"

Lying just seemed more effort than it was worth at this point.

"Yes, that's me. An invitation from whom? And for what?"

"From the archbishop William de Laurent. Apparently, you made an impression at your first meeting. He's quite anxious to speak with you at your earliest convenience."

Widdershins blinked. "He . . . I . . . *Why?*"

Maurice shrugged. "I couldn't say. He told me to deliver his request; he didn't confide his motives, and I don't make it a practice to ask."

"No, you wouldn't." Widdershins shook her head, finally sheathing her rapier with a hiss that masked the monk's sigh of relief. "How did you *find* me, anyway?"

"His Eminence told me what part of town to start with." The young monk raised his eyes heavenward. "I wouldn't dare speculate on the insights made available to the archbishop in times of need, but I imagine that knowing your name and, uh, profession was helpful. After that, I asked around until someone mentioned that you frequent this establishment."

"You . . . you just went around Davillon's poor neighborhoods asking random strangers about a *known thief*?! You're suicidal, yes? I knew taking the cloth had to do bad things to the brain."

"The gods watch over me," Maurice said stiffly. "I was in no danger."

Widdershins wondered how the man could fit that much naïveté into a frame that skinny. And yet—here he was. Nobody had harmed a hair on his tonsure.

All she could was shrug; given what she'd seen Olgun do, it wasn't as though she had any real standing *not* to believe. "All right, fine. Is there a particular place he wants to meet me?"

This, Maurice had been warned, was where it could get difficult. "The archbishop, unfortunately, is watched by too many eyes to go anywhere without being noticed. He apologizes for the inconvenience, but he fears you'll have to come to him."

"At some House estate?" Widdershins's voice could have shattered glass. "Is he insane?!"

"He expressed his utmost confidence in your ability to arrange such a rendezvous, mademoiselle. Apparently, your ability to reach him the first time impressed him."

"Yes, but that was *before* someone made an attempt on his life, Brother. He's being watched more closely than a free exhibition at a brothel and—oh." Widdershins blushed, remembering belatedly to whom she was speaking. "Umm, sorry."

"No trouble," Maurice told her, hoping the heat in his own face didn't show. "I do understand your concerns," he continued, "as does my master. But he assures me that this is most important, and there simply is no other way."

"There never is." Widdershins sighed.

She couldn't just sneak in. The repercussions if she was caught were too severe. Madeleine Valois could just ring the bell, but it would mean revealing her noble alter ego to the archbishop, and she didn't know how far she could trust him. So how to . . . ?

Ah.

"His Eminence has nuns in his traveling entourage, yes?"

"Why, yes, but what difference does that—?"

"You," she told him with a smirk, "are going to help me pick up a new habit."

Maurice choked as understanding crashed down upon him. "Oh, gods. I'm going to hell."

"Probably, but you're the one who invited me, and now I'm too damned curious to ignore it."

The monk deflated in his robes. "Fine. I'll get you what you need."

"Excellent. Don't be in *too* much of a rush." She eyed the door to the Witch one last time and then sighed. "I'm going to go home and grab at least a few hours' sleep, or else I'm likely to collapse on His Holiness's lap.

"Where *is* the archbishop, anyway? I'm sure they hustled him out of Rittier's house like it was on fire. Who's he staying with now?"

"The gentleman's name is Alexandre Delacroix."

Widdershins didn't even blink. "Of course it is," she said.

※

Had she not been so distracted, so overwhelmed by worry, so utterly exhausted, Widdershins might just have realized that someone had followed her from the Flippant Witch to the ramshackle flop in which she was currently staying. Or maybe she wouldn't; the man was no slouch himself.

Louvel—or Scarface, as she knew him—rose from the corner on which he'd been begging, allowing himself a clear view of the Witch's front door, and shadowed the little thief all the way home, practically bursting at the seams. Brock would be delighted, Eudes would be avenged, and Louvel himself would earn himself a nice, fat bonus. Just a quick detour back to his own apartment to shed his beggar's garb and pick up some heavier blades, and he'd be ready to report back to—

"Don't move a muscle."

He froze, one hand on the latch to his door, and glanced over his shoulder. Coming at him from both directions down the dilapidated hall were uniformed Guardsmen led by an officer with a thick brown mustache. Half a dozen flintlocks, and even a pair of blunderbusses, gaped open in his direction.

"In the name of Davillon, Vercoule, and Demas," the officer continued, "you are under arrest for arson, conspiracy to murder, and being an accomplice to the murder of a City Guard." The officer stopped just beside him, jabbing his flintlock into Louvel's side hard enough to draw a pained grunt and leave a bruise that wouldn't fade for some time.

"Just so you know," the man whispered gruffly, "I had myself a friendly chat with your Shrouded Lord the other night. You, my friend, are on your own."

The thug visibly sagged.

"And if it's all the same to you," the Guardsman continued, "I'd really like you to resist."

Louvel decided, rather wisely, not to oblige. And all he could think, as the Guardsmen led him away in manacles so heavy it was all he could do to shuffle along, was *Brock's really not going to be happy when I don't show.*

*

Alexandre Delacroix was not in a pleasant mood. The archbishop's early arrival to his home had upset a very delicate timetable and inconvenienced a great many people. Parties and balls needed rescheduling; appointments had to be pushed up, pushed back, or canceled; other projects and endeavors postponed. His servants had scurried about the house and the city, light or dark, rain or shine, for days on end, preparing for the churchman's untimely, and possibly extended, stay. Claude, who really should have been here doing half a dozen different tasks, was instead out and about in the city performing a

dozen more and leaving the master behind to deal with all manner
of bookkeeping that Alexandre had not touched in years.

Thus it was, when he heard the door chime that particular evening,
he hunched his shoulders, gritted his teeth, and ignored it. *Another
damned highborn fop*, he'd no doubt, *come to petition the archbishop for some
favor or other that His Eminence will politely refuse.* Such it had been since
the day the clergyman arrived: petitioner after petitioner, most in the
guise of social visitors for Alexandre himself, but all inevitably asking
if they might take just a moment to "pay their respects."

With a shudder, he directed his attentions back to the desk. For
over an hour, he'd attempted to balance a set of numbers that refused
to properly add up. He rubbed at the bridge of his nose and glanced
again at the report. "Gains and Losses in the Wool Market, as Per-
tain to Our Interests in Outer Hespelene."

Shutting the ledger with an angry thump, Alexandre shot from
his desk, oblivious to the fact that his chair knocked over a potted
plant by the window, and stalked from the room.

Recognizing the conflagration in his eyes and the glower on his
face, the servants hastily cleared his path. He stomped as he walked,
shoes mercilessly crushing the carpet. He wished one of the servants
would say something to him, block his path, do something, *anything*,
to justify a screaming fit. He felt guilty—most had gone above and
beyond the call in recent weeks—but only a *little* guilty.

So preoccupied was he, he almost missed it.

Alexandre halted so abruptly that his shoes snagged in the
carpet. He had just passed by an open door, and he'd seen . . . No.
He couldn't possibly have seen what he *thought* he had.

Backtracking, he peeked his head around the door frame. There,
seated in a small tea room, was the guest heralded by the recent door
chime. No empty-headed aristocrat, as he'd expected, but a Church
nun in the traditional blue and silver, presumably here to speak to
His Eminence on some ecclesiastical matter or other.

Except Alexandre knew that this was no more a nun than he

was. She'd made a reasonable attempt at disguise: Her skin was duskier than Alexandre remembered it, her lips fuller, her cheeks more sunken.

But even beneath the makeup, and wrapped in that ridiculous wimple, Alexandre would have recognized that face anywhere. It was a face carved so deeply in his memory that it ached, a face he'd seen in a thousand dreams.

Alexandre slammed the door fully open, his pace carrying him into the center of the room before it rebounded from the wall. A livery-clad servant, leaning down to serve the guest, bolted upright, nearly over-turning both the carafe and the goblet upon his silver tray. For her own part, the young nun rose and curtsied deeply, her head bent low.

"Forgive me, my lord," the steward stammered, steadying his shaking tray with a white-gloved hand. "I wasn't expecting you, and you'd ordered us not to disturb you with visitors to His Eminence, and . . ." The slender fellow swallowed nervously as the master continued to ignore him.

Gamely, he tried again. "My lord, this is Sister Elspeth, here for a conference with the archbishop. Sister Elspeth, this is—"

"Get out."

"But, my lord—"

"I said *get out*. If you haven't heard from me in ten minutes, or if you hear any hint of a disturbance from this room, you are to summon the guards—both my own and the city's—immediately."

"But—"

"*Go!*"

The young lady kept her head low, even after the door drifted shut, briefly serenading the room with an audible, and slightly ominous, click.

"It's truly a privilege to meet you, monsieur," she began, her voice low. "I've heard so much about—"

"Give a feeble old man *some* credit, Adrienne. Did you really think that disguise would fool me?"

With a resigned sigh, Widdershins raised her head. She couldn't help but notice how many more lines were laid across his face, how truly old he seemed.

"I was actually hoping," she admitted slowly, "that I wouldn't run into you at all."

"In my own house?" He sounded moderately incredulous.

"Maurice told me you were keeping to yourself and all but ignoring the archbishop's visitors. You picked a rotten day to change your routine."

"Maurice? The archbishop's attendant?"

Widdershins nodded. "I'm here by invitation, Alexandre."

"Right." The old man tensed. "I suppose His Eminence is tired of living?"

Had Widdershins not frantically grabbed for the back of the chair, she might well have fallen. His words hit her harder than Brock's hammer ever had.

"They issued a description of you, you know," the aristocrat continued. "'Widdershins,' they said your name was. But there are so many brown-haired girls, it didn't occur to me . . ." Angrily, he shook his head. "Well, this is where it ends, Adrienne, or Widdershins, or Elspeth, or whatever you want to call yourself. I've kept my household guards ready since His Eminence arrived, and the constables are only a shout away. You can't escape, not this time."

"Alexandre . . ." Adrienne found herself physically reaching out, had to stifle a cry when he flinched from her outstretched fingertips. "Gods, you *can't* believe this!" she demanded softly, imploringly. "You can't honestly think I killed all those people! Our *friends*!"

"You disappeared, Adrienne," he replied flatly. "I didn't believe it then, but you never came back. Never came to me." His mouth twitched, a buried expression struggling to escape his cold façade. "I kept telling myself, 'She'll be back any day. She'll be back, and we'll straighten all this out.' But you never came back, Adrienne."

"I was scared, Alexandre! I was frightened of the Guard, I was

frightened of the—the *thing* that killed my friends. . . ." A tear ran
down her face, threatening to smear the careful and precise applica-
tion of makeup that was *supposed* to have kept her unrecognized.
"And I didn't want to drag you down with me!" The older man
blinked. "I didn't know what else to do!"

"So you went back to the streets," Alexandre snapped angrily.
"You went right back to stealing, and doing everything I spent years
teaching you to avoid." He frowned thoughtfully, curious despite himself. "Why didn't you leave Davillon, start over somewhere else?"

"I don't know anything outside of Davillon," Widdershins admitted miserably. "I wouldn't have known where to start. To me,
everything more than a mile past the city walls might as well be the
Outer Hespelene!"

Alexandre couldn't help but smile, thinking back to his ledger.
Well, no danger of boredom now, at least.

"Adrienne," he said, his voice thawing, "I want to believe you.
I've wanted to believe, for the past two years. But I don't know if I
can, and I can't imagine what I might do about it now. If you'd only
come to me then!"

Widdershins nodded glumly. "Alexandre," she said simply, "we
can talk about this—we *have* to talk about this—later. But something
more is happening here, something important. It has to do with the
people who *did* try to kill de Laurent. They're the same people who
killed our friends! I really am here by invitation, and I've *got* to talk to
the archbishop. Please . . . *please* just give me a little time."

For long, long seconds he stared, motionless, unblinking. And
then, so slowly she was certain his neck must snap, he nodded once.

"I'll escort you upstairs myself," he told her, almost firmly
enough to mask the maggots of doubt that wormed their way
through his voice.

Widdershins's breath rushed from her lungs in a veritable gust
of relief. "Thank you. You've got no idea—"

"Adrienne," he interrupted, "understand something. If you're lying to me now, if so much as a single thread on His Eminence's frock is ruffled . . ." He clasped her arm with bruising force, his gaze burning with the gods' own fire. "I will have my guards right outside his door. Should anything untoward befall him, the only question will be whether they kill you quickly before I get my hands on you. Am I perfectly, crystal clear?"

Widdershins nodded dumbly. Ignoring the perplexed servants, they swept up the stairs, several of the manor's guard falling into step behind them.

They wandered halls through which Widdershins had strode, run, danced in happier years. Upon each, as it truly was, she could see phantom images of what had been, overlaid in strokes of shadow and pigments of memory. Here, what she recalled as a bare wall was adorned with brilliant tapestry, a golden griffin swooping from a sapphire firmament to sink bronze claws through an emerald serpent. There, the bust of Alexandre's great-great-grandfather, which she remembered as perfectly polished and maintained, lay covered in cobwebs and grime. And over there, in what had always been Andre's post while on duty, stood a stoic, grim-faced man she'd never seen. But most disturbing was the *smell*. Nothing overpowering, nothing disgusting, but the manor's background scent, something of which she'd never been consciously aware, had changed, transformed by the passage of time.

Something deep within her wilted, just a little.

And she noticed, too, the lions—everywhere, the lions.

Alexandre nodded as he glanced back, saw her eyes flickering this way and that. "I stopped worshiping Olgun that night," he told her softly. "How could I continue, after everything that had happened?" He smiled despite himself. "Claude was thrilled when I started showing enthusiasm for Cevora's services again. I guess it's good *someone* was made happy by what happened."

They walked the rest of the way in silence, for neither Widdershins nor Olgun seemed to know how to respond.

Finally they reached the door, and Alexandre tapped once loudly on the heavy oak.

"Enter!"

The chamber was plain, almost oppressively so. Off-color squares on the faded walls showed where paintings had recently been removed, and the shelves were empty of their accustomed trophies and knickknacks.

De Laurent, arms crossed before him in folds of black cloth, sat behind a large desk. His iron-hued hair was swept neatly back; his symbol of office hung perfectly from his neck. The desk was covered in numerous stacks of paper, neat and orderly piles that could only be the result of a prodigious lack of work. Behind him, fluttering nervously as a mother bird, hovered Brother Maurice, draped in another of those ubiquitous brown robes.

"Good evening, my dear," de Laurent offered, a raised brow his only comment on her choice of wardrobe. "I'm so pleased you found it in you to accept my humble invitation."

Widdershins curtsied—a tad awkwardly, truth be told, preoccupied as she was—and strode through the open doorway.

"A pair of guards will be posted directly outside the door, Your Eminence," Alexandre said from behind her. "If you have the slightest problem, or the first *hint* of the slightest problem, they can be inside in seconds."

"Your concern is touching, my son," de Laurent told him with a vague *pooh-poohing* wave of his hand (and despite the fact that Alexandre could possibly have been the older of them), "but I don't believe I'm in any danger from this young lady."

Alexandre frowned. "There are those who would strongly disagree, Your Eminence."

"True, but they don't have my gods-granted wisdom, you see." He shrugged. "Not meaning to sound immodest, of course, and I'd be lying if I said I *felt* particularly wise, but that's what the Church says, so I'm required to believe it. Bylaws and whatnot. I'm sure you understand."

For a fraction of an instant, a grin flickered across Alexandre's face. Then, with a final longing look, he faced the young woman. "Adrienne, please prove me right." And then he was gone, the guards noisily and obviously taking up their posts outside.

"Soldiers," de Laurent muttered with a holy headshake. "I swear, sometimes I think they confuse their swords with other, more diminutive parts of their—"

"Eminence!" Maurice protested.

"Oh, relax, Maurice. The Church doesn't allow me to admit to having such things; it doesn't say I can't acknowledge that other people do." He twisted in his seat and winked at the new arrival. "Unless I'm disturbing the young lady with my undignified speech, though I doubt this is the first time she's heard the like."

Widdershins, too, couldn't help but grin. This man was definitely not what she'd expected. "I've run across a little profanity in my time, Your Eminence."

"I thought as much. Please take a seat, my dear. You're hurting my neck. Maurice?"

"Yes, Your Eminence?"

"Please pretend that I've given you some practical-sounding errand to run, in order to assuage your wounded pride at being excluded from this conversation, and leave the room."

Widdershins feigned a coughing fit. She liked the young monk, and was afraid she'd hurt his feelings if she laughed openly.

"But . . . Your Eminence, I don't think it's a good idea. That is, I'm not entirely sure it's . . . well—forgive me, mademoiselle—safe. For you to be here. Alone, that is."

"I'm not alone, Maurice. The gods are with me."

The monk opened his mouth to protest, but nothing emerged save a strangled squeak.

"Maurice," de Laurent said more kindly, "go. If the young lady truly wanted to kill me, I'd not have survived her *first* visit to my boudoir, let alone a second. More to the point, she could kill the both of us as easily as she could one, and still be through the window before the guards could open the door." He smiled at her. "*If* half the stories I hear are true, of course."

"But—"

"Thank you, Maurice. That will be all."

His face forlorn, and with many a backward glance, Maurice went.

"He's such a good boy," de Laurent commented. "Another decade or three under his belt, and he'll be going places. He'd make a pretty good bishop himself one day, if I could talk him into changing orders."

"Your Eminence," Widdershins began, unsure how to proceed, "I'm really not here to hurt you." She wasn't consciously aware of her fingers pulling at the hem of her sleeve, nor of the fact that she was chewing idly on a lock of her blonde wig. "I—"

"I know that, Adrienne. That *is* what Delacroix just called you, yes?" De Laurent's smile held no mischief this time, merely the comforting expression of a gentle old man who knew more about the world—and probably about you—than you did. "It's such a pretty name. May I ask why you changed it?"

Widdershins, who'd expected to be the one asking questions, found herself caught off guard. "Adrienne is . . . wanted for some pretty awful crimes, Your Eminence. Widdershins is just a thief. Though I suppose you think stealing is bad enough."

"I'm not here to judge you. And as long as it's just the two of us, you might as well call me William. 'Your Eminence' gets so unwieldy. 'Excuse me, Your Eminence.' 'If you say so, Your Eminence.' 'Hey, Your Eminence, can you pass the mustard?'"

Widdershins laughed. It was a clean sound, pure, washing away at least a tiny portion of the past weeks. De Laurent smiled gently.

When her laughter faded, he spoke again. "Aren't you going to introduce me to your other friend?" he asked softly.

Every muscle in Widdershins's body locked up. "Excuse me?"

"My dear, I'm an archbishop of the High Church. I've been

known, on occasion, to ask a favor of the gods, something the common man might think of as magic. A nudge of good luck here, a flash of insight there. These events are not the result of sorcery, but neither are they simple manifestations of chance. Sometimes the gods even nudge things for me without my knowledge. Little coincidences—such as, for instance, a thief appearing at just the right moment to save my life from some particularly bold assassin.

"I know the presence of the divine, my dear. And you have a god looking over your shoulder."

"His . . . his name's Olgun," Widdershins admitted, uncertain how many more surprises she could stand in her life.

"Olgun. He's not a god of the Pact, or I'd have heard of him."

"Do . . ." She swallowed. "Do you have to, I don't know, report him or something?"

De Laurent smiled. "Worship of a pagan deity is frowned on by the Hallowed Pact, but it's not forbidden. So long as he doesn't work *against* the Pact, or flaunt the fact that he's not abiding by all of its strictures, I see no reason why either the Church or our gods should see him as an enemy."

She nodded. "I sort of picked him up at the same time I . . . stopped being Adrienne."

"Do you want to talk about it, child?"

Without entirely knowing why, for the first time since she'd told the whole bloody and painful tale to Genevieve, she did.

"It was about six years ago," she began, her voice fading, carried back across the sea of years to a far but never forgotten shore. "I was just a pickpocket on the streets, really. One day, I was watching the shops in the marketplace . . ."

*

Claude maneuvered through the front door as best he could, arms laden with parcels, and glowered at the servants who had taken so long to admit him. "Find a place for these," he demanded, shoving the packages into the chest of a startled doorman, and suggesting by his expression just where the fellow might stick them. Barely waiting long enough for the man to take the weight, he spun and strode up the stairs, taking them two at a time in his long-legged stride.

Even as he approached the master's office, his scowl deepened. No doubt the old coot would have something else that needed doing, some new banal task that would occupy time Claude really didn't have. But he wasn't about to overtly disobey, and he *certainly* didn't want anything to go wrong with the archbishop's arrangements . . .

But Alexandre was neither hard at work on the books, nor shouting instructions to this servant or that. He sat behind his desk, staring dreamily off into space, a strange grin flittering about the edges of his mouth.

"Sir?" Claude asked, gently shutting the door behind him. "What's wrong?"

"Nothing's wrong, Claude." Alexandre turned to him, still smiling. "I think . . . We have to keep this secret, of course, at least for now. Until we can make things right."

"Um, of course, sir. Keep what secret, exactly?"

"She's alive, Claude. She's alive, and maybe . . . maybe she'll come back to me."

The servant's eyes widened briefly, then narrowed. "Perhaps, sir, you'd better tell me everything."

And he stood, listening, with his hands clasped behind his back so Alexandre couldn't see the violent clenching of his fists.

✴

The candle guttered madly, little more than a floating wick in a pool of gooey wax by the time the young woman's narration finally ended. She'd left out almost nothing—nothing save Alexandre's own worship of Olgun, for that was not her secret to tell. Her throat was raw, and she was surprised, albeit only mildly, to discover that her cheeks were damp once more.

William de Laurent leaned back in his chair. He folded his hands in his lap to prevent himself from overstepping the bounds of propriety, for at that moment all he wanted was to reach out and comfort this poor girl who had suffered so much, persevered through hardship and horror the likes of which few could imagine.

"You are truly blessed," he said at last, his own voice hoarse with suppressed emotion.

She couldn't help it; she laughed, loudly and bitterly. "You have a unique sense of fortune then, William." She punched the name ever so slightly, as though pointedly reminding him that he'd given her permission to use it.

"You misunderstand me, Adrienne. Yes, I said *Adrienne*. You no more stopped being Adrienne when you took the name Widdershins than this desk"—here he thumped a fist against the solid wood—"would become, say, a mule, just because I were to call it one.

"But what I mean is that you have a strength about you that enabled you to come through all this. *That* is a blessing. And more to the point, it amazes me utterly that Olgun—and I mean no offense to your god, you understand—hasn't gotten you killed by now."

"What?" Widdershins blinked twice, her own mounting indignation both channel and counterpoint to the deity's own sudden ire. The air around her tingled. "Olgun's saved my life more times than I can count! He's gotten me out of some unbelievably tight spots, and he's usually the one trying to talk sense into me! What could possibly drive you to say something like that?!"

"Again, you misunderstand." The archbishop leaned toward her, resting both elbows on the desk. "Adrienne, Olgun never told you the full import of what you did for him two years ago, did he?"

Her stomach tightened, and for a frantic moment she fought a sudden urge to flee. "What do you mean?"

"You saved Olgun's life."

This time, the laughter died before it left her throat. It sounded absurd—save a god's life, indeed!—and yet, it felt right.

"Adrienne, there are a great many theories and philosophies within the High Church. Sitting around and debating the unknowable is something that overeducated old men like me enjoy so much, we've made it part of our official ecclesiastical duties. And one of the things on which we choose to speculate is the nature of the gods themselves.

"Why do you suppose the gods seek our worship?" he asked her. "What do you suppose they would do—they would *be*—without us?"

"Olgun?" Widdershins asked hesitantly. There was nothing, nothing from the god save an embarrassed silence.

"Consider that most of the gods of the Pact come to us from the scattered tribes and communities before the founding of Galice. That a god of great import in one city might oversee a single blood-line or guild in another. That they are older than modern society, and yet so few of them—or at least, of those we still acknowledge—demand observances that would be considered immoral to contemporary thought.

"Some of us in the Church believe that our worship actually *shapes* the gods—not so much as they shaped us, of course, but what traits the bulk of a god's worshippers believe he has, he has. What emotions we believe he feels, he feels. And without our faith, without mortals to honor and revere him, he would cease to be. He would . . . Well, in all ways that matter, he would die."

"No."

"You are Olgun's last living worshipper, Adrienne. If you perish, so, I fear, does he."

"But I'm *not* the only one who believes in him!" Widdershins insisted, half lunging from her seat, all but tripping herself in the folds of her gown. "*You* believe in him now!"

"I believe, but I do not worship him. That's what they need from us. Devotion, not simple acknowledgment."

Widdershins wanted to scream, to lash out, to cry, to deny it all, and she couldn't quite figure out why. Was it just the idea of bearing such an enormous responsibility? Wasn't it enough that she was liable to get herself killed by her own thoughtless actions? She had to take responsibility for the life of an "immortal," too?

"If I'm the only one keeping him alive," she said, brightening as she saw her way clear of the archbishop's smothering web of revelation, "then he'd be doing everything in his power to protect me! So what the figs is all this about him getting me killed?"

De Laurent smiled gently. "Listen to what I've been saying, Adrienne. Our worship gives them life, power, and *personality*. I would imagine that the fewer worshippers a god has, the more each individual shapes his nature. Your relationship is, if you will, monogamous. Just you, just him; something, I might add, that is absolutely unique in my experience. Neither of you is consciously aware of it—well, I'm sure you're not, though I guess I ought not speak for a deity—but you've been shaping each other's disposition since the day of the murders."

The thief rocked backward, found herself sprawled crookedly across the plush, upholstered cushions. *I don't want to hear this!*

"You're a risk taker, Adrienne. You told me you always have been. You also told me it's gotten worse in the recent past, that you've been taking chances even when you knew they were dangerous, even stupid."

"Because of Olgun," she whispered, hands clenched at her sides. "I've made *him* more prone to taking risks . . ."

"Which he has been, albeit unintentionally, channeling back into *you*," de Laurent concluded. Then, at the look of betrayal that shone so clearly on her face, he quickly added, "You should hold no malice for Olgun over this. I doubt he was any more aware of this than you." He paused long enough to give a hefty shrug that lifted his entire cassock. "And even if he knew, there's little he could've done about it. Even the gods can no more escape what they are than can man."

"Is that true?" Widdershins demanded, her attention clearly focused elsewhere. De Laurent felt nothing at all, but the young woman nodded slowly, accepting whatever silent response she'd received.

"All right," she said a moment later. "That explains a lot of what's happened to me—not least of which is my attempt to rob you, which has to qualify as 'stupid' if anything I've done ever has. But it doesn't get us any nearer to figuring out what's going on, or who's trying to kill you."

"You seem awfully convinced it's not your thieves' guild," de Laurent noted, stroking his chin. "Are you so certain?"

"I was there, William. I told you, I saw no evidence of ritual in their chapel. More to the point, they didn't have the first clue what I was talking about when I accused them of sending that *thing* after me."

"These *are* thieves, Adrienne. I'm sure lying is something at which they're more than a little proficient."

"*I'm* a thief, William," she retorted. "Telling when thieves lie is something at which *I'm* more than a little proficient."

"I see."

"Besides, why would they want to kill you? That would draw exactly the sort of attention that the guild usually bends over backward—and bends *other* people over backward—to avoid."

"Maybe." The old man leaned slightly forward, as though suddenly intent on memorizing the patterns of swirls and whorls in the polished wood of his desk. His fingers idly traced the designs, over and over.

Widdershins remained patient for almost a full minute. "You," she blurted out finally, "are trying to work up the nerve to tell me something."

De Laurent smiled sheepishly. "It's not that I don't trust you at this point, especially given what you've confided in me. It's just that this is a Church matter, not one I can discuss lightly with anyone." He paused again, considering.

"I'm not in Davillon to determine whether it's time to appoint a new bishop, and which of the various candidates I should recommend. Oh, I'll do that while I'm here—it's well past time anyway. But that's an excuse, nothing more."

"Then why—?"

"There are ways other than worship," de Laurent told her, apparently changing the topic, "for a god to draw power, though none as long-lasting or as steady. That's why people offer tribute, or sacrifice animals, and why some of the more vicious cults still practice human sacrifice, for all that the Hallowed Pact forbids such travesties. An item, or a life, dedicated to a god brings that god power."

"I'm sure that's very interesting, but—"

"Recently, the pure of faith in the High Church have felt something, Adrienne. We've received dreams, visions, omens. There is, at the risk of sounding terribly melodramatic, a dark power growing in Davillon, and I can assure you it's not because someone's been successfully proselytizing. And I'm now all but certain that it is this power that spawned the inhuman minion hunting you, and sent it to destroy Olgun's cult two years ago. I've come to learn what it is, and if possible, to deal with it." He frowned. "And yet, beneath its darkness, there's an almost familiar—"

He clamped his teeth together as his guest bolted upright, head cocked as though listening to a voice he couldn't hear—which, no doubt, she was. In a flash, she was standing beside the window, back pressed firmly against the wall. Taking a quick breath, the thief made ready to sneak a peek, but first she needed a favor.

"Olgun," she whispered, "it's kind of dark out there."

It was more than just a request for help. It was her way of saying she'd already forgiven him for anything he'd done, deliberately or not, her way of saying, "Things are the same as they always were."

And Olgun replied, a torrent of relief and more than a little joy coloring the rush of power she felt as the air took on its characteristic charge.

Widdershins crouched before the window. With only the top of her head exposed, she rapidly scanned the ground. Her vision, sensitive as a cat's thanks to Olgun's efforts, ranged over topiary and stone-cobbled path, over bushes, around trees.

There!

Advancing up the walk, in what would have been full view if there had been a sun in the night sky, came a column of City Guards led by Julien Bouniard. They moved at a brisk march, hands on hilts, and Widdershins had no doubt at all why they were here.

Had Alexandre betrayed her after all? Had he allowed her to stay just to stall her while he yelled for the Guard? Panic tried to force its way up her throat like a bad meal, and she swallowed hard to keep it down.

No. No, that wasn't him. If he'd planned to turn her in, he'd have done so, confidently and openly. But however they knew, they were here now. Time later for asking questions.

"A problem?" de Laurent suggested from behind her.

"Major Bouniard and a whole mess of constables. Which I guess, yeah, is a problem."

"They may not be here for you at all."

Widdershins smirked. "You break any laws lately, William?"

"Stay," the archbishop all but begged. "I'll speak for you, Adrienne. Maybe I can help you reclaim your life."

She stared, and for a moment, she almost agreed. But, "No. No, I can't risk it. Maybe later.

"And William? Thank you." She reached out, rested a hand fondly on his arm.

Just like that, she was gone, scampering down the outside walls and vanishing into the trees, well out of sight of the constables on the path. Pieces of habit and wimple fell away, revealing her ubiquitous black, as she vanished into the night.

And all the archbishop could think to say, wrapped up as he was in worry for Widdershins's safety, was, "At least she *opened* the window this time."

*

"Claude!"

The servant halted, his feet on two different steps, and allowed his lord and master to catch up to him on the stair. "What is it, sir?" he asked blandly.

"There are Guardsmen on the premises, Claude!" His voice lowered into a conspiratorial hush. "How could they have found out so swiftly that she was here?"

"I couldn't say, sir. But we'd best check on her and His Eminence, don't you think?"

They darted up the stairs, trying to keep themselves to a brisk walk, rather than the headlong charge that would alert the other servants that something was amiss. They had perhaps a minute before the Guardsmen reached the door, maybe two or three more before the soldiers talked their way past the doormen and made it upstairs. Teeth grinding in impatience, Alexandre flitted down the hall, Claude on his heels. They swept past the hanging paintings and the various idols of Cevora until finally they reached the men assigned to watch the archbishop's door and burst as one into the room. Eyes alert for danger, the two men-at-arms followed them inside.

De Laurent turned away from the open window. "Missed her by just an instant, I'm afraid. But I don't believe she'll have any trouble eluding the soldiers outside."

"Delighted to hear it," said Claude, even as Alexandre broke into a relieved grin.

And then, before the archbishop's horrified eyes, the servant turned and sank a long-bladed dirk into the aristocrat's gut. Alexandre's eyes grew wide and he clutched at the blade, hands fluttering like wounded birds, before he toppled to the floor.

Claude grinned a horrid grin, and a second blade appeared in his fist even as Alexandre's men converged on him. . . .

✸

William de Laurent knelt over the bloodied guard, lips moving in heartfelt prayer for the man's departed soul. He felt the blood soaking into his cassock, the ugly warmth on his knee, but he would not rise until he was done.

"I'm impressed, Your Eminence," Claude told him. "You're handling this with remarkable aplomb."

"No more impressed than I," the archbishop retorted as his prayer wound to a close. "Your god must be sneaky indeed, to have hidden the stain on your soul from me. You know that what you've set in motion is a violation of the Pact."

"Only if we're caught, Your Eminence. And of course, that's where you come in. You and dear old Alexandre."

Slowed by grief and aching bones, gazing longingly at the broken staff of office that lay across the chamber, he rose.

"Thank you," he said, "for allowing me to offer final rites."

"I had no personal quarrel with these men, Your Eminence," said Claude, Apostle of Cevora and former servant of Alexandre Delacroix. "Nor with you. I'll make it swift."

William did not want to die, not here, not now that he knew who and what it was he had come to Davillon to find. He briefly eyed the window, but it was a useless thought. Adrienne possessed the speed and grace to pull it off. Even in his youth, he himself had not.

So he held himself straight, determined to face his end with dignity. Who was Death, after all, if not another of the gods of the Pact?

He felt the first of the cuts as a fire in his gut. And William de Laurent died praying. Praying for the soul of the man who killed him, and for the life of a young woman who had already suffered enough.

Claude was long gone, leaving the room empty of all but corpses, before Bouniard and his constables made their way upstairs.

CHAPTER SIXTEEN

ONE YEAR AGO:

Renard Lambert leaned precariously back in his chair, ankles crossed atop the table, and sipped absently from a goblet of wine of a far better vintage than the bottle indicated. Somebody, somewhere in Davillon, was going to be *very* disappointed with the contents of their forty-mark bottle.

Or maybe they wouldn't be. Not everyone could have as refined a palate as he did. It's what made label-switching a profitable venture. Which reminded him, he needed to swing by the Mahaut vineyards before the end of the week, make sure that they . . .

So lost was Renard in his thoughts, senses ever so gently clouded by the wine he'd already consumed, that it took him a moment to recognize the faint but insistent tapping at his door, a moment more to realize the implications.

Who the hell knows where I live?

The thief shot to his feet, one hand darting to the rapier hanging on the coatrack by the door. Slowly, deliberately, he slid aside the brass cap blocking the peephole.

"Hsst! Lambert! I know you're in there! Let me in!"

Slack-jawed, Renard opened the door, stepping aside as the girl flitted past. Sweat plastered her hair to her cheeks and forehead, and she carried a large and lumpy sack over one shoulder.

He stared at her; she stared at the room. Thick carpeting, polished brass-and-silver fixtures, bright paintings of random scenes and portraits of random faces—all were arranged in a display of opulence that obscenely straddled the line between tasteful and tacky.

"It's absolutely you," she said, turning to face her host.

"Widdershins, what the—?"

She frowned, lips curling into a pert little moue. "You said I should come to you if I had any problems or questions," she reminded him.

"Well, yes. The guild can be a difficult home to settle into. Most newcomers have a guide or a patron for their first few—"

"Then why do you look so unhappy to see me?"

"I—you—Widdershins, *how do you know where I live?*"

"Oh, *that*." Widdershins made a dismissive gesture with one hand, dropped her sack to the floor with a loud clatter, and slid into the chair Renard had so recently vacated. A brief sniff at the goblet, and then she swiftly drained off its contents before he could protest. "I followed you a few weeks ago."

"I—you . . ." Renard had the vague sensation he was repeating himself. "That's not possible!"

"I'm here, aren't I?" She shrugged. "If it makes you feel any better, you're *really* careful. You almost lost me twice."

His face turning peculiar shades of red, Renard hauled a second chair to the table and sat across from his guest. "*Why* did you follow me?"

Another shrug. "I figured if I *did* need to take you up on your offer of advice, I might not want to do it at the guild. In case, you know, it was *about* the guild, yes?"

All right, that *at least makes sense*. "So what's your problem, then?" he asked, calming down.

"Well . . ." Widdershins nudged the bag on the floor with her toe, just enough for a smattering of coins and the tip of a solid gold candelabrum to tumble out. "There's got to be thousands of marks' worth of goods here. Maybe tens of thousands. I just—I didn't know if maybe there were different procedures for reporting and delivering the guild's share of something this big. And I'm a little nervous about just walking into the guild with that much hard currency. I

know we're all supposed to be able to trust each other, but . . .
Renard, are you all right?"

No, he was pretty sure he wasn't, given that his eyes were
doubtlessly about to pop from his skull like champagne corks.
"Widdershins, where in the gods' names did you *get* this?"

"Oh, I hit the d'Arras family tower. You wouldn't believe how
difficult it—"

"You *what?*" The foppish thief literally felt the blood drain from
his face.

"Don't tell me it was off-limits!" Widdershins cried, a twinge of
fear in her voice. "I checked the lists, I swear I did! There was
nothing—"

"No." Renard shook his head, thoughts tumbling drunkenly
over one another—though he himself was now *quite* sober. "No,
d'Arras Tower isn't on the forbidden list."

"Then what . . . ?"

Months, maybe even years *of planning.* He knew, because she'd
bragged to him about it enough times. *Oh, but she is* not *going to be
happy when she hears about this. . . .*

"Widdershins, how much do you know about the guild's
taskmaster, Lisette Suvagne?"

"Oh, is *that* who I saw there?"

Renard dropped his head into his hands and groaned.

CHAPTER SEVENTEEN

NOW:

Clouds smeared the stars into glowing will-o'-the-wisps, orbiting the aura of the waning moon. The sky remained dry, its tears spent in the drenching rains of the previous night, though the air smelled heavily of more to come in the days ahead. Even the predators—the rats, the cats, and the two-legged variety—huddled shivering in their hidey-holes and contemplated staying in.

Beneath those apathetic clouds, Widdershins drifted, equally silent. Utterly lost in thought, barely cognizant of her surroundings, she darted through the city, alley to alcove, shadow to street corner, in an invisible dance. The streets slipped by, Widdershins drew ever nearer a destination that she hadn't yet realized she'd chosen—and still she remained focused inward, pondering the night's endeavors.

She couldn't decide precisely how much that little visit with the archbishop might have accomplished. She felt better, certainly: for her new confidant, for her greater understanding of her link with Olgun, and, perhaps most vitally, for her chance, however slim, to finally make things right with Alexandre.

So yes, the visit had been worthwhile in its own right. But she was nowhere nearer to solving her more immediate problems, or learning who was trying to kill her and William, who had slaughtered Olgun's cult.

"Help me, Olgun," she whispered, her voice lost in the chilling breeze. "Tell me what I'm supposed to do!"

But the deity, as she'd expected, could tell her nothing at all.

She was still muttering peevishly when she rounded the next

corner and realized she'd been heading, all this time, toward the Flippant Witch.

Widdershins stopped, her heels skidding on the dew-slicked cobblestones, and briefly debated going the other way. Someone could well be watching her—especially considering Bouniard's unexpected appearance at the manor—and she absolutely did not want to put Genevieve at any more risk.

But Olgun seemed certain she was in no immediate danger, and she really, *really* needed a friendly ear. Too much had happened to sort through by herself. With a deep, calming breath, Widdershins set out across the market square.

When she spotted the small but irritable crowd milling about out front, what poise she'd gathered shattered like a fallen vase. The usual drunkards and other flotsam that washed up on the tavern's doorstep every night—there was nothing unusual about them, save that they were *outside*, when the ale and beer and wine were *inside*. Her heart hammering at her ribs, Widdershins pushed past the belligerent lurkers and leapt the steps to the front door.

"Might's well give it up," one of the ruffians behind her growled as the latch refused to budge beneath her grasp. He was a particularly brutish specimen, with dark blond hair matted into spiky clumps, a thin growth of beard sporting rust stains from an old razor, and clothes that hadn't been cleaned since he was last caught in the rain.

"I tried already," he continued, the noxious fumes of his breath suggesting that he'd recently inhaled a plague rat. "They ain't open t'night, damn 'em all!" He leered a gap-toothed grin. "Means I got me a few extra marks tonight, and no good place where to spend 'em. You got a few free hours, you could earn 'em."

Widdershins turned her back on the man and shook the latch until not only the door, but the nearby windows rattled in their housing.

"I just tol' you—," the oaf began irritably.

"Go away! We're closed!"

Widdershins recognized the voice. "Robin? Robin, it's Widdershins! You open this door right now! Open this bloody door, or I'm
coming through it!"

When no response was forthcoming, Widdershins dropped to
one knee and examined the various locks. Ignoring the foul-smelling
fellow peering in fascination over her shoulder, she pulled a few
wires and probes from her pouch and went to work.

The new locks were good; it took Widdershins five minutes to
open the lot of them.

Widdershins began to push through the now more pliable
portal, only to stop and glower as she felt the man behind her step
forward.

"This is private," she told him, her voice ice. "They're still
closed."

"Like fun!" he barked, his breath nearly knocking her through
the doorway. "You're going in, I'm going in! Ain't nothing you can
do to—"

Widdershins introduced her knee to the drunkard's gut, and the
last of that foul air escaped his lungs in a single overpowering *whoosh*
as he toppled from the steps. Widdershins was inside, the door
slammed and locked behind her, before he'd finished bouncing
across the cobblestones.

"Robin? Robin, where are you?" She was frantic; she knew it,
heard it in her voice, and she didn't care. "Where's Gen?"

The tavern was unbelievably dark. The fireplace was cold and
empty, the lamps quiescent. Only a handful of torches cast tiny fingers of illumination through the ebon depths of the common room.

It took Widdershins a moment to orient herself. Slowly, hands
stretched before her until her vision fully adjusted, she crept toward
the bar.

"Robin? Gen?"

A soft sniff called to her across the darkened gulf. Slowly, as her
vision adjusted, the furniture began to loom from the shadows.

There! At the very edge of the room, a slender figure hunched over one of the tables. Widdershins recognized Robin's slim build and boyish hairstyle. Heartbeat all but echoing through the empty chamber, the thief skidded to a halt beside the serving girl.

"Robin, what's happened? What's wrong?"

The girl blinked up at her, and Widdershins paled at the unfocused look in her eyes, visible even in the insignificant torchlight. "It's Genevieve," Robin said, her tone puzzled, hollow.

Widdershins found it impossible to breathe. *No. Gods, please, no . . .*

"What . . . what about Genevieve? Robin, *what about Genevieve?!*"

"It's the wine, Shins," Robin said almost dreamily, pointing down at the table, her expression glazing even further. "Genevieve's spilled her wine, and she won't move to let me clean it up."

Only then, staring hard through the looming shadows, did Widdershins see the figure slumped over the pocked wooden surface, facedown in a glistening pool of slowly spreading red.

There was no anger in her scream when it finally erupted, no fear, for there was nothing left for the world to throw at her that she'd not already suffered. There was only pain in that pitiable sound, the terrible wail of a lost and despairing child.

Widdershins didn't remember falling to her knees. Hands shaking wildly, blinded by tears, she reached out to the cooling corpse of the only person she had left, truly called friend, truly loved.

"Olgun?" The god cringed, horrified at the terrible pleading in her voice. "Olgun, please, please, you have to help her! I *need* you to help her! Please . . ."

But save for weeping in his own peculiar way, there was nothing even Olgun could do.

The lingering torches continued their dance, oblivious and unabated, as a tiny portion of the world ended within their feeble glow.

✳

It might have been minutes, or hours, before Widdershins finally looked up from where she'd buried her face in Genevieve's hair, cradling the woman's head without thought to the blood that now coated her arm and chest. She'd sobbed until her muscles ached and her lungs burned for air, cried tears enough nearly to wash the bloody table clean. But all her sorrow, all her prayers to every god whose name she could recall, couldn't restore the life-size doll she held, that once moved and talked and laughed and loved with the soul of Genevieve Marguilles.

And finally, though it took a lifetime, her tears slowed, slowed and stopped, and the sobs that racked her body faded away.

There was no sign of Robin. Widdershins had a faint memory of sending her upstairs to get some sleep. The girl was utterly over-whelmed, and Widdershins could only hope that the vague tint of madness in her eyes was a temporary thing.

She couldn't bear the thought of losing anyone else tonight.

Steeling herself against the pain, biting her lip until it bled, Widdershins moved the lantern closer, looking for details she didn't really want to find.

She didn't have to look hard. The wound that had taken Genevieve away from her was a simple stab, directly over the heart—but the poor woman had suffered before that merciful thrust, her legs broken multiple times with a heavy instrument.

An instrument that Widdershins herself had felt on more than one occasion.

She rose, her body shaking like a leaf in a storm, and she *hated*. She hated the Guardsmen who had stopped her from killing Brock in that alley; hated herself for failing to end his life when she had the chance.

For Brock, she could spare no hate—because so far as she was concerned, he was already dead. Widdershins knew, beyond a shadow of a doubt, that she could find it in her to kill.

She turned to leave, to hunt, and the door opened at her approach, long before she reached it. And there he was, as though delivered by the hands of the gods themselves.

She had been right: He *was* already dead, a neat gash stitched across his throat by a thin blade. Like an enormous sack of meal, he hung limp between two hard, scruffy thugs. Behind them stood a third man, slender, his carefully groomed mustache and garish clothes contrasting sharply with the rapier at his side and the knives in his boots. Widdershins could see that the crowd she'd left outside was gone, perhaps having moved on to more worthwhile alcoholic pursuits—or else having been forcefully shooed away.

She should have fled, should have panicked, but she'd simply run out of emotion. Widdershins stared at them blankly—and then turned, slow and unblinking, when the kitchen door squeaked open as well. From within emerged a third ruffian, accompanied by the soldier whose hand she and Olgun had crippled so many years ago.

If she'd had it left in her, she'd have been surprised to see him.

"Perhaps you should take a seat, mademoiselle," said the dandy in the doorway, pulling the portal shut behind him.

Widdershins didn't move.

"I am Jean Luc. I believe you've already met Henri."

"Brock?" she asked dully.

"Who? Ah," he realized, following her gaze, "yes. We found him here, when we returned to wait for you. He was trying to, ah, encourage your friend to tell him where you might be. Apparently he'd been watching and waiting on and off for days, and had simply grown impatient.

"For what it's worth, dear Adrienne—or Widdershins or Madeleine, it's quite confusing, no?—for what it's worth, we made certain she suffered no more at his hands."

Widdershins showed no reaction to the recitation of her various names. "Then I'll try to make sure you all die as easily," she told him.

The thugs snickered and dropped Brock's corpse in the corner. The entire tavern shuddered with the impact.

"Perhaps," Jean Luc said dismissively. "But first, my employer would like a word with you."

The door opened once more, in what could only have been a deliberately orchestrated dramatic entrance. No matter the coat, no matter the bandages that wrapped his head and hands, Widdershins knew the demon for what it was.

"Yes, Adrienne," it gloated in that crushed-gravel voice. "I'm delighted to see you again, too."

But it was the human beside the hellish thing to whom Widdershins turned her attentions.

"Claude?"

"Hello, Adrienne." He shut the door, wiped a bit of dust from his heavy cloak. "It's long past time we spoke, I should think. Henri," he added, looking across the room, "leave us."

"But, sir—"

"I need someone keeping an eye on the investigation. Go."

With a sullen nod, the former Guardsmen departed.

"Investigation?" Despite herself, Widdershins felt her voice quiver.

"Why, yes, into the deaths of William de Laurent and Alexandre Delacroix. Which will, of course, eventually be pinned on you."

She couldn't weep again, not so soon—it was just too much. Only Olgun's strength kept her on her feet as the world swayed around her.

But inside—inside she cried, not merely for the loss of friends, of love, but of a future she had almost thought she might regain.

"I don't understand," she whispered. "Gods, Claude, do you truly hate me so much?"

"You?" Alexandre's former servant actually laughed. "My dear child, this was never about you at all. This is about your *friend*." The hatred suffusing that last word was nearly heavy enough to cast its own shadow.

And Widdershins saw it all as clearly as though someone had painted her a diagram. "You knew!" she accused. "You knew about Olgun all along!"

"Of course I did," Claude told her, suddenly snarling. "I knew from the moment Alexandre betrayed our god for that barbarian idol! He couldn't hide his heresy, not from Cevora and not from me!"

Widdershins's jaw hung slack at the fanaticism she saw in his eyes, blazing to shame the lanterns. And it wasn't even his own household god!

"After all Cevora had done for him, for his family, to turn away over a few years' misfortune? The bastard! Ah, but I knew better, didn't I? I knew the lion could never be tamed. I knew from the old texts that Cevora was a hunter, a predator, from the days before the Pact! And I knew that he had laid upon me the task of shedding the blood of those who had drawn Delacroix from his embrace!"

"And your pet demon, Claude?" she demanded, ignoring the creature's rough chuckle at her description. "How does Cevora feel about *that*?"

But the Apostle merely shrugged. "Those gods hostile to the Pact were cast down into darkness, and their servants with them— but not all those servants are so content to remain in hell. How does Cevora feel about me calling one of them up? So long as the demon remains loyal to him, rather than its former master, I doubt he cares one way or the other.

"It shouldn't have been necessary," he continued, a bit more calmly as he realized that even Jean Luc and his hired thugs were gawping at him somewhat askance. "I'd hoped that when you and your ilk were dead, he would turn himself back entirely to Cevora."

"But he did!" Widdershins protested. "He abandoned Olgun!"

"His heart was never truly in it. I don't think he'd ever have accepted his part in restoring Cevora to his rightful glory. I suppose I should thank you, in a way. Had I not had to eliminate your tawdry little sect anyway, I would never have had the opportunity to do what Cevora demands be done. And speaking of what must be done . . ." Claude raised a hand, and the demon tensed, awaiting his command.

But Widdershins's mind was racing faster still, spinning over every unanswered question, every detail left unspoken.

And in her mind, she heard a voice. Not Olgun, no; for all their years, he'd never come to her with actual *words*. She didn't think he could.

No, this was the voice of William de Laurent. And whether his spirit was truly with her still, or Olgun was using another's words as his own, or she was simply recalling what he'd had to say, they resounded within her soul.

A *dark power in Davillon. The gods of the Pact.*

Sacrifice.

And Widdershins knew.

"You're not murdering *me!*" she exclaimed, understanding finally how truly mad Claude must be. "You're murdering *Olgun!*" She felt her patron's outrage mix with her own, the fury of an immortal contemplating his end.

Despite himself, the Apostle of Cevora grinned, and for an instant stayed his hand. The demon grumbled, but made no move.

"Go on," Claude said, sounding almost eager to see if she'd figured it out.

"Your god is stagnant," Widdershins continued, stalling desperately for time. "You can't exactly spread his worship. Alexandre has no heirs and his heart's not in the faith, and you've got no pull with Cevora's worshippers beyond House Delacroix. Maybe you sacrifice a few people here and there, but that's a pretty big risk for very little reward.

"But if you kill me . . ."

"*You are Olgun's last living worshipper, Adrienne,*" William had told her. "*If you perish, so, I fear, does he.*"

"*He's* the sacrifice," she concluded firmly. "You're sacrificing a god to a god. No wonder the High Church sensed this coming. That must be an *enormous* amount of power!"

"Bravo, Adrienne. Alexandre really was right about you."

"Yeah, maybe. I'm no priest, Claude, but even *I* know that sacrifice is a violation of the Pact, no matter who or what the victim is. I've got to think killing a *god* is another one, even if he's *not* part of the Pact."

"It is," Claude agreed. "That's why de Laurent had to die."

Widdershins actually smiled, though it was a smile that could have frozen saltwater. "So it looks like an attack on the Church and the gods of the Pact from outside. I kill the archbishop, my god and I come after you, and you kill us in 'self-defense' while everyone else in the Church is looking for an enemy that doesn't exist. By the time anyone knows otherwise, Cevora's got his influx of power, and it's not worth the trouble to try to boot his faith out of the Pact."

This time, Claude actually applauded. "I expect Cevora to be potent enough that the others *cannot* take action against him—but otherwise, correct again! I never did give you proper credit, I'm afraid."

"You," Widdershins told him pointedly, "are insane. Stark-raving. Six heifers short of a herd."

"So say all who cannot see. I'd hoped to offer Cevora the power of the sacrifice years ago, but of course, you spoiled that by escaping."

"So sorry to inconvenience you."

"Indeed. But you're here now, and—"

"No, I didn't mean then. I meant now. Sorry to inconvenience you, but I'm *not* Olgun's last worshipper. Killing me gains you squat."

For the first time, Claude seemed shaken. "What? What are you talking about?"

"Oh, come on, Claude, what happened to giving me due credit?" The man scowled, but still he listened. "It's been a couple of years," Widdershins reminded him, as though hammering home a simple concept to an even simpler child. "Do you really think I've kept Olgun a secret from *everyone?*" She paused thoughtfully, as though mentally tallying sums. "There's at least, oh, eight or ten of us now. After seeing the boons he grants me, how could they not believe?" It was her turn to shrug, doing her best to ignore Olgun's startled bleat. "Not a large following, even compared to his old one, but quite large enough to royally muck up your little plan, yes?"

The Apostle went rigid, and then laughed aloud. "Oh, Adrienne, you had me going for a moment there. But—"

"I'm quite serious, Claude. And either way, can you afford to risk it?"

The scowl returned, tenfold. "I could just let my pet kill you. Cevora would know instantly that you lied, as he fed on Olgun's essence."

"And if I'm *not* lying, I'd be dead, and you'd have no way of finding the others." Widdershins smiled.

Claude drummed his fingers on a nearby chair. "Are you offering to lead us to them, Adrienne?"

She shrugged. "This has always been about survival. You go after them, not me, I renounce Olgun, like Alexandre did, and everyone's happy. Maybe I can even help you in running the Delacroix businesses—for a percentage, of course."

Please, Olgun . . . please understand. . . . Trust me. . . .

"Agreed!" Claude said instantly, holding forth his hand.

Widdershins took it, and for a moment they stared into one another's eyes. Both of them were lying, and both of them knew it. Claude only needed to know *how much* of what she'd told him was a lie.

"I'm looking forward to it, Claude." She gestured toward the northwest. "If you leave the market heading that way, you go about seven blocks, make a—"

She stopped at his sudden laughter. "Oh, I don't think so, Adrienne. I'm not remotely that stupid. You'll lead us to your *former* brethren. Personally."

Ah, well. It'd been worth a shot.

"Of course," she told him. "Whichever."

"And you'll be leaving Alexandre's rapier here, as well."

Widdershins just shrugged, struggling to keep all emotion from her face. "It's a ways across town; I hope you're all in the mood for a walk."

✱

The Apostle craned his neck, wrapping his heavy cloak around him to fend off the late-night chill. He watched for a long moment, scowling at the peeling walls and missing shingles.

"A pawnbroker's, Adrienne?" he asked skeptically.

"Why not? The company's not doing well, so they've plenty of extra room for rent. It's as good a shrine as any."

"Oh, please." Jean Luc stepped forward, giving the demon a wide berth. "This is the Finders' Guild, sir."

"Is it indeed?" he asked, turning to Widdershins.

She shrugged and offered up a nervous smile. "Well, where else would I be sharing my faith, if not here?"

This was it. If Jean Luc knew too much about the guild's practices, about its faith, she was dead.

A long minute passed before the Apostle nodded, and Jean Luc said nothing more. Widdershins all but quivered in relief.

"Very well," he said. "Are there any guards?"

"One outside," she admitted, her voice reluctant. "Dressed as a vagabond. Not sure how many might be inside. It varies based on who's got what assignments."

Claude made a calm, collected gesture, as though ordering a servant to fetch him a drink. The demon darted from the alleyway, elongating to its full height as it moved. Widdershins could only hunch her shoulders, her stomach twisting in knots, and try to ignore the abbreviated shriek, and the horrible tearing, snapping, splashing sounds to follow.

Holding her breath against the sudden stench of blood and

human waste, Widdershins stepped through the front doors as though she had every right to be there, setting foot, for the second time in two nights, in the very heart of the Finders' Guild.

✳

On they came, first in ones and twos, then larger bands. With rapiers and crossbows, then with flintlocks from behind heavy doors and ad hoc barricades, the thieves of Davillon fought to defend their home.

And they failed. The hall grew thick with smoke; the walls gleamed with blood. Weapons careened from the creature's hide, flesh tore beneath its talons, bones broke betwixt its jaws, and those who followed behind slipped and slid in the rising gore.

Even the beast of Cevora wasn't fast enough to slay them all, however. For every corpse it left in its wake, three or four of the Finders' Guild fled through passages twisted enough to confuse even a god's emissary.

Widdershins forced herself to watch, flinching but refusing to look away as rapier, claw, and blood flew. And when she saw that the hideous beast was not invulnerable, that the occasional blade bit through its hide, the occasional ball left its mark, her spirits dared, ever so slightly, to rise.

So they continued through twisting halls and sliding doors, ever deeper into the catacombs, and the inhuman thing cavorted along beside them, now ahead, now behind, an anxious child at carnival eager to rend more unsuspecting souls limb from limb.

Until, mere steps from her goal, Claude reached out a hand to stop her. "I think that's enough, Adrienne," he said darkly.

"I beg your pardon?"

"We've already slain a great many thieves, sent a great many more fleeing in terror. And not once have I seen, or has my pet sensed, the sorts of abilities we know you possess. I don't think anyone here shares your beliefs after all."

"Oh? Then how do you explain——?" and she was off, bolting so abruptly that even the demon was caught briefly by surprise. Hair flying out behind her, she ran as though the hounds of hell were at her heels, for indeed one of them was. She knew full well, as her pounding feet echoed off the stone walls, that she couldn't keep ahead for long, but maybe for just long *enough* . . .

When the fiend appeared from around the corner, Claude's fastest men just steps behind, they stared in puzzlement at what they found. Their quarry had vanished through another sliding door, hiding somewhere in the peculiar room beyond. They peeked inside, stared at the towering shape across the chamber.

Claude, chest heaving and forehead glistening with sweat, emerged from behind his minions and glared around him. "You wait outside," he said, gesturing to one of the men. The others, along with Jean Luc and the demon, followed him inside, their boots muffled by the worn carpeting.

The door slid shut behind them, but their sight adjusted rapidly to the sickly light of the uneven lanterns and torches, the artificial gloaming that presaged the fall of a night that never came. Claude quickly recognized the chapel for what it was, and his gaze slowly traveled across the humanoid form of the idol, coming to rest upon its heavy hood of black cloth.

"Here," Widdershins said, appearing from behind the statue. "Your proof." With an almost contemptuous flip of her wrist, she sent the mask drifting unevenly down to the floor.

The chapel filled with horrified screams, as men and monster looked upon the unveiled face of the Shrouded God.

Beneath the upraised hand that shielded her eyes, Widdershins saw the assassin Jean Luc collapse to his knees, screaming until his cheeks had reddened and his eyes bulged. All around, she heard other men following suit, though she dared not look.

And as it seemed he could scream no more, that his lungs must collapse for lack of air, his voice took on a horrible, liquid tone. Jean

Luc thrashed on the floor, vomiting everything in his gut, heave after heave until there was utterly nothing left.

Still it refused to stop, for the curse of the Shrouded God was nothing less than the most primal font of thievery itself.

Need. Want. *Hunger*.

When she could actually *see* the flesh, the meat, the muscle fading—when his skin sank ever nearer his bones with each purge, as the substance of his body was eaten away, almost *deflating* before her eyes—Widdershins finally had to look away, her own whimpers scarcely audible above the hideous gurgles that had once been screams.

Only when the noises finally stopped and the chamber began to reek of purged and rotted flesh did she open her eyes. Bodies lay strewn across the room, gaunt as famine victims and glued to the matted carpet by a viscous sludge. Even the demon lay sprawled, its leathery hide clinging to its bones. It moved, struggling to rise, apparently too potent for the curse to slay, but for the nonce, at least, it was vulnerable.

Keeping her eyes carefully downcast and her back to the idol, Widdershins reached down and, with a shudder of revulsion, peeled the statue's hood from the carpet where it lay. She felt her way along the sculpture until she finally found the head, and gasped audibly in relief as she pulled the hood back over its face.

All right, all she had to do now was find some way to keep the demon down, and—

Olgun's scream was almost too late. A long, wide blade flickered from the darkness, and Widdershins's desperate forward roll might have saved her life, but only just. Fire flashed through her as the steel punched into her back just above the kidney, and her blood rained down to mix with the vile mire soaking into the carpet.

Struggling through the pain and the crawling of her skin as she rolled across the foul floor, Widdershins rose to her feet and spun, hefting the rapier that had fallen beside the body of Jean Luc.

Claude stood before her, sword in hand. A trickle of blood running down one side of his chin was the only sign of the Shrouded God's curse. Perhaps the Apostle had averted his eyes before the magics had taken hold—or maybe, just maybe, he had taken shelter behind his own divine protection.

"Well played," he growled, the tip of his sword slicing abstract patterns through the air before him. With a scowl, he shrugged the cloak from his shoulders. "You almost had us. But Cevora protects his own, and none can stand before him."

"I'm not standing before him," Widdershins grunted, rapier steady in one hand even as she pressed the other to her bleeding wound. "I'm standing before *you*."

She lunged, ignoring the tearing in her back. She had to end this fast, turn her attention back to the demon before it recovered its strength.

The Apostle's blade, though far heavier than her own, swept up with astounding speed to meet the assault. They stood a moment, steel against steel, the stares they exchanged sharper than any sword.

Widdershins's rapier was gleaming lightning, striking from one direction almost before she had completed her thrust from the last. It whistled as it cut through the air, and the ring of metal on metal was so rapid it became a single prolonged screech.

But through it all, Claude's blade intercepted even the swiftest strike. His heavy sword was more than enough to turn her weapon away, yet quick enough to slice through the gaps opened by his over-whelming parries. Widdershins bled from half a dozen wounds, tiny scrapes that sapped away her swiftly fading strength, yet she delivered none in return. Sweat poured down her face and his, gleaming in the light reflecting off the flashing blades.

Claude was good, but he wasn't *that* good; not as skilled as Lisette had been. But in that earlier struggle—gods, had it been so recent?—Widdershins hadn't been weighed down so terribly, by grief, by exhaustion, by the pain of her vicious wound.

She hadn't faced a foe who, just perhaps, had his own god guiding his hand, even as she did.

And she knew, she *knew*, that this was a fight she could not win.

Widdershins spun, wincing at the pain of her injury even as she ducked under a slash that would have opened her scalp had it connected. Dropping almost into a crouch, she reached out with her empty hand and—struggling not to think about what she was doing—scooped up a handful of the semiliquid remains spread across the floor and hurled it at her foe. Claude saw it coming, turned his face away to avoid getting the horrible stuff in his eyes and mouth—but it was enough to halt him in his tracks, if only for the briefest instant.

Widdershins was off at a limping sprint, standing at the door before the Apostle had taken a single step. With desperate speed she hauled it open, sliding it into its stone moorings, and came face to startled face with the guard Claude had left outside.

For a heartbeat they stared, she having utterly forgotten he was there, he having heard nothing of the conflict within, thanks to the heavy walls and door. And then he was yanking his flintlock from his belt, bringing it up and around with expert speed, finger already tightening on the trigger . . .

Widdershins hissed Olgun's name, and the deity reached out to caress the weapon—not to stop it, not to blow it to splinters, but to ignite it *early*. The flint slammed down without the trigger's urging; black powder flashed and sparked. The thug's eyes had only begun to widen as the lead ball hurtled harmlessly past Widdershins's shoulder—and sank, with a dull tearing sound and a horrified grunt, into the chest of the man charging up behind her.

The soldier stared in growing horror, Widdershins in shock, Claude down at his chest in bewildered disbelief.

"I don't understand," the Apostle whispered, tears forming in his eyes. "Cevora . . ."

And then he fell, first to his knees, then facedown in the putrid carpet.

Widdershins stepped forward, kneed the remaining guard in the groin as he stood stunned, and cracked him over the head with the pommel of the rapier for good measure.

"*Nice* shot, Olgun!" she crowed, laughing through her pain. She felt the god within beaming with pride.

"Don't let it go to your head, though," she added. "I don't want to still be hearing about this a month from now."

She *swore* she could feel him stick his tongue out at her.

Widdershins wanted nothing more than to leave. She hurt all over, she'd begun to feel slightly faint from exertion (and probably blood loss), and she knew it was only a matter of time before the thieves regained their courage and came hunting for whatever had invaded their home. But she'd come here for a reason, and that purpose remained undone.

Leaning over the unconscious thug, she carefully removed the powder horn at his waist and made her way back into the reeking chamber of horrors that had lately been a shrine.

It wasn't dead. The inhuman form had survived a three-story plunge back at the tenement, waded through a barrage of bolts and bullets, refused to be slain by the curse of a god not its own. But it lay, grunting and twitching, struggling to regain the strength that had been ripped from it. Some hideous viscous sludge of a color that Widdershins had never before seen—she could describe it only as some hideous combination of blue and death—oozed across the floor where the demon had puked it up, slowly bubbling and eating away at the carpet.

Moving as rapidly as her aching body would allow, keeping half an eye on the demon at all times, Widdershins skittered about the room, packing the horn with all the black powder carried by every one of Claude's thugs. Then and only then did she lean down beside the demon.

"Go back to hell," she whispered.

Widdershins shoved the horn unceremoniously into the beast's upturned mouth, as far down its throat as it would go, and fled the room. She paused once in the doorway, just long enough to yank one of the torches from the wall and hurl at the writhing, choking form, before slamming the door.

The thunderous blast made her ears ring even through the normally soundproof portal. Carefully she cracked it open once more, peered into the chapel just to be certain, and smiled.

And twenty-six souls, hovering in the ether around Adrienne Satti for two long years, drifted away to their long-sought rest.

"*Now*," she told Olgun exhaustedly, "would be a good time to go home."

Even as she spoke, she realized that she knew exactly where "home," from now on, had to be.

It was the very last respect she could pay.

EPILOGUE

SEVERAL DAYS FROM NOW:

"Well," the girl began hesitantly, voice husky with suppressed grief, with tears long since cried, "I guess that's the end of it." Robin looked around her, gripping the haft of the broom as though she sought to prevent the tool, and all it represented, from disappearing.

The common room looked good, better than it had in months. The employees, and Robin in particular, had done a marvelous job of cleaning up. The floor was free of dust and debris, and scrubbed so that all but the most stubborn stains had given up in despair. For the first time in years, the twin scents of alcohol and sawdust were stronger than the lingering aura of stale sweat. The tables, too, were cleaned and polished to within an inch of their lives. . . . All the tables but one. That one was gone, Widdershins having fed it piece by piece into the blazing hearth.

The serving girl still didn't know, really, what had happened. Part of her wanted to push, to demand an explanation, but she'd never do that to her friend. Shins would tell her the entire story if and when she was ready, and not a moment before.

"It looks good, Robin," Widdershins said softly from behind her. The girl felt a comforting hand close over her shoulder. "She'd have been proud of what you've done with the place."

With a piteous wail, Robin dropped the broom and fell against the newcomer's chest, sobbing miserably. Widdershins clasped her arms around the girl and let the spell subside.

Even once it had, she kept a worried eye on Robin, watching for a relapse of the near madness that had gripped her the night

Genevieve died. She'd suffered no similar attacks since, but Widdershins walked on eggshells around her, terrified that she might set off
another episode.

But it was more than the memory of her lost friend that had
Robin so distraught. As the sobbing wound down, Widdershins distinctly heard a muffled, "What am I going to do?" from the tousled
black mop of hair against her breast.

"What else would you do, Robin? You'll pull yourself together,
organize the others when they get here, and get this place ready to
reopen. You've got no idea the amount of business we've lost already."

Robin jerked back from her friend's embrace as though she'd
been shoved, her red-rimmed eyes wide. "Shins," Robin began,
trying to keep her voice steady, "there's not going to be any
reopening. You know what Gen's father thought of this place! He'll
probably just close it down, or maybe sell it, and in either case—"

"Robin, what makes you think Monsieur Marguilles has any say
over what happens?"

The girl blinked, and despite her grief, Widdershins laughed at
the befuddled look.

"Genevieve's will explicitly grants ownership of the Flippant
Witch to someone else."

"But Gen didn't *have* a will!" Robin exclaimed. "She kept putting it off."

Widdershins smiled sadly. "You're forgetting the kinds of
people I work with, Robin. By the time Marguilles gets here to take
possession of 'his' tavern, I'll have a will so perfect that Genevieve
herself wouldn't have recognized it as a fake."

"Is . . . is that right?" The girl sounded doubtful. "I mean,
would Gen have approved?"

"More than she'd have approved of her father selling her home
to some stranger, I think."

Robin felt herself starting to smile as well, for the first time in
almost a week. "And this new owner would happen to be . . . ?"

Widdershins casually buffed her nails on her vest. "Of course," she finally admitted, "I don't know the first thing about running a tavern, so that's pretty much going to be your job. It means, I'm afraid, that I have to insist on paying you more, but I'm sure you'll underst*ooof!!*"

Trying her hardest to gulp in some much-needed air, Widdershins gently disentangled herself from the world's most aggressive hug. "I take it you're happy with the decision," the thief croaked.

"You could say that," Robin replied.

"Is that why you tried to crush me to death just now?"

Startlingly, the girl's smile grew wider. "I thought it might be best to get you out of the way before you changed your mind."

For a long moment, Widdershins just stared at her, and then nearly collapsed with laughter.

"Which reminds me," Widdershins remarked afterward, tousling Robin's hair fondly. "I have a thing or three I've been putting off, myself. Now that the bar's taken care of . . ." *And you, too*, she added silently, "I really ought to get to them. You get this place ready to open by tomorrow night or it's coming out of your pay, you hear me?"

Even from outside, Widdershins could faintly hear the young girl whistling as she once more swept the already pristine floor of the common room.

✸

Standing in the midst of a filthy bedroom, heaps of clothes and assorted bric-a-brac hiding the old, termite-eaten floor, Henri Roubet desperately shoved the pieces of several outfits into a satchel already bulging at the seams.

He wasn't entirely certain how it had all gone wrong, but he knew that it couldn't possibly have gone any worse. The Apostle was dead, his men were dead, and Widdershins had not only seen his face but *heard his name*! He'd flinched even then, when Jean Luc introduced him, but he'd figured it didn't matter. She was going to be dead, and he was going to be rich.

Well, so be it. He was still good at his job, bum hand notwithstanding, and the Apostle had paid him more than enough over the years. He could start over in some other city without difficulty, live for quite some time before he even had to worry about finding a new position. In fact, much as he'd have enjoyed the riches promised him, this might even prove the better option. In another city, the weight of his past and the suspicion of the Guard wouldn't be hanging over his shoulder. He just needed to—

He froze, satchel falling from limp fingers at the feel of the cold metal mouth kissing his skull. Nobody could have snuck up on him here! Just dropping a damn pair of trousers made the floorboards in this pesthole squeak! And yet there the man was, visible just out of the corner of Roubet's eye, flintlock pressed to the back of his head.

"Why?" the former Guardsman asked softly.

"Because Widdershins isn't a murderer," Renard Lambert said to him. "And Genevieve would never have wanted someone like *you* to turn her into one."

Henri Roubet closed his eyes tightly as the hammer fell.

❋

Renard glared for a few moments at the corpse of Henri Roubet, then casually stuck the flintlock back in his belt. He tugged briefly on the fingers of his glove, blew on them to clear them of any excess powder, and turned toward the door.

Widdershins would be angry when she heard; she doubtless still believed that she actually wanted to find Roubet and kill him herself. Well, let her believe it. Renard knew better. And he knew that someday she'd understand, maybe even thank him.

Genevieve certainly would, looking down from wherever she might be.

He grinned suddenly, even as his hand touched the latch. It wasn't like him to be so spiritual. That's what he paid the guild priests for.

One last glance behind, taking in the cluttered room that reeked of unwashed clothes (and, with a growing insistency, spilled blood), and Renard sighed. Damn, but that girl was awfully hard to watch out for. As it was, the Finders would be expecting some sort of punishment—quite a lot of punishment—for her part in the recent massacre. He'd have to make sure he and the priests were on the same page, explain that her actions had prevented the rise of a power that might have threatened the guild, even the Shrouded God himself. Most of them wouldn't believe it, but at least it would quell the uproar. Still, maybe he should ask her to consider lying low for a few weeks . . . As though there was a chance in hell she'd agree.

And there was so much else to do, as well: rebuilding the guild's membership, appointing a new taskmaster, figuring out what to do with Lisette now that she'd proved herself utterly untrustworthy. . . . Perhaps she'd make a good public example, show the others the dangers of working against their leader, but that might just entice her followers and allies to further conspiracy. . . . Gods, but the work never ended! Sometimes, Renard wondered if it had even been worth taking the damn position in the first place.

Renard Lambert, Shrouded Lord of the Finders' Guild, disappeared into Davillon, grumbling over the inconveniences of love and duty.

✸

With a low groan of exhaustion, Major Julien Bouniard of the Davillon City Guard tore his gaze from the mounds of paper littering his desk like so many bird droppings, and clasped two fingers to the bridge of his nose. It was late, long past the end of his shift. The candles and lanterns guttered, the low background hum faded as the day shift trickled out to go home, the night shift out to their assigned patrols.

Julien knew that he could have, should have, given up and gone home, taken a fresh crack at this in the morning. It had been going on for days, now, form on top of form, briefing on top of briefing. But he'd ordered his men to get this whole mess done and over with as rapidly as possible, and Julien Bouniard wouldn't ask anything of them that he wasn't willing to do himself. So, with a frustrated shake of his head, he determined to return to work for at least another hour, opening his tired eyes—

And nearly leaped out of his skin through his own mouth when he saw that the thin wooden chair across from his desk was no longer vacant.

"That was an interesting yelp," the Guardsman's visitor said dryly, prodding at one ear with a finger. "I think you've just deafened every dog within two city blocks."

Julien glared, one hand clenched at the tabard covering his chest, the other on the butt of his flintlock. "Gods above, Widdershins! If you're trying to kill me, pull steel and have done with!" A few deep breaths seemed to calm him; at the very least, he stopped clutching at his breast as though he was having heart palpitations. "I'm not as young as I used to be," he told her more steadily.

You have no idea, she thought with a touch of bitterness. What she said was, "Really? I am. I gave up aging a few years back. Nothing to be gained from it, really."

"Indeed. Did you have any particular reason for coming here, in gross disregard of all logic and common sense? Or were you just hoping to startle me into an early grave?"

"Tempting as that may be," she said, "no, that's not why I came." She frowned. "Actually, Julien . . ." The guard's eyebrows rose. Any time she called him by his first name, he felt the irresistible urge to count his money. And perhaps his teeth.

"Yes?" he prompted.

She sighed. "I wanted to find out if you're still determined to pin de Laurent's and Al—um, Delacroix's deaths on me."

Bouniard frowned. "If I am, you took an awful risk in coming here to ask me."

Widdershins laughed aloud. "Julien, you've not even the vaguest comprehension of the sorts of places I've been recently. No disrespect to your abilities, or those of your men, but this place holds no real fear for me anymore."

"What makes you think," Bouniard asked slowly, his voice deliberately noncommittal, "that we have any reason to suspect—"

"Bouniard, please don't waste my time. We both know you've suspected me since I escaped your stupid prison. We both know that you were looking for me within moments after finding out that William—that is, the archbishop—was dead." The Guardsman filed that little slip of the tongue away for future study, but chose not to interrupt. "And we also know," she continued, suddenly angry, "that you've found, or at least should have found, if you're doing your job, enough evidence in Delacroix's house to implicate the real killer! So kindly stop stonewalling me so we can both get on with our respective evenings!"

All gods damn the woman, how did she *know* about these things?! Yes, the Guard had searched Delacroix Manor—gingerly, reluctantly, forced into it by the murders therein. They'd found evidence indeed, and to spare: a hidden shrine, devoted to a worship of Cevora far older and more primal than his modern, Pact-approved incarnation. And they'd found a number of disturbing writings, as well as ritual workings whose purpose Julien couldn't comprehend, but which the Guard priests told him had been banned since the earliest days of the Church.

Was there enough to convict anyone for the murders of Alexandre Delacroix and William de Laurent? No, not really; but there was certainly enough to draw a number of conclusions.

All of which was a moot point. None of this was public information, not when it involved a family as powerful as Delacroix was—or, well, had been.

"I can neither confirm nor deny anything you might have heard, Widdershins," Bouniard said stiffly. "I can, however," he continued hastily as she drew breath for another tirade, "assure you that we've no longer any reason to assume it was you. You're free and clear. Of this, anyway."

The young woman all but deflated in her chair. "Thank you," she said softly. Then, "How's Maurice?"

"Maurice? Oh, the monk." Julien shook his head. "Heartbroken. Still, I think some small good may have come of this. Last I heard before he left, he was talking about petitioning his superiors to transfer orders. Planning to become a priest, I understand, follow in de Laurent's footsteps." The Guardsman shrugged. "I think the Church could do worse."

Widdershins smiled faintly. "That they could," she agreed. "Well, I must be off." She paused yet again. "Unless you're planning to arrest me for breaking gaol?" she asked, only half teasing.

Bouniard's mouth twisted in an odd moue, trying to smile and frown at once. "I should," he admitted. "But . . . just maybe I was a bit, ah, overzealous in arresting you in the first place."

Widdershins's eyes widened, and it was her turn to clutch at her chest melodramatically.

"Don't push it," he warned. "I'm suddenly wondering where you're off to in such a hurry."

"Nothing sinister, Bouniard—not that I'd tell you if it was. My tavern's reopening tomorrow night. I want to make sure it's ready."

"Your tavern?"

Widdershins's face fell. "Genevieve left it to me."

Bouniard nodded. "I'm sorry," he told her, and Widdershins was startled to realize that he meant it. "I know you were close."

"We were."

"If it helps at all, Widdershins, we've arrested Brock's surviving partner. Fellow named Louvel, part of the break-in at the gaol as well. He'll get whatever justice I can bring down on him, I promise."

"Thank you," she said softly.

Feeling an intense need to break through a suddenly awkward moment, Julien said, "If you own a tavern now, does that mean you won't be stealing anymore?"

She grinned, brightening at least a bit. "It might, Bouniard. You never know."

"I hope so, Widdershins. I don't want to catch you doing anything illegal again, understand?"

"Oh, I understand perfectly," she said, gracing the Guardsman with an impish grin. "I promise, you won't catch me."

Despite himself, Julien couldn't help but laugh. By the time he stopped, the young woman was gone.

It was strange, really. He felt better now, after talking to her, than he had in days. She was definitely a bright spot in the week—which might actually have said less about her and more about the truly awful week, but there it was. Julien took one last look at the paperwork awaiting him and decided it could wait until tomorrow after all. He was going to lock up the office, go home, and get at least one good night's sleep, even if it meant a demerit for coming in late tomorrow.

Now where the hell had he put his keys?

✳

Widdershins shook her head as she slipped through the corridors of the Guard Headquarters. She didn't really need to sneak, now, seeing as she wasn't currently wanted for anything, but old habits and all that. She was glad Bouniard had cleared her of killing poor William and her fath—Alexandre. But she'd hoped . . .

Widdershins sighed. She still didn't know if Claude had just been a zealous lunatic, or if Cevora had truly guided his hand, but either way, she'd hoped he might have left some solid evidence behind. Maybe even, unlikely as she knew it was, something relating to the tragedy two years ago. She had hoped that the Guard might have cleared not only Widdershins, but Adrienne Satti. For all that had happened, she missed being Adrienne, sometimes.

She didn't even realize when Olgun sent a wave of confidence through her soul, of acceptance, of peace. No, she couldn't be Adrienne Satti anymore, not now, maybe not ever.

But there were worse people to be than Widdershins.

"Let's go home, Olgun," she said softly, in that tone that only he could hear. "I think it's time we start spreading you around a little bit, wouldn't you agree? I wonder how Robin feels about religion. . . ."

Chattering happily to her patron god, Widdershins idly spun Julien Bouniard's key ring around her finger as she emerged from the Davillon City Guard, stepped into the dancing shadows cast by the flickering streetlights, and was gone.

ABOUT THE AUTHOR

Ari Marmell is a fantasy and horror writer, with novels and short stories published through Spectra (Random House), Pyr, Wizards of the Coast, and others. He has also worked as an author of role-playing-game materials for games such as Dungeons & Dragons and the World of Darkness line. His earliest novels were written as tie-in fiction for the games Vampire: The Masquerade and Magic: The Gathering. His first original (that is, non-tie-in) published novel was *The Conqueror's Shadow*, followed by a sequel, *The Warlord's Legacy*. Although born in New York, Ari has lived the vast majority of his life in Texas—first Houston, where he earned a bachelor of arts degree in creative writing at the University of Houston, and then Austin. He lives with his wife, George; two cats; and a variety of neuroses.

You can visit Ari online at http://mouseferatu.com.